THE TREASURE OF RODOLFO FIERRO

The Treasure of Rodolfo Fierro

ST. GEORGE COOKE

A DOUBLE D WESTERN
DOUBLEDAY
New York   London   Toronto   Sydney   Auckland

A Double D Western
PUBLISHED BY DOUBLEDAY
a division of Bantam Doubleday Dell Publishing Group, Inc.
666 Fifth Avenue, New York, New York 10103

Double D Western, Doubleday,
and the portrayal of the letters DD
are trademarks of Doubleday, a division of Bantam Doubleday
Dell Publishing Group, Inc.

All of the characters depicted herein are fictitious
and have no resemblance to any persons living or dead, except
for those personalities of the Mexican Revolution
mentioned by name, who are now on the pages of history.

Library of Congress Cataloging-in-Publication Data

Cooke, St. George.
    The treasure of Rodolfo Fierro/St. George Cooke.
        p.   cm.—(A Double D western)
    I. Title.
PS3553.05575T7   1990
813'.54—dc20   89-48670
CIP

ISBN 0-385-23856-8
Copyright © 1990 by María Concepción Gómez Cooke
ALL RIGHTS RESERVED
PRINTED IN THE UNITED STATES OF AMERICA
May 1990
First Edition

For María Concepción Gómez Cooke, my wife,
who taught me all I know about Mexican women.
And then some.

And for Lee Florin,
who helps me polish gems as I learn.

THE TREASURE OF RODOLFO FIERRO

IT WAS THE FOURTH OF JULY, 1923, and it would be a scorcher of a day in southern New Mexico, thirty-five miles north of the Mexican border.

Richard Henry Little leaned out of the top half of the vestibule door, watching the town of Deming grow on the horizon as the train approached that station. Called "Tiny" by his friends, he stood six feet six in his stocking feet. His body was thin and angular, giving the impression of all bones and no meat. His arms were long. His broad-palmed, slender-fingered hands were thrust deep into the pockets of his tan whipcord trousers. His face was narrow and thin to match his body. The eyes, watching the passing scenery, were wide set in deep sockets. They were of an astonishingly deep blue. At the eye corners were lines radiating outward toward the temples, worn into his flesh by years of squinting into bright sunlight. Other lines on his face, particularly about his full mouth, indicated he laughed a lot. Richard Henry Little was an adept student of the human race: he found much to amuse him.

The black train, with its puffing engine pulling a line of black Pullman cars, began to slow down. Steam shot into the air as the engineer pulled the whistle cord to announce its arrival. The Pullman cars began to rock more gently on the tracks as the clatter of the wheels slowed. The rhythm was broken as the truck of his car and the one ahead crossed a switch, then resumed their regular, steady clatter. Wind, hot in the July air of southern New Mexico, ruffled his graying hair, blowing it in all directions until his head resembled an uncontrollable mop. A slight frown crossed his high forehead. Behind him the door to the Pullman opened, and the porter stepped into the jolting vestibule. He joined the tall man who was leaning, cross-armed, on the lower half of the partly opened door.

"Sorry, suh," the porter said in a soft southern voice, "I've got to open th' door for th' station."

Richard Henry Little nodded, then pushed open the door and entered the coach. From the seat in his compartment he picked up a Gladstone bag and returned down the swaying aisle to the vestibule.

"You're from Chicago, suh?" the porter asked politely to pass the last remaining minutes before the station.

"Virginia, Mr. Randolph. But I was in Chicago doing some research."

Mr. Randolph nodded. "There's not much to find hereabouts, Mr. Little, exceptin', maybe, a little history."

The tall man shook his head. "Lots of history," he emphasized. "Could be something hidden in those mountains yonder."

"A gold mine?"

Little nodded. "Maybe."

"Good luck to you, Mr. Little."

The tall man smiled. "I'll need it."

The porter nodded wisely. Then: "Sorry, suh, I've got to open the door for the station."

The tall man stepped back, watching the porter open the bottom half of the vestibule door, placing his foot on the catch to release the part of the platform which swung up revealing the steps. The porter went down halfway; taking a rag from his back pocket, he wiped the handrails outside the coach. He looked forward past the engine. He returned to the vestibule. " 'Bout a minute an' a half, suh," he said. The tall man nodded. He reached into a pocket. "That was a good ride, Mr. Randolph," he said, pulling out a bill. "For your courtesy and trouble." He handed the gratuity to the porter.

The colored man glanced down at the bill. "That's too much, suh."

"It's my pleasure."

"Thank you kindly, suh," the porter said, the bill disappearing into a black trousers pocket beneath the white linen jacket. "It'll be hot here, suh," he said, taking off his stiff black cap.

"I'm used to heat, Mr. Randolph. It won't bother me." The train began to crawl. "I'd better put my own bag on the platform."

"Yessuh, Mr. Little."

The red-bricked apron of the station platform appeared at the bottom step. The train moved forward slowly, stopping with a shudder; the sound of air hissing and the sudden clunk of heavy metal against heavy metal filled his ears. Richard Little picked up his Gladstone bag from in front of the opposite vestibule door. He put on his white Soldier Stetson which had been on top of the bag. The porter placed his yellow step-box just in front of the Pullman's bottom step, and the tall man was on the platform. Several passengers were coming out of the day coaches up front. He was the only one from the Pullmans. Men were lining up a large-wheeled baggage wagon near the open door of the express car and began taking sacks and packages from the coach mail. Little watched while they wrestled what appeared to be a very heavy rectangular box onto the wagon. At the end of the train the brakeman was standing on the platform looking alternately at his watch and forward to where the conductor was also on the platform, watch in hand. In less than five minutes the conductor called " 'Board!''; the brakeman crossed his arms three times over his head. Mr. Randolph picked up Little's step-box. He swung onto the Pullman steps just as the train started to move with a clanking jerk. The conductor and brakeman had disappeared into the train. The porter, closing the bottom half of the vestibule door, waved a farewell to the tall man as the engine picked up speed and puffed black smoke into the clear air in great gouts. Next stop west, Lordsburg.

"Carry your bag, meester?"

The tall man took his eyes from the departing train to glance down at the source of the accented voice. He saw a small brown-skinned boy with black matching hair and eyes. A round face, and white gleaming teeth smiling up at him. The boy's clothes consisted of short pants and what could have been a shirt at one time. At least they were cleaner than his bare feet.

"Think you can?"

"Oh sure, *señor.*"

"Then pick it up, son," Little said softly, smiling.

The boy reached for the handles of the Gladstone, started to straighten his back, and grunted. He tried again. A look of disappointment crossed his face. "I cannot do eet, *señor.* Eet is too heavy."

Two men pulled the baggage wagon across the platform. Their backs were bowed. The wheels creaked, the iron rims clattering over the bricks.

A flash of silver arched in the sunlight. The boy deftly picked the dime out of the air with a broad smile. "Where's the taxi, *muchacho?*" Little asked.

"I weel show you, *señor.*"

"What is your name?"

"Paco, *señor.*"

"Good, Paco. *Vamanos.*"

The tall man leaned down and picked up the bag without effort. The boy ran ahead of him to the corner of the station, the man following with long easy strides, stopping for a minute at the Railway Express office. A Model T touring car was parked in the shade of the building, its driver in complete repose except for alive black eyes. The driver's bulk almost filled the front seat, the steering wheel just missing his large belly by a half inch. The boy opened the rear door as the tall man hefted his bag onto the backseat before climbing in and seating himself, arranging his long legs into a position of comfort. "What's the best hotel?" he asked the driver.

"I'll take you there," the driver said. *"Muchacho!"* he yelled at the boy, "crank us!"

The boy went in front of the Ford, reached down, giving the crank a turn. The driver moved levers under the wheel and the engine sputtered into noise. The dusty car backed into the dirt street, then lurched forward.

Richard Henry Little allowed his body to ride easily as the car's wheels bounced in and out of holes. The streets, save one they crossed, were dirt. On his journey the tall man observed more horses and wagons than automobiles. He began to classify the town. Agriculture. Ranches. Feed stores. Farm machinery. Hardware. They passed the two-story First National Bank of Deming building on a corner. He saw more men than women on the streets. Most of them wearing bib overalls or Levis. Some wore strong clod shoes and others high-heeled range boots. Most of them had on broad-brimmed hats. The women he saw wore long skirts and blouses. The day was hot. They passed a drugstore, then an empty building that had a faded sign above the door which read PALACE SALOON. Here and there, on the fronts of some of the buildings, hung a limp flag in the dead air, reminders of the Glorious Fourth.

After turning several corners, the Model T pulled up in front of the Baker Hotel.

"How much, *señor?"* the tall man asked as he got out of the car.

"Twenty-five cents," the Mexican answered.

The tall man lifted out his bag. He slipped a coin into the hand of the driver.

"Gracias, señor."

"De nada," the tall man answered, picking up his bag and entering the hotel.

Behind the desk stood a young man in shirtsleeves. He wore a stiff collar and tie and looked uncomfortable in the heat. The lobby was small, filled with heavy furniture. From the ceiling two fans were circulating the air with no diminishing of the temperature in the lobby. The young man was blond, his hair combed carefully, parted on the left side. He looked up at the approaching customer, spinning the register around. "What can I do for you, sir?" he asked pleasantly.

"Do you have a corner room overlooking the street?"

"Sure do."

The tall man picked up the pen and dipped it into the inkwell. He hesitated a moment, then wrote with a bold hand on the next empty line in the register: *Richard Withers.*

The clerk read the signature upside down. "Where are you from, Mr. Withers?"

The tall man murmured, "Sorry." He finished the registration: *Santa Fe, New Mexico.*

"We're mighty pleased you're visiting us, sir," said the clerk. "My name's Charles Elliott, at your service. How long do you intend to be with us?"

Richard Little, alias Withers, smiled. "Depends on how soon I can finish my work here. How much?"

"Two dollars a day, payable in advance."

"I'll take a month's worth," Dick Little said. He reached into his pocket, pulling out a roll of bills. Peeling off one he placed it on the counter.

The clerk glanced at the money. It was a hundred dollars. He became flustered.

"If—if you're staying that long," he stammered, "we'll give you a rate."

"Very well," Dick Little said, "figure it out and give me the change later." He placed a stub on the counter. "I have a trunk over at the station. Have it brought here and put it in my room."

"Yes, sir!"

"It's heavy. You'll need a couple of strong men to bring it upstairs. Pay them from that," he said, indicating the bill.

"Yes, sir!"

"Is there a saloon in town?"

The young man shook his head. "There's Prohibition, sir."

"Some place a man can get a drink if he wants one?"

The clerk smiled. "There's Gunny's, sir. Run by a man named Gunny."

"Gunny's?"

"Yes, sir. It's a—well, sir—you can get a drink there if you want one. It's illegal, you know."

The tall man sighed. "I know. Can you get me a bottle?"

"I think so, sir."

"Good. Bourbon, if you can. The best brand available. Old Crow, if they have it. Bring it up to my room with some ice."

"Yes, sir. Anything else, sir?"

"Is there a livery stable in town?"

"Three, sir."

"Which has the best horses?"

"O'Conner's, sir. About two blocks down this street and a block over to your left." Charles Elliott indicated the direction with his hands.

Little nodded. "I'll find it tomorrow. Now, show me the room."

They climbed the stairs to the second floor, turned down the hall where the clerk unlocked a door, standing aside to let the tall man enter. Little set his bag down and looked around.

The room was large and plain. There was a double bed with a heavy oak headboard. Four windows made the room gleam with light. Two faced one street and two another. Little walked over to them, looking down on the corner for some time. He opened a door which led into a deep closet. He opened the drawers of the dresser, the one in the table beside his bed, the one in the desk. He switched the goosenecked desk lamp on and off. He flicked on and off the light hanging down from a cord in the ceiling. He tried the overhead fan switch, watching it turn faster and faster, then he turned it off. He turned the water off and on in the sink—the single tap. He noticed a phone on the bedside table. "Does that work?" The clerk nodded. The tall man opened two of the windows from the bottom, pushing them up as far as they'd go. He pulled down the shades, letting the room grow dark with only filtered sunlight. He nodded. "Where's the bath?"

"Last door down the hall," the clerk answered.

"Shower?"

"No, sir. Tub only."

Dick Little sighed. "It would be. When do you change the sheets?"

"Mondays and Fridays. You get clean towels then, too, sir."

"Good enough."

"Will that be all, sir?"

Dick Little smiled. "One more thing. Get me that fat Mexican who drives the cab. I'll be ready in fifteen minutes. Then get the Bourbon and put it on the table beside my bed. Is the water from the tap pure?"

"The best in the country, sir," the clerk said proudly. "Here in Deming it is 99 percent pure. You'll have no trouble with it, sir."

"Good. Thank you very much."

"Yes, sir."

"I'll be down as soon as I freshen up a bit."

"Yes, sir. Here's your key, sir. I'll have your trunk brought over as soon as possible, and the bottle brought up for you right away. I'll have to make a couple of phone calls for both of them, sir."

The tall man was looking at one of the shaded windows. "You do that, son. You do that," he said absently.

The clerk went out, shutting the door behind him. For a moment Dick Little continued to stare at the darkened window. "Gunny's," he said softly to himself. "Well, well, well!"

He snapped out of his thoughts, picked up his bag, putting it on the bed. From his pocket he took out a ring of keys. He unlocked the bag, spread open its large mouth and dug into it, taking out his shaving kit. In a minute he was heading down the hall toward the bath, being careful to lock the room door behind him. He was whistling through his teeth.

Eufemio Martínez was a practical person. He wore only those clothes necessary to cover his body, and a hat to keep the sun off his head. The wide-brimmed straw sombrero had seen better times long ago. His shirt was clean, but there were buttons missing, allowing the great expanse of his stomach to push an undershirt out into the open. The undershirt was not all that clean. He wore a pair of cheap trousers held up by a piece of rope thrust through the belt loops and tied tightly under his stomach: this made him bulge even more. His feet were covered by a worn-down pair of huaraches made long ago below the border in Mexico. The one big love of Eufemio's life, since his wife had run off with a smuggler from Casas Grandes, was his Model T taxi. On this car he lavished all the love he had once given to his wife and was very content the car did not argue and scold him as she had done constantly. He loved to drive his car, his one big possession, and had often dreamed of having just such a customer as the one who now rode beside him, his long legs curled up, one foot on the dashboard and the other hanging over the door. The tall man was smoking a hand-rolled cigarette.

"Where is the best place to see the countryside?" he had asked before they had pulled away from the hotel.

Eufemio had gestured vaguely to the southeast.

"Good," his passenger had declared. "Let's go that way."

They went that way. South first, to circle behind the county courthouse, then southeast onto a wagon road. As they bumped along, Martínez acted as guide, throwing his arms about in grand gestures, forgetting

the wheel of the car for long moments at a time while he told stories of
the country.

Once, by accident, he had lapsed into his native tongue. He realized
then his passenger had also changed his language to Spanish. Martínez
was very pleased. They drove slowly along the road for an hour. Dick
Little was much taken with the countryside. It was a green, rolling land,
good, he could see, for growing things if there was water available.
There were long vistas to look at and nearby mountains jutting suddenly from the plains areas. They were not of a chain of mountains, but
seemed to have risen abruptly from the ground, ragged, edged with
sharp rocks. To the north the mountains had an older look, but the ones
they were near were much newer. They had a bluish cast on them, and
the ridge ran almost due south toward Mexico.

"What are these mountains?" he'd asked.

"The Floridas. They are little mountains. They are good for nothing.
Just to look at," Martínez had answered.

Dick Little grunted. He watched them closely, noting the sharp
rocks, the little canyons cut into the sides. He saw stone on stone
balanced ready to crash and roll down to the plains at a touch. There
was small vegetation growing on the sides, but he was not close enough
to identify it at firsthand. He was content to make himself as comfortable as possible in the jolting, swaying seat of the car. He enjoyed the
rugged beauty of the land.

At last, Martínez announced he had driven as far as he could. He
turned the Ford around, heading it back down the road they'd traveled.
"It is indeed beautiful country, señor," he said. "I am content to live
here the rest of my life."

"Driving a taxi?"

Martínez shrugged. "Why not?" he said. "It is a quiet life. I have
seen too much of blood and death in my day. Now, all I want is to be
left to live my life as I please."

"May God grant you your wish," the tall man said quietly.

"Thank you, señor."

They drove along the road for a couple of miles before Little broke
their silence.

"How far is it to Columbus?"

"Thirty—forty miles," Martínez answered.

"Can you take me there someday soon?"

"I can, señor, but it will be all day. The road is not very good."

"Is there a place to stay there?"

"Under the stars, *señor*. There is little left since General Villa burned the town seven years ago."

"That bad, eh?"

"It never has been the same. When would you wish to go?"

Dick Little shrugged. "One day soon, Señor Martínez."

"Please be kind to let me know so I can prepare for the trip."

"I will surely do so."

The Model T Ford touring car rocked and bucked along the road, leaving a plume of dust behind them to settle slowly back to earth.

O'CONNER'S LIVERY STABLE read the sign over the wide doors of the barn. Dick Little sat in the cluttered small office which smelled of leather, hay, sweat, and manure. A small sandy-haired man sat across the desk from him puffing on a cob pipe, sending clouds of smoke roiling about his head. His face was the map of Ireland. "So what'll ye be wantin' a horse by the week for, bucko?"

Dick Little suppressed a smile. "Why, Mr. O'Conner, to ride about the countryside, of course," he answered, managing to put a little brogue into his speech.

O'Conner's sharp eyes peered at the tall man across the desk. There was a trace of suspicion in them.

"Ye wouldn't be pullin' me leg now, would ye?"

Little smiled. "I might be wantin' to ride all the way down to Columbus on a campin' trip," he said innocently. "I'd be wantin' a nag with a bit of bottom an' stayin' power. That is," he added, "if you'd be havin' one of the likes I'm after."

The little man snorted through his pipe, sending sparks and smoke shooting toward the ceiling. He hastily brushed pieces of glowing tobacco from his shirtfront. Leaning forward he closed one eye, raised an eyebrow, pointed a finger under Little's nose. "What'll ye be payin', bucko? Cash, or the promise to pay at the end of the week? We take no domned promises here, ye hear?"

Dick Little reached into his pocket, pulling out his roll of bills. "How do ye want it, boy-o?" he asked innocently.

O'Conner sat back in his chair quickly. "Well, now—" he breathed. His eyes glittered. "A man after me own heart, says I," he said. "Can ye really ride one of the domned things?"

"I've been known to," Little smiled. "I'll let you pick the one for me."

"Knowin' horses," O'Conner said, "don't mean I have to like the sons o' bitches."

"What's your deal?"

"Ten Yankee dollars a week, five for the saddle."

"Three," Little said.

O'Conner waved his pipe. "Skinflint," he said. "Three for the saddle." He sucked smoke from the pipe. "And one for the saddle blanket," he added blandly.

"None for the blanket," Little said. He held up a finger hurriedly. "And three belts of pure Irish up in me room at the hotel the first time you catch me there."

O'Conner sucked in a long breath. "Real Irish?" he whispered.

Dick Little nodded. "Real Irish as sure as me mither's grave is in County Cork." It was a lie, but he couldn't resist it.

The little man sighed. "I don't give a dom where ye mither's buried, God bless her soul! Name your own price, bucko, and let's get the hell down to th' hotel afore I change me mind."

It was dark when the little Irishman happily left the room. Dick Little looked at the remains of the bottle of Jameson's he had dug out of the vitals of his Gladstone. The corners of his mouth turned up slightly. He walked to the switch beside the door, turning off the overhead light. Going to one of the windows he raised the shade, looking down on the dirt streets crossing at the corner below his room. A small movement in a building shadow caught his eye. He stared at the spot for several long minutes before he saw the movement again. There was a man standing across the street in the dark. For an instant he glimpsed the white of an unrecognizable face lifted toward his window. He slowly pulled down the shade. He crossed the room and sat on the edge of the bed. For a moment he stared at the remains of his drink in the tumbler he was holding. Who the hell in Deming knew who he really was? That is, well enough to be standing in the dark watching his window?

He drained off the remains of his drink in one quick gulp.

FOR THE NEXT THREE DAYS Dick Little rode horseback around the countryside. Whenever he met someone he'd stop to talk and ask questions. He became familiar with the names of the jutting hills and mountains which surround Deming: the Cobres; the Little and Big Burro; the

Victorio and Cedar. He could distinguish them individually: Red Mountain; Grandmother; Black; Cooke's Peak; Dragon Ridge; Navajo Bill Hill; Arco del Diablo; Snake Hills; and Las Tres Hermanas, the Three Sisters. One person he stopped to talk with was a geologist who was puttering about on the sides of the Floridas. He was wearing a pith helmet, a canvas hunting jacket, olive drab khaki hiking britches, and puttees above heavy blucher shoes.

"Yes, sir," the geologist said in a thin voice, "this is mighty interesting country hereabouts. Look over yonder to the northeast. That's Black Mountain. Volcano at one time; just to the left are the Grandmothers. Volcanoes also. Over there are the Burro Mountains, Little and Big Burro. They're of granite along with igneous and metamorphic rocks. They're old rocks. Much older than the rocks we're standing on now. These Floridas are volcanic, too. They're younger than most of the other volcanic heaps around here; that's why they are so jagged and rough; they haven't had the time to wear down as the others have."

The tall man said something about exploring the Floridas.

"If you do," the geologist said, "be mighty careful. There's a lot of old abandoned mines up here in these hills. You don't go exploring in them just for the fun of it. They could come down on you just like that!" He snapped his fingers. "Or you could step in a hole you didn't see, break a leg maybe, and never be able to crawl out alive. Even if you did crawl out, how many persons pass through this section of the country in a day? Maybe not more than fifty the whole year."

Little allowed he wasn't about to enter an abandoned mine by himself.

"Look at this hunk of rock," the geologist said, sweeping an arm in a gesture to include the whole mountain. "Volcanic tuffs and breccias. Lots of gemstones hereabouts."

"Gems?"

"Semiprecious stones."

"What kinds?"

"Silica minerals mostly," the geologist answered pedantically. "Quartz crystals, red jasper, gray to black perlite, pitchstones, spherulites, or spheroidal nodules formed in glassy volcanic rock by local crystallization of minute particles of feldspar and silica. Thunder eggs, the agate-cored nodules, are a particular variety of spherulite. I've found many around here."

"You sort of lost me on the first turn." Dick Little smiled. "I thought

I knew words, but you've thrown a few at me today I never heard
before."

The geologist laughed, cackling. "I'm sorry," he said. "Geology is my
life and I'm caught up in it. I teach geology, you know."

"I didn't know, but I suspected as much. Is there anything special
you're looking for here?"

The geologist shook his head. "Just looking," he said. "This is very
interesting country for me. You might say I'm doing a little prospecting
on the side. I've visited some of the abandoned mines. Nothing much to
be found. On the tailings I find manganese minerals such as manganite,
pyrolusite, psilomelane, wad, and manganiferous calcite. Not much
else."

"I guess not," Dick Little said to be saying something. He was completely ignorant when it came to minerals and rocks. "How about the
plants around here? Know what they are?"

"Oh yes," answered the geologist proudly. He started to point to
various bushes and growing things. "This is construed as a semiarid
country so you'll find such varieties of cacti as the sotol, or desert
spoon; there is yucca, the one with the tall stem growing from the
middle. It blooms once a year. Very pretty. We're standing amidst
prickly pear. Over there is a small barrel cactus. Those whiplike
branches are of an ocotillo. The stunted treelike bushes are creosote
bush, juniper, mesquite, scrub oak, and hackberry."

Dick Little laughed. "I can tell many a jungle plant from another but
I'm lost on these."

The geologist smiled. "If you stay around them long enough they'll
become very familiar to you. You'll be able to tell one from the other
with just a glance."

"I suppose so," Little said, "but I don't propose to stay here that
long."

"Are you vacationing, too?"

"It could be called that. I've had a rough year behind me. I'm here to
relax; do some riding; lots of reading and not much else. Well, sir, many
thanks for the course in geology and botany. It'll help make my rides
about the country that much more interesting."

He shook hands with the geologist, mounted his horse and rode off
toward town. About half a mile away he stopped and turned his horse.
He took a pair of field glasses from their case strapped to his saddle and
focused them on the geologist. The man was bent over, walking slowly
across the ground, peering at the earth. He would kneel down, pick up a

rock, examine it, throw it away, stand up and repeat the process. Little watched him for ten minutes. He saw the geologist take off his pith helmet and wipe his head with a handkerchief. After the helmet was replaced, another rock was picked up, this time to be put into one of the oversized pockets of the man's canvas jacket. The geologist was so absorbed in his search, he never glanced back. The horse and its rider had been completely forgotten.

The following morning Richard Little rode to the north and east of Deming. He was in no hurry; the day was beautiful, as had been all the days since he'd arrived in the area. The sun shone in a cloudless sky. It was hot, but the prevailing easterly wind provided a touch of coolness that was more imaginary than actual. Little was following the railroad tracks, letting the horse pick his own pace as long as it was not a slow walk. He was a good horseman, knowing how to suggest to the horse the direction and speed of travel without wearing down either the animal or himself. To his right, the Floridas rose abruptly out of the plains wrapped in a blue haze; to his left the highest point in the area grew closer and closer: Cooke's Peak. It jutted above the surrounding mountain mass, resembling a bent thumb pointing eastward. Being a casual student of military history, Dick Little had read the book Colonel Cooke had written about his adventures as commanding officer of the Mormon Battalion. *The Conquest of New Mexico and California* was, in the opinion of Richard Henry Little, one of the best accounts of a U.S. military operation ever set to paper.

Cooke had been given the command of the Mormon Battalion in Santa Fe. He had disciplined the undisciplinable and had marched them from Santa Fe, New Mexico, to San Diego, California, building the first road for wheeled vehicles across the continental divide from east to west. The Mormons, under Cooke, had marched as a military unit farther than any other orderly military unit in history, without losing a man. Cooke had been a strict disciplinarian, but he tempered his sternness with a sense of humor.

Desirous of gaining fame as his fellow West Point classmates were doing in the war with Mexico, Cooke found himself diverted from the war to command the Mormon Battalion across the western part of the United States-to-be. His commanding officer, Stephen Watts Kearny, had already conquered New Mexico for the United States in that year of 1846, and was ordered to continue on west to conquer the rest of the land area in the name of the growing country. It was the year of the country's Manifest Destiny when it was to grow and expand from sea to shining sea. California, here they came!

At the time of the march, Cooke had no idea how important his command would be to the history of the country as a whole. It was to lay claim to all of Mexico's possessions to the north of the Rio Grande and then some. The fact was, after the war the United States had to buy a tremendous tract of land from Mexico in order to keep Cooke's road within the borders of the growing nation.

Cooke had raised the first American flag over Tucson, Arizona, and had arrested John Charles Fremont in California for trying to set up his own empire while under orders of the President of the United States and its Army to behave himself.

Dick Little was of the opinion Fremont was as big an ass as two other fools who had been given command of troops: Fetterman and Custer.

In spite of the great results of the march of the Mormon Battalion on history, Cooke at the time was more concerned over his lost chance in the war; not realizing his was the greater glory, proven by time. Since, Cooke told himself, I am not in Mexico making a name for myself in the military annals of war, I will, at least, put my name on the map. Therefore, the tallest peak in all of the mountains we have encountered since leaving Santa Fe—and the tallest peak we are likely to encounter on the way west—I shall name after myself.

Such was his reasoning and deed.

Little's mind was filled with thoughts of that tough army officer and his accomplishments as he rode along the railroad tracks.

When he reached a point where the tip of Cooke's Peak was in line with the tallest ridge of the Floridas, he stopped his horse where a road turned off toward the peak. There was a galvanized rural mailbox set on the top of a post. The wide world reached even to this isolated place, he thought. Dismounting to stretch his legs and to allow his animal to crop at the sparse range grass, he rolled a cigarette and lighted it.

The silence was deep at first until he became aware of the noise insects were making as they buzzed about unseen; of the cry of a high flying bird; of the sounds of his horse's teeth grinding against grass and bit. He hunkered down on his heels, slitting his eyes, taking in the massive scenery of the peak, and the faraway mountains on the other side of the plains.

Near Cooke's Peak, Little knew, were the remains of Fort Cummings, the only walled fort in New Mexico during those bygone days of Indian depredations. Cooke's Spring was also over there near the fort. It was being used by the railroad, which piped the water to the tracks for their engines. He could see the water tank up the line a ways. Before coming to Deming, he had read everything about the area he could put his hands on: when he could, he always scouted through literature those places he knew he was going to visit. In his mind's eye, he almost could see the stagecoaches of the Butterfield Overland Mail Company crossing the plains behind four to six mules, heading for Cooke's Spring out of Mesilla. He could visualize the ancient Folsom hunters tracking down the Pleistocene bison some ten thousand years ago. Perhaps a later Indian culture had settled near the spring to plant corn and other agricultural crops, and to form a small village. Behind the mountain, and to the west, other Indians had settled along the Mimbres River. There they had planted. They also had created beautiful decorated pottery.

The early Spanish had crossed these plains and mountains looking for great conquests and for riches: God! King! Gold! was their credo.

Dick Little had read of the discovery of a great hoard of copper not too far north. This metal had been mined and sent to smelters on the backs of mules, forming miles of pack trains, to Janos in old Mexico.

The plains where the stagecoaches had run were soaked with the blood of Spanish, Anglo, and Indian, for this was the country of the Apache who resented the intrusion of all strangers. Mangas Colorado, Cochise, Victorio, the great chiefs, knew this country. The Apaches fought hard to keep it theirs. But the white eyes were too many, too strong. The Indians disappeared into the dusty pages of history, or on to reservations of the white man's choosing.

The faint whistle of a train brought Dick Little out of his reverie.

He picked up the trailing reins of his horse and mounted. He held the animal still while the train approached. Larger and larger it grew, writing of its passage with a long line of black smoke. The train thundered by. Little waved at the engineer, receiving a wave and a sharp toot on the whistle in return. He patted the neck of his horse to quiet it down, then watched the passenger cars hurl past with a swirl of disturbed air and the clickety-clack of the wheels. He waved at the people seated on the deck of the observation car. They waved back. The train would stop in Deming in a few minutes; he had hours to ride back. Throwing a salute at Cooke's Peak, he turned the head of his horse toward civilization.

Someone had ransacked his room. His bed had been pulled apart. The mattress and pillows had been slashed with a sharp knife. The feathers and ticking had been thrown all over the room. Drawers from the desk, table, and dresser had been emptied, thrown on the floor. Clothes from the closet were crumpled, discarded. His Gladstone had been ripped open with the knife. It was no longer useful. The case in which he kept his toilet articles was open, its contents thrown carelessly about the room. Dick Little swore under his breath, reaching for the phone on the table.

"Who has been up here?" Little asked angrily when the young clerk came into the room.

His eyes were wide, startled. His tongue wet his lips. "I—I—I don't know, sir," he stammered. "Who could have done such a thing?"

"I'm asking *you*," Little stated simply. "Is there a back stair?"

"Yes, sir. Somebody could have sneaked in," the clerk said. "I wasn't on the desk every minute. They could have gotten in through the lobby while I wasn't there. They could have done that. Is anything missing?"

"I have nothing to miss. Besides, they couldn't get into the trunk." He pointed to the rectangular metal box beside the desk.

"I've never seen one like that before," the clerk said.

"Maybe you never will again."

"It took four men to bring it up the stairs. There's no lock on it, and you can hardly make out which side is up."

"That's right. Had it made special for me in the Orient. I'm the only one who knows how to open it. Even a good safecracker couldn't do it."

The clerk looked around the room. "I'll get the woman to come up and clean up this mess. We'll have the room fixed up quickly."

"Fine," Little said. "I'm going over to O'Conner's stable. If you need me for any reason, send somebody over."

"Yes, sir."

When the clerk left the room, Little went to the table beside the bed. He picked up the bottle of Bourbon. "Son of a bitch!" he said to himself. "The lousy bastard drank half my bottle!"

She saw him first. Standing within the open stable doors in the shade, she was invisible to anyone approaching. Her dark eyes widened slightly with interest. She saw a very tall, spare man with a slight stoop about his shoulders walking toward her. He wore a white Soldier Stetson, tilted slightly forward. His face was lean and strong. Broad shoulders covered by a twill Norfolk jacket, with breast pockets and two oversized pockets on the sides. The jacket was tightly belted, showing the man had a flat stomach, as the cloth was not wrinkled. His trousers were gray whipcord, fitting his long legs tightly. He wore black cavalry boots curving snugly over the calves of his legs. His feet were not small, yet he walked lightly in spite of the high riding heels and blunt rounded toes. His arms were long; his hands large with long delicate fingers. She had the impression that this man could be dangerous if he wanted to. As Dick Little came closer she could make out his straight nose and wide, deep-set eyes. His stride was long. He covered ground easily and quickly, almost silently.

At last he saw her. His eyes did a quick up and down glance which registered her in his memory for the rest of his life. She was tall for a woman, yet her head came only up to his shoulder. Her face was olive, clean-featured, full-mouthed. Her hair was drawn back into a bun at the nape of her neck: it was as black and shining as obsidian. She was wearing a Spanish riding costume: a short jacket, open in front to reveal a white pleated shirt, the collar buttoned at the neck. About her slender waist was a wide black belt. Her skirt was of a brown material, long, to her mid-calves which were covered by black, soft leather riding boots. The skirt was split to allow the wearer to straddle the horse Spanish style, or ride sidesaddle comfortably as did society women back East. Dick Little saw her figure, noting her full breasts, and that she was sufficiently well rounded in back to fill out her body in the most pleasing way.

"Buenas tardes, señorita," he said to her. She took note that his voice was deep, melodious: that his Spanish was almost without accent.

"Buenas tardes, señor," she answered. Her voice was also deep, husky.

"Is Mr. O'Conner around?" he asked, still speaking in Spanish.

"Not at the moment, señor," she answered in the same language. She was aware he was looking deeply into her eyes.

He noted the black, broad-brimmed, round Spanish riding hat on her, tilted slightly to one side, the cord slipped up to her chin and held by a clasp of deep blue turquoise. She tapped her quirt impatiently into the palm of one of her gloved hands. "I have been waiting for him to return," she said.

He lifted his hat. "My name is Richard"—he paused slightly— "Withers. May I wait here with you?"

She inclined her head slightly. "I'm María Luisa Isabel Gutiérrez y Velasco," she announced, raising her head proudly.

"Pleased to meet you. About twenty-seven, I'd say."

Her eyes became puzzled. "What?"

He smiled. "A joke, *señorita*. Please pay no attention."

She returned his smile, showing strong, white teeth. "You are new to Deming?"

"Yes, *señorita*. I arrived only five days ago. It is beautiful country. Are you from around here?"

"I am paying a visit to my uncle, *señor.*"

"You are from Mexico?"

"Yes, *señor*. From San Luis Potosí. Do you know of it?"

"I have spent many wonderful days in your city, *señorita*. It does not please me that we have not met before."

She lowered her eyes. "You are most complimentary, *señor*, but I do not live in the city itself. My family and I have a ranch just a few kilometers outside of San Luis. I spend most of my time there."

"Gutiérrez," he mused. "I have heard that name many times in Mexico."

"It is not uncommon, *señor*, in my country."

"But you are. You are very beautiful."

He could see her blush.

"Perhaps, Señorita Gutiérrez, if you plan to wait for Señor O'Conner, you would be so kind as to tell him I will be needing my horse about ten tomorrow morning. I plan to ride a few miles south."

"I will deliver your message, *señor.*"

"You are very kind, *señorita.*" He made her a little bow, put his hat back on and left her, striding his long strides. She watched him with interest until he disappeared around a corner.

Her eyes narrowed slightly. "So *that* is the man," she said softly to herself.

The July night was warm. The billions of stars overhead appeared to be close enough to pick from the sky. Dick Little left the restaurant, standing in front of the door just long enough to light his cigarette. He glanced up at the stars, feeling a sense of inadequacy at being so infinitesimal in the scheme of things. Yet he was strangely happy with a tranquility he hadn't felt for a long time. His thoughts were still on the lovely señorita. After he had left her, he'd returned to his hotel, taken a long bath by somehow folding himself into the short tub, shaven himself, and had put on clean clothes from the skin out. After dressing, he poured himself a stiff drink of Bourbon and stretched himself catty-cornered across the bed, his head held up by the pillows. For a long time he allowed his thoughts to dwell on the lovely Señorita Gutiérrez. He cast fantasies about her; her family; her ranch; about her uncle in Deming. He dozed a little until it grew dark, then he left the hotel for supper.

He was heading back to his room to take a book from his trunk and read until he felt sleepy enough to go to bed. As he was passing in front of a store he heard the bark of a pistol!

He threw himself to the ground, rolling quickly into the darkness of the store's doorway. The glass window of the store shattered under the impact of a second bullet.

He could see nothing across the street in the shadows. He could hear footsteps running from the spot the shot had come from.

He was swearing quietly to himself as he returned to the Baker Hotel, and his room.

RICHARD LITTLE was putting on his jacket when the knock came. He crossed the room, spun the key in the lock, and opened the door.

"Mr. Withers?" The voice was pleasant.

"Yes."

"I am Sheriff Chucho Armijo of Luna County. May I come in?"

Little stood aside as the sheriff entered. He closed the door.

The sheriff was simply dressed: a broad-brimmed black hat with a round, flat crown; white shirt, open at the neck; tight-fitting black trousers; high-heeled boots. On the left breast of his shirt was pinned a six-pointed star of brass engraved with the words *Sheriff, Luna County, New Mexico.* When he removed his hat he revealed his dark curly hair. His face was squarish; eyes dark, and a thin mustache over tight lips. He was of a type women were attracted to in spite of the black gun belt he wore about his slender hips, weighed down by the heavy Colt .45 Peacemaker. "I am sorry to bother you this early, Mr. Withers," he said, "but I hear you were shot at last night?"

Dick Little shrugged. "He missed."

"Did you see the man?"

"Saw nothing; heard nothing until the shots. Then, all I heard were his footsteps as he ran away."

"You have no idea who it was?"

"None."

"Or why?"

"No."

The sheriff shrugged. "That is not much help."

"I don't suppose it is."

"Do you know who ransacked your room?"

Little shook his head. "Again, no."

The sheriff twirled his hat by the brim. "I don't understand it," he said. "You arrive in town a stranger. You take rides about the country, minding your own business; then, all of a sudden, your room is wrecked. You are shot at. Why would anyone do that to you, Mr. Withers?"

"As I said, Sheriff, I haven't the slightest idea. It is uncomfortable, though, to be the pigeon without knowing why."

The sheriff smiled broadly. "I'll be looking into it."

"Why not the city police? Why the sheriff?"

"The city police—" he shrugged. "I have told them I would look out for you, and not to interfere. They follow my orders. Besides, you intrigue me a lot. There's something going on around you I know nothing of. I'd like to find out what it is."

Little smiled. "So would I, Sheriff. Now, if you will excuse me, I'm going out for a horseback ride."

"May I inquire in which direction?"

"Why not?"

There was a silence in the room. "Well?" asked the sheriff.

"South."

"Ah. In that case I will know where to keep an eye on you."

"By all means. Now, if you'll excuse me."

"Certainly, certainly." The sheriff put on his hat, and strolled leisurely through the door Dick Little had opened. The tall man listened to the sheriff's footsteps going down the stairs, then he shrugged. He left the room, locking the door behind him.

The country below Deming was flat plains, with the exception of the Floridas rising suddenly on the left. To the right were other mountains, but they were scattered and isolated. Way off to the west was a range of hills, but they were indistinguishable in the distance. The country was laid out in farms with wheat, corn, and cotton beginning to mature in the hot July sun. This was irrigated land, as there was no water visible on the surface. Dick Little knew good farming country when he saw it. He was pleased at the sight of clean fields and growing things.

The road south was packed dirt. His horse kicked up a little dust as they took a slow pace. Time passed; miles passed. Almost dead ahead, in the distance, three pointed peaks began to take shape. They were clustered together, standing alone in a family group. These were the Three Sisters, Las Tres Hermanas.

As he passed a grove of trees, beside a water tank, he heard his name called.

"Señor Withers!"

He reined his horse, waiting while Señorita Gutiérrez rode up beside him. He raised his hat. "You are very lovely this morning," he said with a smile.

She smiled. "Thank you. Do you mind if I join you?"

"Not at all. It will be a great pleasure."

They headed their horses, side by side, down the road.

Dick Little was very conscious of her presence. She was dressed as before, the same type of riding habit, but the colors were different. He glanced toward her. She was staring straight ahead.

"I heard about last night," she said, startling him with the abruptness of her statement.

"You heard what about last night?" he asked.

"Someone shooting at you. Deming is a small town. News such as a man being shot at, mysteriously, travels quickly. We hardly need our weekly paper."

He laughed. "Whoever it was wasn't a good shot."

She turned her head, looking at him levelly. "Perhaps he wasn't shooting at you. Perhaps he wanted to warn you."

His eyes narrowed as he looked at her. "Warn me of what?" he asked slowly.

She shrugged. "I cannot tell because I do not know."

"What do you know about me, Señorita Gutiérrez?"

"Nothing."

"Yet you are interested about my being shot at last night."

Looking straight ahead, she replied, "I am interested always in knowing why one man would want to kill another—or warn him of a danger to himself. I am curious as to why you are here in Deming. I am curious as to where you came from. I am curious as to who and what you are." She paused. "It is the prerogative of a woman to be curious."

He laughed. "At least you've put it on the line. Where do you want me to begin?"

"Wherever you like."

Looking at her he admired the roundness of her bust, the straightness of her back, the tilt of her head, the beauty of her face. "Very well," he said. "I was born in the eastern part of the United States. In Virginia, as a matter of fact. My parents were landowners, so I had the good fortune to be raised in a comfortable family. I went to the University of Virginia, first, with the idea of graduating; of becoming a pillar of society; a gentleman farmer. I changed my mind, however, and went to medical school."

She turned her head to him. "You're a doctor?"

"No," he said. "I learned a little of medicine. I also learned something of engineering. For a few years I was what is known as a professional student. I went to several colleges. I was always studying different fields to find out what I really wanted to be."

"What did you decide on?"

"Nothing."

"Nothing?"

"Nothing. I am a gentleman drifter. My family in Virginia provides me with my wants. They'd rather not see me about, so to speak. I am what the English call a remittance man."

"I do not believe you, *señor.*"

He shrugged. "Why not? Our place in Virginia is large. We grow many crops, principally peanuts to feed our razorback hogs. On our place we make the most delicious hams in the world. I have a married sister. She and her husband are in the business of selling our hams. Since I have little interest in commerce, they would rather I not be around doing nothing while they work hard. They pay me to stay away."

"Why did you come to Deming?"

"Why not? I have been in New Mexico for several months. I find it a fascinating place. I have stopped in Taos, Santa Fe, Albuquerque, Las Vegas, Socorro, Magdalena, Lincoln, Alamogordo, Las Cruces—you name it. I visit a place and stay as long as I like. When I tire of it, I move on to another. As I said, I'm a gentleman drifter."

"You have also been in Mexico?"

"For a long time, yes. Also in Central and South America, Europe, Asia, and Africa. You see, I get around."

"And Deming?"

"One of the places I had not visited in New Mexico."

"Do you plan to stay long?"

"Who knows?" he asked. "I haven't gotten tired of it yet."

"Even with people shooting at you?"

"That," he said quietly, "I cannot help. I will find out someday who did it and why."

"Unless they kill you first."

He laughed. "That is a possibility, too."

They rode a half mile in silence. "Señor Withers," she said abruptly, "you realize, of course, that I do not believe you, what you have told me of yourself."

"I am sorry, Señorita Gutiérrez."

"I am sure I know why you are here in this part of the country."

"I would be happy to hear your explanation, *señorita.*"

She bit her lip. "Perhaps I have said enough already."

"Enough of what, *señorita?*"

She shook her head. "Please. I have said too much."

"I'm not sure I understand you, *señorita.*"

"I—I—," she started to say.

"Yes?"

"There is a man here. He is in Deming. I have seen him."

"And—?"

"I have seen him before—in Mexico."

"So—?"

"He was a Villista."

"Pancho Villa?"

"Not the general. One of his men. I told you, I had seen him before. In San Luis Potosí."

"Where is he now?"

"I do not know. I saw him in Deming a few days ago, riding out of town. He passed very close to me, but did not see me. It gave me a cold feeling to know he had been so near me. He is a cruel man who would stop at nothing, even killing if he felt like it."

"Do you know his name?"

"I have heard him called El Gallo, 'The Rooster.' "

"El Gallo?"

"Yes, he was one of General Villa's Dorados, his personal bodyguard of picked men."

"I have heard of Villa, of course, and also of his Dorados. Are you sure?"

"I am sure."

Dick Little took a long look at the Three Sisters simmering in the distant haze. His face was impassive. "Would this man be hunting me?"

"I do not know, Señor Withers."

"But why?"

"Perhaps, *señor,* you could tell me. I do not believe the story you

have told me. You are much more than you appear to be. I believe you
are not, as you say, a gentleman drifter. You are in Deming for a purpose. You and others?"

"What others?"

"It is only a feeling." She shrugged. "In the past few weeks I have
felt an atmosphere of danger. I feel as if I am living in the center of it. I
do not know what it is, but I am afraid."

"Why should you be afraid?"

She looked at him steadily. "I am very sensitive to feelings, Señor
Withers. I feel you are not what you say you are. I feel there is something in this part of the country which is evil; and when an evil man
appears, my feelings are strengthened. What it is, I do not know. Do
you understand me?"

"Yes," Dick Little said slowly, "I think I understand. Shall we turn
back?"

She nodded assent. Little cast another look toward the Three Sisters.
He turned his horse around just as she did hers. They spurred to a faster
pace, returning to O'Conner's stable with scarcely a word between them
during the entire ride back.

Walking from the stable toward the hotel, Dick Little thought about
his casual meeting with the lovely and mysterious Señorita Gutiérrez.
Was the encounter accidental, or had she ridden out especially to meet
him? Well, he hadn't revealed much to her that wasn't the truth: perhaps a slightly bent truth. Anyway, she was, indeed, interesting. And
she certainly was very lovely. Lovelier and more exciting than the ma-
jority of women he had met during his life of roaming about the world.

He shrugged as he lit a cigarette.

He had a sneaking feeling he'd better keep a sharp eye on her.

Her being there today, and the other time, meeting him almost as if
she had been waiting for him to appear.

He inhaled and felt as if he had been dealt a pat hand by a professional gambler.

"Cynic," he said aloud to himself.

Still, there was that slight uneasy feeling.

The young clerk at the hotel handed Dick Little a crumpled envelope
as he came up to the desk. On the face of it was written in a penciled
scrawl the one name *Withers.*

"Who's this from, Charlie?" Little asked.

"A stove-up old cowboy came in this morning right after you left. He asked if I had a man here who was tall and skinny. I told him yes, and he asked your name. I said Withers. He asked for a sheet of paper and an envelope and copied your name on the envelope. Then he went over to that lobby table and wrote you a note. Took him over half an hour. When he finished, he handed it to me and left."

"Know who he was?"

The clerk shook his head. "I've seen him around once or twice, but I don't know who he is."

"Thanks, Charlie," Little said.

He went to his room, opened the envelope and, stretching out on the bed, translated it from the crude scrawl.

deer dik, it read, *plese com too see me at st ranch i ned too talk too u. i seen u rid out but u didno see me. i ned help an u can giv it too me. i loked all over town fer u i fond u. ples com as son as u can. i wil be watin fer u. ure ol pal billy thomas.*

Billy Thomas? Dick Little thought. Where in hell did I meet a Billy Thomas? He sighed deeply. The name had struck a bell, but the tone was too soft.

He picked up the phone. Charlie answered. "Do you know of an S T Ranch near here?"

"Yes, sir," Charlie answered. "It's out near Cooke's Peak. Take the road along the tracks to Florida, the watering tank; turn left toward the peak and follow along about three miles. You'll see a mailbox on the turnoff road leading to the ranch house."

"Thanks," Dick said, hanging up the phone.

He stretched out again. In a moment he was on his feet, striding toward his trunk. He reached into his pocket, taking from it a piece of metal. Placing it against the trunk, he moved it slightly, then opened the lid. Reaching in he took out a soft chamois bag. He opened it over the bed. A stream of gold coins clinked merrily on the coverlet. Quickly, Dick Little counted out a handful, replacing the rest in the bag, and the bag in the trunk. He closed the lid, moved the piece of metal, putting it back in his pocket.

Downstairs, in the lobby, he picked up a copy of the weekly *Deming Graphic.* Riffling through the pages, he found the advertisement he was looking for: *Studebaker Big Six, Seven Passengers, 126-Inch Wheelbase, 60 Horsepower, Cloth Top, $1,750, J.S. Kerr, Agent.* He'd passed the place earlier on one of his walks about town. It wouldn't be hard to find again.

Leaving the hotel, he went to the Studebaker salesroom, looked up Mr. Kerr, and dickered. In a short while fifty-dollar gold pieces changed hands; there was a flurry of paper signing. Dick Little hadn't paid any seventeen hundred and fifty dollars for the automobile, nor was Mr. Kerr dissatisfied with the money he'd received. It didn't take long to fill the tank with gasoline and load into the backseat extra metal containers, also filled. The oil was checked. The motor barked into life. Dick Little backed the automobile through the shop. He was pleased with the cloth top, keeping the hot sun off his head.

He raced the engine, tried the clutch and brake pedals, ran the stick shift through its paces. He took off down the street, cautiously at first, then faster and faster as he fed gasoline to the engine. He picked up the way he had ridden down the day before. Soon he was bouncing down the road.

As he was driving along, humming to himself, he suddenly remembered who Billy Thomas was.

THE RANCH HOUSE was of a wooden-brick construction, one story with a peaked red roof. A covered porch ran across the front of the building. It was painted white, glaring in the summer sun. Near the house were the other buildings of the ranch: the barn, bunkhouse, blacksmith shop, corrals, all of naturally weathered wood. Strong pole fences enclosed the working areas. Dick Little drove up to the gate of the white fence surrounding the house. He shut off the motor and sat for a moment looking around to orient himself. There was not a tree in sight although there were bushes and green vines in the yard, clinging to the fence.

He got out of the automobile, standing beside it, stretching his legs. The front door of the house opened. A young woman crossed the porch, came down the three steps and along the walk leading to the gate. Little watched her with interest. She was not tall, but she was well formed. She had an oval, pretty face, a sensuous mouth, a determined chin. She wore a checkered apron dress of gingham which came down to her mid-calf and was tied in back with a large bow. Her figure was very apparent beneath it. Her blond hair was pulled back and tied with a ribbon. Her eyes were green. Dick Little took off his hat, waiting for her to near the gate.

"Can I help you?" she asked pleasantly.

"Good afternoon," Dick said. "Is this the S T Ranch?"

"Yes, it is."

"My name is Richard Withers. I was wondering whether you might have an old friend of mine working here: Billy Thomas?"

"Yes, Billy works here," she answered politely. "But right now he's out on the range somewhere. He won't be in until suppertime."

"That will be several hours yet," he mused. "Do you think I could drive my automobile out to where he is?"

The young lady smiled. "I don't think so. The land at the foot of the mountains is very rough. It's really horse country."

"I don't suppose I could borrow a horse?"

The young lady gave him a cool appraising look. "What did you say your name was?"

"Richard Withers."

She smiled suddenly. "I'm Stella Townsend. My father is the owner of the S T. He isn't here right now, but I think he'd approve of your request."

"Thank you, Miss Townsend."

"You'll find a horse in the barn. There'll be a saddle or two around you can choose from. You're familiar with horses, of course?"

"I've ridden them all my life, Miss Townsend. I certainly appreciate your generosity."

"I'm glad to be of service."

"Where would I find Billy?"

"He's riding fence today, over there." She pointed in the general direction of Cooke's Peak. "He shouldn't be too hard to find."

"I thank you again."

She smiled at him. "When you get back my father will most probably have returned by then. We have so few visitors out here I'm sure he'll be pleased to meet you."

"Thank you, I'll do that," Little replied.

She turned and walked back to the house. He heard the screech of the screen door closing behind her. He put his hat back on as he headed for the barn.

The horse he chose was not up to the one he rented from O'Conner, but it was the best available. It did not take him long to saddle up and ride out of the corral toward the peak. As the horse and rider covered the ground they scared up into sudden activity several rabbits, kangaroo rats, lizards and, once, a covey of quail. The horse shied at times, but Dick calmed him down with a firm hand on the reins.

After four miles of riding he came to a three-strand barbed wire fence. Little stopped the horse and stood in the stirrups, turning his body to look both ways down the fence. In the distance, to his left, he made out the moving dot of what could be a man on horseback. He headed his animal in that direction.

In time the other rider's shape grew more distinct. As he drew closer, Little could make out the figure of the man clearly.

Billy Thomas was indeed a stove-up cowboy: a bantam of a man, lean and hard in body, his face and hands burned brown by the sun. His face was deeply wrinkled beneath his battered Stetson. He hadn't shaved in several days; his beard covered his chin and jowls with wiry gray stubble. He wore faded Levis and a disreputable shirt. About his neck was tied a red, not very clean, bandana. His boots were old, run-down at the heels, almost as cracked and rough as the skin on Billy's gnarled hands.

Dick Little rode up to him. "Howdy, Billy," he said, offering his hand in greeting. "Long time no see."

"Long time, Tiny," Billy snorted, taking Little's hand.

"I got your note."

Billy smiled, showing ragged tobacco-stained teeth. "She-it!" he said. "You're hard to find."

"But you found me."

"Hell, yes, I did!"

The two men dismounted, ground-reining their horses. They hunkered down on their heels. Dick Little took out papers and Bull Durham. He handed the makings to Billy. In spite of his clumsy-looking hands, the old cowboy rolled his cigarette with astonishing speed. He handed the makings back as he took a wooden match from the band of his dirty Stetson, flicking fire onto it with a broken fingernail.

"I done seen you with m' glasses," he said. "I seen you ridin' yestiddy an' when I throwed m' glasses on ya I recognized who ya was. I rode in town this mawnin' ta see if I could catch ya."

"I got your note," Little said again.

"I ain't up ta writin' much."

The two men smoked in silence.

"Ya still writin' fer them newspapers?" Billy asked suddenly.

"Still writing."

"Ya changed ya name?"

"Just here."

"Why?" Billy was watching him sharply from under the brim of his battered hat.

"Didn't want to be recognized."

Billy nodded sagely. "Ya come lookin' fer th' money?"

Little hesitated a long time. "What money?" he asked.

"She-it! Ya done come to Deming an' ain't lookin' fer th' money?"

Little shook his head. "I've heard of it. I thought it might make a good yarn. After all, it's been eight years since the story started."

"There's some others lookin' fer it," Billy said softly.

"Who?"

"She-it!" he said. "Me fer one!"

"You believe in the story?"

"Damned right I do! I know it's hereabouts. Somewheres." He looked off in the distance toward the Floridas. "I know it's here."

"What makes you so certain?"

Billy shifted his position. "I got m' reasons, that's all."

Little broke the silence. "Seen Gunner?"

Billy looked at him, startled. "How d'ya know?"

Little shrugged. "Somebody dropped his name. Seen him?"

"She-it! Yes! Damned son of a bitch! I seen him. Everytime I goes inta his joint he tries ta get m' drunk. She-it! He ain't done it yet."

"You haven't changed so much, Billy, that you're against getting drunk, have you?"

The old cowboy laughed. "Not soz ya noticed. Gunner thinks I got somethin' he wants."

"What?"

"Ya ain't gonna spread it aroun' iffen I tell ya, are ya?"

"Scout's honor."

"She-it! Tiny, he thinks I gotta piece of paper he wants."

"Like what?"

"Like I ain't got it." Billy flicked the stub of his cigarette away after carefully pinching out the spark. Little handed him the makings again. "Gunner's got a piece of a map. He done tole me he's got it. Sez it can tell where some money's buried."

"What sort of a map?"

Billy shook his head. "She-it! Ya think that son of a bitch would show it ta me? In a pig's ass he will! Not ta me." He paused, then said softly, "Mebbe I'll tell ya, mebbe not. Ya helped m'out of a real tight spot one time. I ain't fergettin' nothin'."

"That was a long time ago in another world."

"I ain't fergettin'."

"I have."

"I ain't."

The horses cropped grass. "You said you needed help."

"She-it! Yes!"

"What is it?"

"She-it," Billy said softly. He was embarrassed. "Ya remember th' hoss turd who called hisself 'The Rooster'?"

"I remember him well."

"He's lookin' fer me."

"How do you know?"

"I seen him in town. I know he's lookin' fer me."

"Why?"

"Goddamn it! Didn't he almos' had me killed onest?"

Little nodded. "He did."

"She-it! Iffen ya hadn't stopped him that day heeda done it sure as bull's got balls."

"All I did was talk to him."

"An' got me from out in front of a firin' squad. She-it! I still sweat 'bout that."

"So that was years ago. Why would he be hunting you now? And here, of all places?"

Billy Thomas didn't answer. "I jest wanted ya ta know. He don't like ya much neither."

Dick Little smiled. "Just one of my many former friends," he said. "Okay, Billy," he continued, "I'll keep an eye out for him." He rose to his feet. "Anything else?"

"She-it, no!"

They gathered the reins of their horses and mounted. "Nice seeing you again, Billy. If you need me just yell."

"Thanks, Tiny. I ain't gonna spill ya go-by. Say—"

"Yes?"

The old cowboy grinned. "Read one of ya books onest. Took m' three goddamned months ta finish th' damn thing. Thought I owed ya that much."

"And—?"

"She-it! I liked it." With a wave of his hand and a grin, Billy turned his horse and rode off along the fence.

Richard Henry Little watched his friend ride away. He smiled to himself. His go-by. He hadn't heard that word in years. So what name was he going by now? Withers, of course. His mother's maiden name.

As he rode slowly back toward the S T ranch house he thought of

Billy Thomas and the event which had brought them together those many years ago.

Billy was one of those many Anglos who had crossed the border into Mexico seeking adventure and fortune in the Revolution. Some of the fortune hunters were highly skilled in the arts of warfare; Sam Dreben, for instance. Some really didn't know what they were getting into; Billy Thomas, for one. For him the war was romantic with the good chance of picking up some loot. But he had crossed tempers with El Gallo. Poor Billy, not knowing much Spanish, found himself up against the wall in front of a firing squad. If it hadn't been for some fast talking by Dick Little, plus the threat he would personally dehorn The Rooster, plus the biggest threat of all—reporting to General Villa the incident, with the promise it would be publicized worldwide—Billy Thomas would have been shot and his bullet-riddled body rolled into some hole in the ground for a nameless grave.

It took a few solid weeks of doing, but Dick had finally persuaded Billy to return to the States; that wars and revolutions were not his brand of booze, so to speak. Billy had finally seen the light. He'd taken off, crossing the border at Juárez, dropping out of Dick Little's life— until now.

Then there were the cowboy's insinuations of a map which could lead to a lot of money. There had been stories persisting for years that Pancho Villa had buried a treasure somewhere in New Mexico. According to the legends, he had slipped it into the United States and had buried it somewhere to the north, many miles into the state. No one seemed sure when it was buried, or its general location, just that it had been buried. The usual guessable amount was never mentioned, nor where it came from. In short, Pancho Villa's treasure was pure myth.

On the other hand, Little thought, there were too many funny things going on in Deming to turn aside the rumors of a treasure buried nearby. El Gallo, for one. Why was he around? Billy's hints? Gunner being nearby? Señorita Gutiérrez? Should he include her in his thoughts? Then, of course, there was his own presence, his own mysterious activities. Little smiled to himself. Surely his actions alone were enough to raise the suspicions of anyone.

He came in sight of the S T ranch house. Spurring his horse to a canter he came upon the corral in short order. He unsaddled the horse in the barn, rubbed it down, giving it some grain before walking to the house. He was met at the gate by Stella Townsend. "My father's home," she said smiling. "He wants to meet you."

In the cool of the parlor the two men met. They'd shaken hands, appraising each other. Townsend was almost as tall as Little. Gray-haired, gray-eyed, gray-mustached, with broad shoulders and a slender waist. His dark shirt and tight pants fitted him perfectly. Little figured him to be in his late fifties or early sixties. His eyes were keen, his skin darkened by the sun and weather of an active outdoor life. When he spoke, his voice was soft, almost gentle. "Nice to see you, Mr. Withers. Been long in this area?"

"About six days, Mr. Townsend."

"How do you like us?"

"Interesting."

Townsend turned to his daughter. "Stella," he said, "make us a pitcher of lemonade. I'm sure Mr. Withers would like a glass or two after his ride."

"Thank you, sir, I would."

Stella left the room for the kitchen.

"Sit down, Mr. Little," Townsend said.

Dick Little was about to fold himself into a chair when he hesitated. He looked at his host who was smiling at him. He sighed. He seated himself, making himself comfortable. "Where did you know me before?" he asked.

Townsend took a chair himself, facing the tall man. He filled a pipe from a canister on the table beside him.

"In Mexico City," Townsend answered. "Richard Henry Little," he continued, "war correspondent for the New York *Times* and Associated Press. You were there when Zapata and Villa took the city. I read all of your dispatches. I saw you many times—from a distance." Townsend smiled. "You would have a difficult time trying to hide yourself."

Dick Little laughed. "I suppose so," he said. "What were you doing in Mexico then, if I may ask? They were very difficult times. Especially for a gringo."

"I was in business there," Townsend answered. "I'd spent many years below the border doing one thing or another. At that time I was representing several American firms. As you say, they were difficult times. You were with Villa then, weren't you?"

"I was with everybody, Mr. Townsend. I covered Mexico from one end to the other. It was my job."

Townsend struck a wooden match under the table. He lit his pipe, sending up clouds of smoke toward the ceiling. "About the only American correspondent I didn't meet was you. Funny. I had drinks with the others. Let's see," he mused, "John Roberts, Ed Behr, Floyd Gibbons, Norm Walker, and the others. Nice people." He paused, thinking of old times.

Dick Little rolled a cigarette and lighted it. He, too, gave thoughts to the old days, to his associates of the press, remembering each clearly. "You have a nice ranch here," he said after a while, making conversation.

"Yes. I've had it for years. Even before I went to Mexico. My wife and I bought the place about '90; Stella was born here in 1900. My wife took care of the place while I made money in Mexico. She died five years ago. Stella and I have been running it ever since. I've left Mexico behind me."

"What sort of firms did you represent down there, if I may ask?"

"Railroads principally. I was property manager for several of the American companies building railroads in Mexico."

Thoughts crossed Dick Little's mind. "You were there under Díaz?"

"Yes."

Porfirio Díaz, the dictator of Mexico, had been very partial to foreign companies, especially those from the United States, gaining concessions, looting the country of its wealth. Railroads, land companies, mining companies, cattle companies, oil companies—any type of large enterprise was welcome to establish itself as long as it was respectable on the stock exchanges and had plenty of money behind it. They had carte blanche in their operations: their profits leaving the country to swell the coffers of the industrialists who owned the controlling stocks. Díaz had been openhanded with those foreigners. He preferred dealing closer with them than with his own people who lived in abject poverty and peonage. Except, of course, for the very rich.

The railroads had been built slowly across the rugged face of Mexico. The American companies demanded exorbitant sums from the government for each mile of track laid. They wrung from the government thousands of acres of land, establishing cattle ranches, developing mining properties, and so on, with hardly any protest from the Mexicans. The people had no way of protesting until Francisco Madero was elected president. Díaz went into exile to die in Paris. Townsend must have been a very important cog in the railroads' operations.

"Did you find Billy Thomas?" Townsend asked.

"Oh yes. We had a long chat."

"You knew him before, of course?"

"We ran across each other during the Revolution. I hadn't seen him since then."

"A good man to have working for us," Townsend remarked.

Dick Little agreed.

"I understand," Townsend continued, "that you have been assaulted since you've been here?"

Little shrugged. "Someone took a shot at me. As you can see, they missed."

Townsend sighed. "Strange things have been going on around in this area lately. I can't figure it out."

"Strange things? Like what?"

Townsend looked at Dick Little sharply. "Your being shot at, for one thing. Why would anyone want to do that? Then, we've been having strange people climbing our peak lately."

"Cooke's Peak?"

"Yes."

"What for?"

"Gold, perhaps. There are several old mines on the peak. There's an old ghost town up there called Cooke's Camp. It was abandoned when the gold petered out. But I don't think these recent people were prospectors."

"How do you know?"

Townsend laughed. "They sneak in at night, climb about the peak for a day or two, then sneak out at night. We never see them really. Once in a while, through my glasses, I've caught a glimpse of someone moving around. We've found evidence of small camps in hidden places: tin cans, remains of a fire, things like that. But nothing definite as to what they're looking for. I've seen no place where anyone has taken samples. These mysterious wraiths just seem to vanish into thin air." Townsend tapped his pipe on the edge of an ashtray. "As long as they do not steal my cattle or damage my property, I don't worry too much. Once they start doing harm, my men and I will go armed."

Little nodded. "It is a strange situation, sir."

Stella entered the room carrying a tray with glasses and a tall pitcher of cold lemonade.

She poured three glasses, giving her father and Dick Little one each. She sat in a chair near the pitcher, sipping from her glass.

"This hits the spot," Little said with a broad smile. "My thanks to you, Miss Townsend."

She made a mock bow with her head. "You are welcome, kind sir."

They sipped in silence for a while. "What were you two talking about so seriously when I came in?" Stella asked. "You both looked like you were discussing the end of the world."

"Mr. Withers and I were talking about Mexico," Townsend told his daughter. "It seems we were both in the same place at the same time on several occasions."

"Didn't you meet?"

"Unfortunately not, Miss Townsend," Dick interjected. "Your father was in business there and I—I was doing something else. You might say, I was just an observer."

She laughed. "It must have been very exciting during those times."

Little shook his head. "If you consider sudden death, dirt, poor food, poor accommodations, poor everything, exciting, then, I guess, it was. I didn't look upon it as being so."

"They were not places a thirteen- or fourteen-year-old girl ought to be," Townsend interjected seriously. "As Mr. Withers says, they were extremely hard and dangerous times."

A clock on the mantelpiece chimed. "I'm afraid I must go," Dick Little said, rising, placing his empty glass on the tray. "I want to be back in town before dark."

The Townsends invited him to stay for supper, but he politely declined. They walked him to his automobile, examining it, commenting on its powers, its newness, and its potential in ranching country. Once Dick was seated behind the wheel, Townsend extended his hand. "Come back soon," he said.

Taking it, Little said, "Don't worry, I will." He smiled at Stella. "I think I have good reason to." She blushed.

"My name's Sam," Townsend said. "Call her Stella. We're not very formal out here."

"Thanks, I will, Sam," Little smiled. He started the car, putting it in gear. He waved at them as the car began to move.

"Goodbye, Mr. Withers," he heard Stella call. "We'll be expecting you soon."

At the top of a rise just outside the ranch gate he leaned out of the car and looked back. The Townsends were climbing the porch steps, the father's arm around the slim waist of his pretty daughter.

"I've put a full bottle of Bourbon in your room, Mr. Withers," the hotel clerk said, handing him his key.

"Thanks, Charlie," he answered absently.

The clerk hesitated. "Gunny called you earlier," he said.

"This is my day," Little murmured. "What did he want?"

"He asked if you'd come to see him as soon as you can."

"I guess so. Where is his place?"

"The pool hall down on Main Street. You can't miss it."

"I'll go now," Little said, handing back the key. He walked out of the hotel.

Gunner Marks, twisted body, booming voice, greeted Dick Little as he entered the back room of the pool hall. "Tiny! You long-legged son of a bitch! Jesus, it's good to see you again!" He hurled himself on the tall man, enveloping him in a bear hug. Dick Little returned the *abrazo*.

"You're a sight for sore eyes, too, you old bastard! How've you been, Gunner?"

"For Christ's sake, can't you see? Come in! Come in! Come in! Sit at this table here. What'll you have? Beer? Tequila? Or what we mix locally?"

"What's the local stuff?"

"We get one hundred and eighty proof from Mexico for eleven simoleons for a twenty-five liter can. I have to cut it with grapefruit juice."

Little laughed. "Good God, no!"

"Okay, okay, okay! I've got some cold Mex beer. How about it?"

"Sounds good."

Gunner shuffled off behind the small bar. Little couldn't help but think of the man years ago when they'd first met. "The Gunner" they'd called him. A stocky, ramrod straight bull of a man, with a voice like a foghorn. He'd come straight out of Central America into Villa's Division of the North with a knowledge of artillery surpassed only by that of Felipe Angeles. Now Gunner was crippled, limping, body twisted, his face pain-lined. He was a shadow of his former self in all but his bull voice. Little felt a bit of himself dying as he watched his old friend bringing several bottles and two glasses over to the table, his onetime-white bar apron hiding his legs.

"I knew you'd be here. I knew it!" Gunner said, pouring. "Goddamn, I said to myself, I know that skinny old bastard will come." He smiled delightedly. Raising their glasses they clinked them, then drank deeply, exhaling deep sighs of contentment. Gunner reached across the table, putting his hand on Dick's arm. "I saw you at your hotel window. That's why I called you today. Say, remember the time in—. Shit, you don't want to talk about the past. What are you up to?"

"Same old stuff, Gunner. Writing for the newspapers. So that was *you* on the street?"

"Hell yes. Didn't want to disturb you." He paused. "You wrote some books, didn't you?"

"Some."

"That's good. That's good. You're after the treasure, too, ain't you?" Little looked innocent.

"Don't gimme that horseshit, Tiny. I'm after it, too. Old Billy Thomas is after it. There are a few more after it. Gallo's in town. I'll bet my bottom dollar he's in the picture somehow."

"You've seen Billy?"

The Gunner grinned. "He comes in once in a while. I try to get him drunk. He won't buy."

"What's Billy got that you want, Gunner?"

A sly smile crossed The Gunner's face, his eyes narrowed. "There were eight pieces, Tiny. I've got one. I've got one of the eight. Hell, it ain't doin' me no good. I can't make ass or elbow from it. How many you got?"

Little smiled and poured more beer into his glass. "Eight pieces of what?" he asked calmly.

"Fierro's map, you son of a bitch! Fierro's map!"

"That old story."

The Gunner hitched his chair around closer to Little's. "It ain't an old story. It ain't! For Christ's sake, Tiny! I was there when Villa tore the son of a bitch up and passed the pieces around. Goddamn it! I know there was a map!" He leaned closer. "Look, Tiny: you and me, we've been through the ass of the world more'n once. Name the country: China, Cuba, Nicaragua, San Salvador, Guatemala, Mexico, Panama, Chile, Bolivia—shit, we've fought in every one of them goddamned places. You wrote stories about them, and books; but, me, I fought my ass off in them places. Remember the time Lee Christmas took Tegucigalpa? Hell, I was his police chief. You, you bastard, wrote all them stories about me and him. We had a hell of a time. Remember?"

"I remember," Little said, a far-off look in his eyes. "I remember, Gunner."

"So I ain't shittin' an old shitter. I seen the map. I know it's around."

"I saw Billy this afternoon, Gunner," Little said.

"Yeah?"

"He said you had a piece of the map."

"That's just it, Tiny," The Gunner said eagerly. "I do have a piece. I *do* have a piece."

"Can I see it?"

"Sure you can. Hell yes, you can! I'll get it." Gunner limped across the room to the bar. He rummaged around back of it, returning to the table with a wallet in his hand. Seating himself, he opened the wallet, taking out a soiled and wrinkled rectangular piece of paper. He placed it slowly on the tabletop, then palmed his hand over it. "I'm trusting you, Tiny. Goddamn, I'm trusting you!"

"All right, Gunner. I'll be fair, you know that."

"Hell yes, I know it." He raised his hand.

Dick Little bent over the piece of paper. He stared at it intently for a few seconds. Blessed, or cursed, with a photographic memory, and total recall, he burned the lines and letters of that piece of paper forever in his mind.

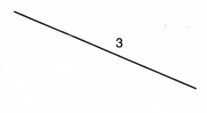

T R O

"Okay, Gunner," he said, straightening up. "What do you make of it?"

The Gunner shook his head. "Not a goddamned thing. Not a thing."

"Tell me about it."

The Gunner went to the bar again, returning with a bottle of tequila and a glass. He sat down, poured himself a glass full of the clear liquid and drank half of it rapidly. He wiped his mouth on his sleeve. "I gotta get some of this in me before I can loosen up," he explained. He drank the rest of the glass of liquor, shuddered, poured another glass full. "Tiny, promise me a good share? Promise?"

"I promise. Provided we find it. Whatever it is."

"That's good enough for me," The Gunner said. "Villa was in Juárez. He'd had the piss beaten out of him at Celaya and León because he wouldn't take the advice of Felipe Angeles. You know about that?"

Little nodded. "I know."

The Gunner continued. "We were at Villa's headquarters having supper. There was the general himself, Felipe Angeles, Fierro, a young captain named Galinda, myself, and three others. Villa never drank, but he was in a good mood. You know how those damned Indians are: up one minute, down the next. Old Pancho was up, way up. He got to talking about how he was going to fight to the finish, an', in the next breath, he was saying he was fixed for life when the Revolution was over. He'd smile at Fierro and Fierro would smile back. Anyway, Pancho got really wound up. He took this piece a' paper out of his pocket, unfolded it an' tore the damned thing in eight pieces and passed them around, handing one to each of us. 'This is for all of us afterwards,' he said over and over. 'We'll get together and be rich!' Anyway, we never did get together again. Fierro drowned; I got blasted open; Angeles was executed; Galinda disappeared; the other three scattered an' old Pancho went into retirement near Parral. That's the story of th' map."

"What makes you think it's in Deming?"

"Because Fierro was up around here before he died. That's no goddamned secret. No secret!"

"Good point. What else?"

"I think Billy has a piece of it."

"Old Billy?"

"As sure as shootin'!"

"What makes you think so?"

"Say it's a hunch, Tiny. I've been trying to get a look at it, but he's cagey. He won't get drunk."

"What about El Gallo?"

"That son of a bitch!" The Gunner spat on the floor. "I hope he comes around. I'll rip that bastard's guts out and throw them in his face!"

Little smiled. "Sounds as if you don't like him very much."

"I'd like to kill the son of a whore!" He drank off his glassful of tequila.

The drink mellowed him. The Gunner began to talk about himself. After that night in Juárez, he had been almost blown apart by an artillery shell. He was run across the border by friends into the army hospital at Fort Bliss where he had fought off death for weeks. The doctors and nurses saved his life, overlooking the fact he was wounded in Mexico, admitting him as an old Army Regular.

Recovering, but horribly disfigured, he wandered about the States

doing anything he could for a living. Three years of that was enough.
He began to think of his piece of the map. He began to believe the
stories of Fierro being around Deming at one time. So he settled in
Deming, taking over the pool hall and bar until Prohibition. He opened
his back room as a bar, paying off the police, they not bothering him as
long as his place was not a center of trouble. Sometimes he would take
off and go out into the mountains hoping to strike it rich, but without
success. His was a hard life. He was going to bed.

Picking up his piece of the map carefully, putting it slowly back into
his wallet, The Gunner staggered off to another back room. Dick Little
finished the last bottle of beer and left.

Good Lord! Little thought on the way back to the hotel, has time
flown by that fast? All of those banana republics of Central America,
plus South America, plus Mexico: how many wars had he seen? Small
wars, to be sure, but men were killed just as dead as in big ones. The
only difference was the terrain and the language. Mexico was the blood-
iest. Neither side believed in keeping prisoners: prisoners were for killing. It was easier to shoot or hang those *pobrecitos* than it was to keep
and feed them.

When had it all started? He was right in the autobiography he had
spun for the Señorita Gutiérrez, but only up to a point. He had found
he liked to travel; he realized he could also write a clean sentence; so, he
had started writing for a small paper, graduating to larger ones, then on
to the *Times* and AP. The writing was not as hard for him as were the
subjects he wrote about: the wars, the eternal wars south of the border
and elsewhere in the world. It was his specialty. He was damned good at
it.

Where the hell had he met The Gunner? Ex-U.S. Army turned soldier
of fortune. One of the best with artillery; he had an instinct with a
cannon some men had with a pistol, or Fierro had with killing. That's it:
Costa Rica. Years, and years, and years ago when they were both still
young; when both still looked upon life as a great adventure. He'd
written books about those times; he'd sent dispatches, from the various
fronts, which overflowed with the golden words of youth and high spirits. Good Lord! His life had been the reality of a Douglas Fairbanks!

The Gunner had been a good friend all those years. They had met
occasionally in strange places. They marched side by side, often sharing
the same tent; more likely the same bottle, or the same *chiquita*. The
Gunner's talents were always in demand, especially from such filibusters

as Lee Christmas, or earlier, William Walker. Then Mexico. The Revolution had drawn soldiers of fortune from all over the world. Villa had himself one company made up of gringos only. Tracy Richardson was one of his captains. Sam Dreben was always where the fighting was the thickest and best. Poor Sam. Dying of syphilis in an El Paso hospital, sent before his time into the nether world by a wrong injection given him by a nurse. Where was Tracy now? Or Dynamite Dick? Or the hundreds of others, the good ones like The Gunner, or the little ones like Billy Thomas? Oscar Creighton had been killed early, at Tierra Blanca. His body had been taken to El Paso to be shipped for burial in his hometown of Boston. He recalled Oscar well.

War was so goddamned useless. Nevertheless, it was necessary to vainglorious bastards like Carranza. Villa had spent a lifetime at war: it was all he had known. Now he was a gentleman farmer, bought off by the government to be set out to pasture for the rest of his days. He had risen so far and had fallen into obscurity so quickly.

Little missed the BIG war in Europe, but he'd seen Celaya after Villa's defeat. At one time he'd given thought to enlisting for the fighting in France, but he realized he was no longer a romantic, that he could see, feel, and smell death just as well in Mexico. It was all the same no matter where soldiers were killed, or how.

Was The Gunner's story of the map really true? Why not? It was not improbable he was at Villa's headquarters for that supper; after all, he was a captain with Felipe Angeles. Even if he had not been there, his piece of the map was authentic. That much Little knew: he'd seen others; he had one; and, above all, he had heard from too many sources the story of the map, of Fierro's trip to Deming, of the buried treasure, to disclaim it as just another story without validity.

How many legends were there in New Mexico of buried treasure? Too many to his liking. Most of them based on the same premise: the treasure-ladened burro train of the priests escaping from the Indian revolt of 1680. They had driven the burros into a large cave, then had collapsed the entrance. Of course, only one priest escaped alive to draw a map while on his deathbed. The next holder of the map searched for years unsuccessfully, then passed it on to another as he was dying. And so on down the line. For one excuse or another, no holder of the map had found the cave. And so, the Treasure of the Padres was lost forever except for an aging map being passed from hand to hand, always at the demise of the holder.

And where had all this gold come from in the first place? The padres were not that rich, nor had New Mexico produced much gold for them. True, there were mines and smelters, crudely built and operated, but the wealth of the Seven Cities of Cíbola, the legendary Cities of Gold, was merely a legend. The Treasure of the Padres never existed. But, then, treasure hunters never gave up. No matter the impossibilities of the existence of such a hoard of gold, the treasure hunter would always believe. No matter the inconsistencies of maps or stories regarding lost loot, the treasure hunter would always have an explanation to fit his belief. And he *knew* it existed. And he *knew* he had the only correct information. And he *knew* he would be the only one to rightly interpret the signs. And he *knew* he would be the only one to find it after centuries of burial. And he *knew* he would be successful. The only thing the treasure hunter didn't *know* was his own ignorance.

Did The Gunner trust him as completely as he said he did? Probably. In view of past experiences, why not? One piece of the map would not lead anyone to a treasure. A line, a three, three letters spelling T-R-O were not sufficient clues to point in any definite direction. The only reason the area might be accurate was due to the presence at one time of Fierro. And that was merely rumor. But it was strong enough to attract The Gunner, Billy Thomas, perhaps El Gallo, certainly himself, and possibly others. And do not discount Sam Townsend's story of the wraiths of Cooke's Peak. Somebody, perhaps many, were looking for the treasure.

The past, the Revolution, The Gunner, the map, were beginning to confuse in his mind. He'd had a long day; he'd traveled many miles and had concentrated for many hours. His brain was weary. He was physically tired.

The bed in his room was inviting. Removing his boots, he poured a shot of Bourbon into a tumbler, added cold water from the tap, and sipped. He sat on the edge of the bed, his body sagging. Placing the glass on the night table he rolled back onto the covers; his last conscious thought was to lift his feet from the floor and stretch out. Crosswise on the bed.

THE RINGING PHONE awakened him. He rolled off the bed, standing up in his stocking feet. He ran his fingers through unruly hair, reaching for the phone. He put the receiver to his ear. "Yes?" he asked.

"Good morning, Señor Withers," the cheery voice of Señorita Gutiérrez greeted him.

He glanced at the shaded windows, noting the strong sunlight trying to penetrate. "Good morning, Señorita Gutiérrez," he answered. "To what do I owe the pleasure of your call?"

She gave a throaty laugh. "I was hoping," she said, "to appeal to your gallantry, to ask you for a favor."

"I'd be delighted if I could be of service to you."

"I understand," she said, "you are planning a trip to Columbus. I was wondering if you are going today, and if you'd be so kind as to take me in your new automobile?"

News certainly travels fast, he thought. "I'd be delighted to, *señorita*. When would you like to leave?"

"Today? This morning?"

"Let me think," he answered her. He'd mentioned to Martínez, the taxi driver, he might go to Columbus. He'd mentioned to O'Conner at the livery stable he was thinking of riding there. Who else? No one. He made up his mind. "Within the hour," he said. "Where may I pick you up?"

"Thank you," she laughed. "For a moment I thought you'd decline." She gave him her address.

As soon as their connection was broken, he had Charlie call the taxi driver. "Do you want to go to Columbus today?" he asked him.

"Of a certainty, *señor*," Martínez replied.

"Can you drive my automobile?"

"I can drive anything, *señor*."

"Very well. Meet me at the hotel in half an hour. Bring Paco along. He might like the ride."

"I will, *señor*."

In thirty minutes, Dick Little met Martínez and Paco in front of the hotel. They climbed into the new automobile, the fat man driving. He had a gleam of pride in his eyes as he started the motor, listening to it critically for a moment, nodding with satisfaction before driving off slowly. The boy, seated beside him, could not hide his excitement.

They stopped at a garage to fill the tank to overflowing. Martínez inspected and kicked each tire to test it with the demeanor of an expert. He made sure the spare on the rear of the car was full of air and in good shape. Next they stopped at the Central Café to buy sandwiches, bottles of soda, and candy. The final stop was in front of the house where Señorita Gutiérrez was staying with her uncle. Although Martínez blew the horn, Dick Little walked up to the door to knock. He led her down the steps, on his arm, to the automobile, opening the door with a gallant gesture, helping her in. Then he followed.

"To Columbus, Mr. Martínez," he said airily in Spanish.

"At your service, sir," was the reply.

Paco cried out, "*Olé!*"

The señorita and Dick Little laughed.

The automobile started off smoothly, gaining speed.

It was another beautiful day in New Mexico. The car surged forward. Martínez guided it expertly around holes in the road and missed as many ruts as he could. In spite of his careful driving the automobile swayed and bounced on the way south.

Many of the miles Little had ridden horseback the day before. It was when they passed the place where he had turned back with Señorita Gutiérrez that his interest began to rise. He scrutinized the country on both sides of the automobile, making mental notes of the terrain, the road, and the blue, jagged Floridas on their left. Occasionally, Martínez had to slow the car down to almost nothing as they crossed dips in the road where waters of long past heavy rains had washed it out. Once across, the automobile would pick up speed.

The wind and the automobile made so much noise it was impossible to converse except in loud voices as if one were trying to make a person hard of hearing understand. Therefore, it was better not to talk; just enjoy the ride.

Dick Little noted the señorita's costume for the day. She had on a long skirt, a white blouse covered by a small long-sleeved jacket, and a hat which was round and sort of flat. A thin veil covered her face. He could see her features through it. She carried a purse and, of all things, he thought, a rolled-up umbrella. Her hands were encased in long, black kid gloves. As for him, the Deming Laundry was providing overnight service when he needed it, so he was dressed as usual in clean clothes of the style he most always wore. Even his jacket was newly washed and pressed.

In spite of the heat, the señorita managed to look cool. Once in a while she would open her purse, take out a small white handkerchief, touching it to her lips and temples under the veil. Dick Little made himself as comfortable as he could in spite of his long legs. Paco leaned over the front door, peering ahead, letting the wind ruffle his hair. Martínez was humming to himself as he drove.

The road had been surveyed as being thirty-five miles from Deming to Columbus; it took them two hours to drive it. They stopped once to open some of the sodas and to stretch their legs.

When they arrived at Columbus there was not much to see except a tall water tank, the Southern Pacific train station, a few scattered houses, some barracks left from Camp Furlong, and many tumbleweeds. The road ran straight ahead toward Mexico.

At one time the town had been bustling, until in the predawn of March 9, 1916, soldiers of Pancho Villa crossed the border and literally burned it to the ground. Many people were killed, mostly Villistas. The soldiers of Camp Furlong battled bravely, eventually repulsing the Mexicans across the border, leaving hundreds of Villistas dead. They had been gathered, when they could be found, and cremated summarily without bell, book, or candle. Columbus never survived the raid.

Dick Little had heard stories. Villa had been there: Villa had been elsewhere. The debate was strong for both sides without decision. President Wilson had sent an expeditionary force into Mexico to catch Villa. They never did, though they came close once, it was said. The expedition had been commanded by General John J. "Black Jack" Pershing. If nothing else, it trained troops to be ready for the big war which followed.

Dick Little had a theory about that raid. He had heard it expressed by one or two of his colleagues. Knowing politicians and the lengths to which they would go, he was almost convinced the theory was possible.

Wilson, at one time, a few months previous, had tried to call the National Guard in an emergency. Only a very few states answered the call, saying they needed the Guard at home. The President, in his powerful position, knew the United States was drifting irrevocably into the European conflict; he therefore needed a strong Regular Army. But he needed an incident to put the National Guard units under federal jurisdiction. Villa was paid to raid the United States to create an incident. The Congress afterward passed laws federalizing the National Guard at the call of the President. The United States then had an army with which to go to war. There had been too many incidents to back up Little's theory: where was the commanding officer of that military district that night? Or the commanding officer of Camp Furlong? Other key personnel were missing at the time with no strong explanations afterward. The machinations of the politicians and officers before and after the raid had been carefully hidden under a smoke screen of state secrecy. It was a story Dick Little never tried to prove; but, in his mind, he felt strongly he could.

He also had dug up another story: where Pancho Villa had been during the raid. It had been told to him by one of Villa's Dorados whom he had drank with in a cantina in Camargo one night.

"*Sí*, Pancho, *mi jefe,* was there!" the Dorado had boasted. "I was right by his side. When the fighting started, Pancho and me, and others headed to the bank. We tried to open the safe with crowbars and pickaxes. That safe, she was safe. We had to dynamite it!

"The fighting was still going on when we crossed the border into Mexico with the money from the bank. Was Pancho at Columbus? He was, and I was right beside him. We came out of Chihuahua state and hit that little New Mexican town about four-thirty in the morning. We had one hell of a fight with the regular army soldiers stationed there." He shook his head sadly. "We lost a lot of good men in Columbus."

"But why did Villa attack the United States at Columbus?" Little asked.

The Mexican shrugged eloquently. "I'll be damned if I know. We just followed orders. We just followed our general. Pancho Villa. That was enough for us."

The ex-Dorado laughed and tossed off his shot of clear tequila. "We got over thirty thousand dollars from that bank. That little bank. *Caray!*" He lowered his voice. "When the United States sent that General Pershing to find Pancho—ha!—Panchito was in Los Angeles, in California, trying to raise more men with the money we took!"

He laughed again.

"Pancho Villa was a smart man, *hombre.* He hid out in your United States and let Pershing's army chase smoke. That's what he did. *Ay! Cantinero! Dos otros tequilas para yo y mi amigo gringo!*"

Dick Little couldn't help but believe him.

They passed, on the right side of the road, the remains of Camp Furlong and the concrete grease racks where the first motorized transportation used by the Army had been greased for their long journey of supplying the expedition into Mexico. Trucks, from that time on, were the beasts of burden of the supply corps, relegating the long mule pack trains to oblivion. To the left, the flying field at Columbus where the early Army Air Force first used planes against an enemy of the United States. The planes were held together with spit, chewing gum, and baling wire; they often crashed, but they had taken off from Columbus to fly in war against a foreign country: Mexico. Little had written stories about this first air war. He had known several of the fliers, admiring them for their courage in those rickety planes. They'd all crashed while searching for Villa, but none of the pilots were killed.

Weeds grew on Camp Furlong and among the grease racks. The airfield was deserted.

Three more miles to the border straight ahead.

The border was not marked except for two houses catty-cornered from each other. The one on the right was built of adobe and had the Mexican flag flying over it; the one on the left was of wood, the American flag flying from its staff. As the automobile approached the adobe building, a uniformed man stepped out, holding up his hand for them to stop.

"Good morning," he said politely. "Where are you going?"

"We're just visiting Las Palomas for a short time," Dick Little answered. He smiled. "We want to visit a few of your bars."

The border guard grinned. "It has become a big business here, sir. Please pass to enjoy yourselves."

"Thank you, sir."

They drove across the border into Mexico.

Las Palomas was a dusty town of two main streets and three or four cross streets. The buildings were all of one story with the exception of the church and the stone Customs House, which were of two. There was no pavement anywhere. Just dirt, hard-packed. On one side a row of buildings stretched southward. From there on, there was nothing but countryside with a narrow road disappearing over the horizon. Around the Customs House, to the right, was the second street leading south. This was evidently the shopping center, as many of the buildings had words painted on their fronts saying BAR, TIENDA, CANTINA, PANIFI-CADORA, BAR, ABARROTES, BAR, and so on. The small plaza, with its round, covered wooden bandstand in the center, was two cross streets down. The church faced the plaza. Many of the buildings had posters pasted on their fronts announcing bullfights, fiestas, dances; some advertised cigarettes, or brands of beer, or tequila. Official notices were also pasted to the buildings.

The señorita directed Martínez to drive the automobile down the second street and park in front of a house next to a bar called, from the sign over the door, LA CUCARACHA.

She opened the door on her side and got out. "I'll only be a few minutes," she said. She gave Dick Little a quick smile, walked around back of the car, then knocked on the closed door of the house. In a moment it was opened. She entered. The door closed behind her.

There were not many people on the street. One automobile, a Ford, was parked in the block below. Several men leaned against buildings talking in soft Spanish, occasionally glancing at the dusty Studebaker, but evidencing no great curiosity. Most of the men were poorly dressed, nearly all wearing large sombreros and sandals; one or two had serapes thrown over their shoulders.

From behind the swinging doors of the barroom, next to the house Señorita Gutiérrez had entered, came the music of a guitar being played lazily. Once in a while the sound of laughter came from the dark interior. Paco was getting impatient with the quiet sitting in the car. Dick Little felt in his pocket for some change, handing him a coin. "Here," he said, "find yourself some candy or something."

Paco flashed him a big smile, jumped over the door without opening it, and ran down the street.

After long minutes, with the flies beginning to buzz about their heads, Little handed more change to Martínez and pointed to the bar. With a sigh of gratitude the fat man eased out of the automobile, and entered through the swinging doors. For a moment the guitar music stopped. Then it began again.

Little began to feel the indolence of Mexico. He stretched his legs to a more comfortable position, tilted his hat farther over his eyes, crossed his arms over his chest, and dozed off.

How much time had passed until he sat up suddenly, he didn't know, but he had the feeling it was not just a few minutes. He looked around. The scenery hadn't changed much. Men were still leaning against buildings, talking, but they were different men. The Ford had disappeared. He noted the shadows had changed some. Soft music was still being played in the bar, and there was still laughter. The door to the house was closed. He got out of the automobile slowly. He stretched to his full height, yawned, walked to the door, and knocked.

After a moment he knocked again. Then, a third time. He tried the handle of the door. It was loose. He opened it, entering cautiously. He was in a short passageway. Beyond, the sun shone brightly on a patio full of flowers and growing things. The sounds of chirping birds in cages came to him. Little entered the patio slowly. Doors led from it into rooms. He opened one: bedroom. Another: a living room with heavy furniture and photographs of people, singly and couples, hung on the walls in big frames. Another: a dining room. He called. "Señorita Gutiérrez! Señorita Gutiérrez!" The house answered with silence. Even the birds had stopped their cheerful noise. Quickly he searched it from one end to the other. No one was there. He returned to the street, closing the door behind him. For a moment he stood in the sun, puzzled. He entered through the swinging doors into the darkened bar next to the house.

It took several moments for his eyes to become accustomed to the darkness of the barroom. There was nothing special about it. A bar at the far end with shelves of bottles behind it and a dark-skinned bartender wearing a shirt with rolled-up sleeves. Several tables and chairs were scattered about; at one a musician was holding his guitar, his hand poised over the strings, his eyes watching the tall man standing by the door. Several heads turned his way. Eufemio Martínez was leaning on the bar at one end, a bottle of beer in front of him. At the other end, a stocky Mexican was turned his way, his hand upheld with a glass in it. As he recognized Dick Little, his face broke into a smile. "So," he said, his voice slightly slurred, "the big writer comes to visit with us. Are you going to write about us again, Señor Writer?" The voice was snarling.

"Hello, Gallo," Dick said pleasantly, approaching the bar. "I didn't expect to see your filthy carcass so soon. Heard you were around, though."

El Gallo tossed off his drink, setting the glass with a thump on the bar. "What are you doing here?" he growled.

"If I'd known you were here," Little answered, "I'd have gone to a better place. You make this one stink."

El Gallo made a sound in his throat. "I should have aimed better the other night. I am sorry I missed."

"One would expect you to miss, *cabrón,*" Little said. "You were likely drunk as usual. The only men you can kill is when they're tied up so you can put your pistol to their heads. You can't miss then. And, remember, I've watched you do it."

The Mexican threw himself at the tall man. He swung a wide blow. Little stepped in. His right sunk deeply into El Gallo's stomach. With a whoosh, air exploded from the Mexican. He doubled over. Little brought up a knee into his face. There was a sharp crack and the stocky man dropped to the floor unconscious, his crushed nose streaming blood.

Dick Little looked down on him. El Gallo was powerfully built in the shoulders but he was beginning to run to fat about the middle. He had a round face with slit eyes, his hair plastered to a pointed skull, giving the impression he was wearing a tight-fitting cap of gleaming pomade. Little knelt beside the unconscious man. He opened the vest El Gallo was wearing, removing a pistol from a holster beneath his arm. He rolled the man over. Pulling up the back of the vest, he took a long knife from the sheath on his belt. The men in the bar had not moved. Martínez's eyes were wide. He licked his lips.

Little walked to the bar. He picked up the bottle of beer from which Martínez had been drinking, shook it several times with his thumb over the top, then squirted the contents of the bottle in El Gallo's face. The unconscious man moaned. He began to move his head to escape the foaming stream of beer. He moaned again, rolling over. After several tries he sat up, feeling his broken nose gingerly, the blood running down his chin. He looked like some cornered animal who expected momentarily a knife to cut his throat.

"Get on your feet, you piece of shit," Little told him softly. "That was for shooting at me and missing. I'll keep your gun and knife for a while. If you want to kill me, do it like a man, face to face."

He helped the groaning man to his feet and back to the bar. "Give him a wet rag."

The bartender hastened to dip a rag in a bucket of water, handing it to El Gallo. The Mexican placed it carefully against his face, moaning.

Little smiled grimly. "Think of those you've pistol-whipped when they couldn't fight back, son of a whore. Let me give you a warning. Whenever I see you I'll either give you the knee again, or shoot you in a place where it will hurt for a long time. Understand?"

The wounded man groaned, but nodded.

"Now get out of here, son of a pig!" Little said sharply.

El Gallo gave Dick Little a look of pure hatred, but he left the bar, staggering slightly, his hands holding the bloody rag to his face.

"Now," Little said quietly, turning to the frightened bartender, "I want a cold beer and information about the people who live next door. Who are they, and where can they be found? *Comprende, amigo?*"

Fifteen minutes and two beers later, Dick Little had his information. A Señor and Señora Valencia lived next door. They had moved into the house only a month ago; from Camargo, a bit over a hundred miles south of Ciudad Chihuahua, the bartender believed. They kept to themselves, seldom left the house and were very, very quiet. He was an elderly man, his wife about the same age. They had never been in his bar, nor were they seen in the streets after dark. One woman worked for them, but only during the day; she did not live in the house with the Valencias. The maid did all the buying for the couple. Once in a while they would hire a horse and carriage and drive into the country for a few hours. This was their only pleasure outside of their house. They did not go anywhere especially, just drove out and back. They seldom spoke to people, but always very politely. That was all he knew.

Little bought a case of cold beer and a bottle of tequila for Martínez. He paid the bartender, tipping him for his trouble and information. Outside the bar, he discovered that Señorita Gutiérrez was seated in the backseat on her side of the automobile, chatting with Paco in the front seat. Martínez found places to hide the beer and his bottle. He got into the automobile. Dick Little stood by his door until Martínez was behind the wheel, then he opened it and sat down. "I looked for you," he said.

She smiled at him. "I had a little business with a friend of mine," she said. "I'm sorry I took so long."

"How are the Valencias these days?" he asked.

She stared at him. "What do you mean?"

"The bartender told me all about them. Incidentally, our friend, El Gallo, hurt himself badly in that bar not long ago."

"El Gallo is no friend of mine," she said haughtily. "As for the Valencias, they are old, old friends. You had no right to ask questions about them."

He sighed. Martínez and Paco sat quietly on the front seat, staring ahead. "All right, Eufemio," he said, "back to Deming."

Martínez started the engine and the automobile moved slowly forward. They circled in back of the Customs House. At the border the Mexican guard saluted as they passed. A few yards farther on, Martínez stopped the car in front of the wooden house of the U.S. Customs.

The customs officer, uniformed, came from the house. "Citizenship?" he asked.

Martínez and Paco answered, "New Mexican."

Dick Little told him, "U.S."

With a sigh, Señorita Gutiérrez removed a folded piece of paper from her purse, handing it to him. The customs officer unfolded it, read it, and handed it back to her. "You're all clear, Miss Gutiérrez," he said. She returned the paper to her purse.

The customs officer put his head into the automobile, under the top. "Anything to declare?"

"No, *señor*," Martínez said.

"No liquor?"

"No, *señor*," Martínez answered simply.

The customs officer smiled slightly. "I'll bet," he said under his breath. Straightening up, he waved a hand. "Have a good trip. You're clear."

Martínez thanked him, setting the automobile in motion. Each one of the occupants let out a long breath, suddenly smiling.

Outside of Columbus they pulled off the road and got out of the automobile. Dick Little brought out his bag of sandwiches while Martínez opened beer and a bottle of soda for Paco. They all ate with relish, drank from the bottles, then subsided into a quiet state of fulfillment.

Finally, Señorita Gutiérrez asked, "Were you upset I was gone so long?"

Dick Little merely grunted.

She became annoyed, her eyes flashing. "You had no right to make inquiries of my friends!"

Martínez and Paco moved away from the automobile to some mesquite bushes across the road.

"Wasn't asking about *them* so much," he finally answered her, "just was interested where *you* went for so long."

"That was none of your business," she snapped.

"Made it mine," he said.

"You had no right!"

"Made it my right."

"Take me back to Columbus," she said sharply.

"Why?"

She was busily lowering her veil. "I will not ride back with you."

"How will you get back?"

"I'll—I'll hire a car."

"Don't be an ass!"

Señorita Gutiérrez straightened her already straight back. "I'll have you know—"

"That it's a hell of a long way back to Deming," he interrupted. "Relax. Don't get yourself upset. You were gone a long time. I was worried. That's all there was to it."

"You were worried?" Her voice had softened.

"Yes."

"About me?"

"Yes."

She laughed a silvery laugh. "In my own country?"

He smiled slowly. "I hadn't thought of that."

"I am pleased, however, that you did worry."

"How so?"

She shrugged slightly. "To have a man worry over you always makes a woman feel good."

"It depends on the amount of worry, and why, doesn't it?"

"Sometimes."

"And the woman?"

She looked at him and smiled, pleased.

"Well," he said, "now that you're happy, would you change your mind and ride back with us?"

She got to her feet. "I'd be delighted, Señor Withers."

Dick Little called for Martínez and Paco, who came from behind the mesquite, grinning at some secret they shared between them.

If Dick Little had been worried about the señorita's mysterious disappearance he didn't allow himself to show it. He had known many Latin women in his wanderings. He had learned they enjoyed secrets: would disappear for long times and make a mystery of where they had been, and with whom they'd been with, even if they'd been visiting with a girlfriend. To ask questions, he knew from experience, would only produce vague and misleading answers. So he hadn't really pried and pushed the point as to where she had been and whom she'd seen. Oh, he'd sweated inside, all right, but he wouldn't give her the satisfaction of letting her know. He could be as damndably secretive as she was.

The ride back was uneventful. Eufemio and Paco began to softly sing songs of Mexico. The señorita fell silent, listening, letting her thoughts show on her serious face. Dick Little watched the country intently, saying nothing. In Deming, they drove her to her house, Little letting her out with only a few words to her at her door. Dick instructed Martínez to have the tank filled to the top before returning to the hotel. When the automobile was parked outside on the street, he paid Martínez, adding an extra silver dollar for the delighted Paco.

Stretching himself, he entered the hotel lobby.

"Mr. Withers!" It was Charlie.

"Yes?"

"Miss Townsend called. She says it is very urgent."

"To do what?"

"She wants you to come to the ranch as soon as you come in. She said it was an emergency."

"An emergency?"

"Yes, sir."

Little hesitated a moment thinking. "Does she have a phone out there?"

"Yes, sir."

"Call her and tell her I'm on my way. I'll be there within the half hour."

"Yes, sir!"

He sat in the front seat of the automobile a moment, staring down the street. He sighed deeply. The motor roared to life.

He made better time than he thought. He almost missed the turn by the mailbox, but slowed down sufficiently to make it, swaying the car on two wheels. At the house he was met by Sam and Stella Townsend. They were standing by the fence gate waiting patiently, their faces long and solemn.

"What's happened?" he asked when the car stopped.

"Come with me," Sam said, leading him off toward the bunkhouse.

They crossed the corral toward the barn. The bunkhouse was not far from it. A long building with few windows. Sam went through the door. "Stella," he called back over his shoulder, "you stay outside." Dick Little followed the ranch owner down a hallway.

"Each hand has his own room," Sam was saying. "I want you to see Billy's." He opened a plain wooden door, standing aside to let Dick Little enter.

The room was as thoroughly wrecked as his had been a few days earlier. What could have been ripped open was ripped open. Clothes were scattered on the floor, the closet stood empty. The lid of Billy's small army trunk was thrown back, the lock having been twisted off, its meager contents strewn about. Dick Little couldn't help but think of the few possessions Billy had collected. So very few.

"Where's Billy?" he asked.

"Come along!" It was almost a command.

Sam led him to the barn, Stella stopping just outside the door. They went up to a ranch wagon.

"One of the men found him. He was taking some posts out to Billy. All he could do was dump the posts and put Billy in the wagon. He brought him back just like this." Sam Townsend reached into the bed of the wagon and threw back a tarpaulin. Underneath was the bloody body of Billy Thomas. Someone had almost blown him in half with a shotgun. Right through the stomach. The double-ought buckshot killing him instantly.

Dick felt tears filling his eyes. He almost threw up at the sight of the bloody and torn flesh. It was at that instant he felt the power and the urge to kill and kill again if he ever learned who had killed poor old Billy Thomas.

SHERIFF CHUCHO ARMIJO was waiting for him in the lobby when he returned. "Mr. Withers?" he asked politely.

"Yes, Sheriff?"

"Do you have a few minutes to spare?"

"Here, or in my room?"

"I'd prefer the privacy."

"Come along then."

They climbed the stairs. Dick Little unlocked the door to his room, letting the sheriff precede him. "Would you like a drink?"

The sheriff smiled. He took a thin cigar from his pocket and lighted it. "Whatever you have to offer."

As Armijo carefully placed his hat on the desk, Dick poured Bourbon into glasses, handing the sheriff one. "There's water in the tap, but no ice."

The sheriff shrugged. He raised his glass in salute, then drank half of its contents straight. Little followed suit. "Good liquor," the sheriff said. He set the glass down on the night table, seating himself on the bed. "Señor Withers, you have caused me to do a lot of thinking at night."

"I have? About what?"

"You."

"What on earth is making you think of me?"

The sheriff smiled, looking at the ash on his black cigar. "I do not believe you are what you say you are."

Dick Little laughed. "I haven't said anything of what I am."

The sheriff nodded. "That is what I mean. I do not like mysteries in my own county. Mysteries that I cannot solve."

"What sort of mysteries?"

"Well, for one, Señor Withers, you buy a car, paying for it with gold. Why did you do that?"

"I wanted transportation better than horseback."

"Why gold?"

Little smiled. "It is easier to spend, and I like the feel of it."

The sheriff smiled back. "Very true. Why did you fight with El Gallo in Las Palomas this morning?"

"He attacked me."

"Why?"

"I don't know."

"You were out to see Billy Thomas yesterday?"

"Yes, I was."

"Why?"

"He was an old friend. He left word he wanted to see me. So, I went out to see him."

"You talked with him?"

"Yes, I did."

"About what, if I may ask?"

"This and that."

"I see." The sheriff finished off his liquor. He held out his glass for more. Dick Little poured him a generous drink. "*Gracias.*"

"Look, Sheriff," Little said, "I don't know what all of this is adding up to. You have something on your mind. What is it?"

The sheriff took another swallow of whiskey before he answered. "Señor Withers, you know of course, Billy Thomas was murdered?"

"I just came from the S T Ranch."

"I was there earlier. Sam Townsend called me right after lunch when they brought in the body. Sam told me of your visit yesterday. He called me after you left."

"And—"

Again a shrug. "Your reactions seemed normal. However, I am a suspicious man. I do not like strangers I can learn nothing about coming into my territory. I like to know who they are and what they're up to. There's something going on around here I cannot put a finger on, as yet. You were shot at—"

"By El Gallo," Little interrupted.

"Oh?" The sheriff glanced at him sharply. "How do you know this?"

"He told me. But, then, Gallo was always a bad shot."

"Why would he do this thing to you? Do you know him?"

"We have met before—in Mexico. We've had our differences there. I suppose he wanted to settle old scores. I think I've changed his mind."

"Ah, you knew him in Mexico?"

"A long time ago."

"What is this old score?"

"It is unimportant."

The sheriff smoked a moment. He carefully brushed the ash from his cigar into the tray beside his glass. "That brings up another interesting part of your past, Mr. Withers. I did not know you were in Mexico, as you say, a long time ago. During the Revolution?"

"Yes."

The sheriff sighed. "So many people here, now, fought for one side or the other. You're another. Which side were you on?"

"Neither one. I was neutral."

"Isn't that hard to be in a revolution?"

"There were times when you might say it was hard. But I survived."

"What were you doing then?"

"Minding my own business." He took away the sting of his answer by smiling at the sheriff.

The sheriff smiled back. "If El Gallo shot at you, did he also ransack your room?"

"He didn't mention it." Little paused. "Tell me, Sheriff, how is it you know El Gallo?"

"As I have said," he answered, "I make it my business to know about strangers in my county. El Gallo is notorious. He has been in these parts before. But, since I have no reason to bother him, he does not bother me. Unless, that is," he added, "you want to swear a complaint against him for taking a shot at you."

"It wouldn't stand up, Sheriff, if I did."

"Why not?"

"My word against his."

"You have a point there. At the most a small fine. Why do you think he is here?"

Little poured more Bourbon in his glass. "For the treasure."

"Treasure? What treasure?"

"I thought you'd know. I've heard hints of it ever since I came here. Supposedly, somewhere in the vicinity of Deming a treasure is buried. Pancho Villa's treasure."

"Oh yes, that one. I've heard about it, of course." The sheriff knocked more ashes from his cigar. "There are always stories about buried money around here. Everybody looks for it, but nobody locates it. I have prospected a little myself."

"Find anything?"

The sheriff laughed. "Calluses on my hands." He finished off his drink. "Thank you for the booze." He got to his feet, picking up his hat from the desk.

"Leaving?"

"I have a busy evening ahead. I'll have to borrow a truck to bring Billy Thomas into town. Tomorrow morning there'll be a formal coroner's inquest. If Billy is fortunate, we'll bury him tomorrow afternoon."

"Let me know the time of the funeral, if you please. I'd like to attend."

"I'll see you are notified." He added, "Watch yourself carefully. I wouldn't want to be hauling in your body from some place to bury you."

The sheriff put on his hat, letting himself out the door. Dick could hear him whistling down the hall and stairs.

Dick Little stared at the door for several moments. He went to the phone, and picked it up. In a moment he heard Charlie's voice. "Yes, Mr. Withers?"

"Can you send a telegram for me?"

"I'd have to send someone to the railway station."

"Very well. Take it down for me, please."

"Yes, sir."

Dick Little thought a moment. "John Smith," he dictated, "De Vargas Hotel, Santa Fe, New Mexico." He paused. " 'Target sighted.' Sign it, 'Richard.' "

"Yes, sir," said Charlie. He read it back.

"Good. Do you have enough to cover it?"

"Yes, sir, Mr. Withers. I still have a lot from the hundred you left with me."

"Fine. Thanks, Charlie." He replaced the receiver.

Crossing the room, he removed his jacket. As he hung it over the back of a chair a thump reminded him of the contents of one of the large pockets. He removed El Gallo's pistol and knife, holding them in his hands, looking at them. The pistol was a short-barreled .38 Colt Single Action. He placed it in the desk drawer. The knife was long, broad-bladed, sharp on both edges. He flipped it, noting its balance. It was a good throwing knife as well as a sticker and ripper. He stared at it. The knife fascinated him: cold steel, razor sharp, silent in murder, deadly. The bone handle was yellow with age and use. Dick felt a chill run up his spine. The knife had the fascination of a deadly snake ready to strike: a weapon which drew death to it. He couldn't help staring at it, wondering . . . How many times had it been used on a human being? He flipped it two or three times. He was about to put it in the drawer with the pistol when something about the knife caught his attention. The handle felt loose. Dick Little grabbed a towel from the rack on the wall, wrapping it about the blade. He twisted the knife. It *was* loose. Examining the handle closely, he saw the screw holding the handle on the shaft. Reaching into his trouser pocket, he took out a penknife. Opening the little blade, he inserted it in the screw head and turned. In a moment the knife was in three pieces: the blade, the handle, and the screw. He looked into the open end of the handle. He saw something white. Being very careful, using the small blade of his penknife, he worked the paper out and unrolled it. It was the same size as The Gunner's piece of the map. Dick Little stared at it intently, memorizing it.

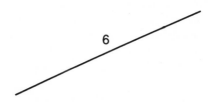

V O M E X

6

He carefully rerolled the paper, placing it back into the handle before reassembling the knife. He tightened the screw until the looseness of the handle was eliminated. He placed the knife in the drawer and hung up the towel.

Slowly he undressed. He cleaned his teeth at the sink. He went to bed, falling asleep almost immediately.

The cemetery was to the east of Deming about three miles from downtown. Waiting at the desk had been a message from the sheriff; the funeral would take place at four in the afternoon. Dick Little took his horse from O'Conner's, riding slowly toward the cemetery, planning to arrive just as the service began. He was on time.

Part of the burial ground was landscaped with stones and monuments marking the prior deceased. In the southeast corner the land was bare of all save a few wooden headboards and a few crosses. Billy Thomas was to be buried in that section. The grave had been dug, the wooden coffin was set beside it; the undertaker and one of his men were much in evidence in their dark clothes and solemn expressions. There was a minister, his face serene above his white turned-about collar. He was standing at the head of the grave. Dick Little ground-reined his horse, walking up to the meager number of people standing in a group at the foot of the hole. There were Sam and Stella Townsend; the sheriff; and three cowboys, in their work clothes, who were lounging behind the group, smoking their cigarettes and talking in low tones. Stella was dressed in black for the occasion, wearing a sort of flat black hat which accentuated her light hair. All of the faces were solemn, fitting the occasion.

The minister took his place, setting his feet firmly, slightly apart. He opened his prayer book and began the service. All of the men removed their hats, staring at the grave or the coffin, each lost in his own thoughts as the minister read from the book in a quiet but firm voice.

He was giving a eulogy: "We do not know much about the departed, Billy Thomas," he said in conversational tones, "except that he was cut off from life suddenly. He had been in our midst for a few years, proving his worth as a man by doing his duty to his employer with devotion and hard work. He was never known to complain about his life. He was loyal and kind to the people he met. His sins must have been small in the eyes of the Lord.

"Billy Thomas," the minister continued, "came to us from nowhere: a drifter. He did not speak of his origins, or of any former friends; but he made friends during his stay among us. He was not a religious man in the sense of attending church on Sundays: he was a religious man in the sense of appreciating the wonders of this earth; those he could feel, those which guided him night and day through all of the seasons of the year. I knew Billy Thomas. I talked with Billy Thomas occasionally. He never apologized to me for not being a churchgoer; nor did he apologize for what he was in his life. He did, on occasion, express to me in his own language how he felt toward the Almighty and to the wonders of God around him. Billy Thomas was a straightforward, direct man, whose friendship I respected. Receive him, O Lord, as he was and as he comes to you: a man of the earth, of the plains, of the mountains, of the days and nights, of good weather and bad: a simple man. Give him a range to ride, fair play, and he will be content in your Heaven. Amen."

The undertaker and his man lowered the coffin into the grave. The minister intoned, "Ashes to ashes, dust to dust—" Stella, eyes glistening with tears, threw a handful of dirt on the wooden box. The others followed, coming to the grave, awkwardly bending to scoop up a fistful of earth. When the minister intoned the final "Amen," the group responded. The minister turned away. The cowboys put on their battered hats, drifting off toward one of the automobiles parked nearby. The sheriff waved a hand of recognition toward Little. He caught it from the corner of his eye as he approached Sam and Stella Townsend.

"I'm sorry about Billy," he said.

Sam Townsend answered him. "We all are. He was just as the preacher said of him. Thanks for coming, Mr. Withers." He strode off to the car where his men were waiting.

"Miss Stella," Dick said, "I'd be obliged if you'd meet me in town in about half an hour. I'd like to buy you a coffee before you return to the ranch."

She looked at him steadily. "I'll be glad to. The Manhattan Café?"

"I'll see you there."

She was waiting for him when he tied his horse to the telephone pole outside of the café. They selected a table.

She used sugar and cream in her cup; he stirred his black coffee, cooling it.

"Those were fine things Mr. Strang said about Billy."

"He was the salt of the earth," Dick said. "A very simple person."

She looked at Dick Little. "Where did you know him before?"

"In Mexico. Billy was seduced by the idea of being a soldier of fortune. He joined Villa's Division of the North. I met him one day when he was in bad trouble. I was able to save his skin."

"What sort of trouble?"

"He was going to be executed."

She gasped. "Executed? For what?"

"A brigade captain thought Billy was the butt of a very bad practical joke. The only thing was, Billy resented the joke and flattened the captain; so, he was sentenced to be summarily shot. I was able to convince the captain that Billy's death would become an international incident. I saw Billy for some time after that; finally, I persuaded him to get out of Mexico. I made him see that being a soldier of fortune was not all it was cracked up to be. That was in '15. I guess he got out, came here, and started working for your father."

She nodded. "He came to us in '17, I think. He was a good man. He was good to me."

Dick Little nodded.

"Who do you think killed him, Mr. Withers?"

Little shook his head. "I've no idea."

"But why?"

Little shook his head again.

"What would anyone want to search his room for?" she asked. "Billy never had anything of value to steal. He owned the clothes on his back, a pistol and a rifle. That's all he had. Would you like to have his possessions?"

"Yes," he said, "I'd like to have them."

"I'll send them in to you." She sighed. "Funny, isn't it?"

"What?"

"How quickly a person can be dead."

He agreed.

"I saw him last, yesterday morning. He was riding toward the railroad tracks. He saw me and waved as he passed. We didn't even talk. The next time I saw him was in the wagon—dead." She emphasized the final word.

"Life is like that," he said. "A group of Roman officers were discussing death in Caesar's tent one night, each one telling how he'd like to die. One of them turned to Caesar and asked him how he'd like to go. Without hesitation, Caesar answered, 'Quickly.' That's the way I'd want it. That's the way Billy went."

"But who could have deliberately shot Billy? Who would want to do that to a harmless old cowboy?"

Dick Little shook his head. "He told me he thought El Gallo was looking for him."

"El Gallo? Who is he?"

"The man who nearly had Billy executed. Billy thought El Gallo was going to kill him."

"But why?"

"Perhaps he was still mad at Billy. El Gallo has been seen around lately."

"Oh no!" she gasped. "Do you really think he murdered Billy for something which happened years ago?"

Dick Little shrugged. "He's capable of it."

"Does the sheriff know about this—this El Gallo?"

Little nodded. "I'm sure he does."

"Why doesn't he arrest him?"

"No proof."

"Well, I think he should!"

"It couldn't be proven. Besides," he said, "a shotgun is not Gallo's weapon. A knife or a pistol, close up, are his specialty. I say that Gallo is a good suspect, but there's nothing to prove it."

"I'll spit in his face if I ever meet him!" she announced boldly.

"And probably get your jaw broken by his fist," Little said. "Or worse. He's that kind of a man. If you can call him a man. He doesn't take insults lightly."

She subsided, finishing her coffee. "Would you do me a favor?"

"Certainly." He brightened.

"Dad and the men are probably at that Marks person's place. Could you tell them I'm here and I want to go home? You do know where it is, don't you?"

"Yes," he said getting up. "I'll tell them. Will you do *me* a favor?"

"Of course," she said, "what is it?"

"Don't mention our conversation about Billy, if you please. His past is his own now."

"If you say so, I won't. To anyone," she added.

He left a tip for the waitress under his saucer, paid for the coffees as he left the café, untied his horse, and rode to the pool hall. He found Sam Townsend in the back room drinking some of The Gunner's alcohol and grapefruit juice. He delivered Stella's message, took a glass of the liquid from The Gunner, and downed it.

"I'll see you tonight," The Gunner whispered to him as Dick set the glass on the table.

Little nodded. He left the pool hall with Sam Townsend.

The cowboys climbed into the backseat of a Model T.

"Bad business, Dick," Sam said.

Little agreed.

"I'm going to miss Billy a lot. He was a good friend."

Little agreed again. "By the by, Sam," he asked, "you haven't mentioned my name to anyone, have you?"

Sam Townsend shook his head. "Not to a soul."

"I'd like to keep it quiet as long as I can. The Gunner knows me. So does one other, but I don't think they'll spread it around. I want to stay incognito as long as I can."

"They won't learn it from me."

"Thanks."

Sam Townsend climbed into the automobile. He started the engine, driving off slowly, making a U-turn in the street. Dick Little watched until the automobile turned a corner, then he mounted his horse, heading for O'Conner's stable.

At the hotel he picked up his key from Charlie. Dick Little looked at him, puzzled. "Isn't there anyone else working the desk?" he asked.

Charlie laughed. "I live in that room there," he said, pointing to a door at the end of the desk. "I'm a light sleeper."

"Seven days a week?"

"Six. We have someone in on Sundays. Oh, by the way," he said. "I picked up a letter for you while I was at the post office this afternoon. The clerk asked me if we had anyone at the hotel by your name."

Dick took the letter, thanking Charlie. On the way up the stairs he read the scrawl on the envelope.

> *Withers*
> *hotl*
> *demin new mex*

It was in Billy Thomas's handwriting.

pard, it said, *i don tol u a li. i no th son ov a bitch is gona kil me. i don tok this ofen a mex i sen kil in mex. he wuz som kine ov a genral. i giv it to u. he sad giv it too roodi butt roodi don got kilt. i had it al th tim. iffn i get kil too u can hav it. i don fergit. ure ol pal billy thomas.*

Billy's last will and testament, Dick Little thought. He stared at the scrawl which took up both sides of the paper. He turned it over a couple of times, looked on the floor, then thought to look in the envelope. He took from it a small torn paper. It was another part of the map.

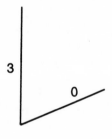

THE GUNNER knocked on the door late that night, entering carrying a gallon bottle of his alcohol and grapefruit juice. Dick Little shuddered, but felt he was man enough to join his friend in a few rounds of drinks.

He rinsed out glasses in the sink, held his for a bountiful libation, and drank manfully.

He sat, propped up with pillows, against the headboard of the bed, while The Gunner smacked his lips appreciatively over his swallows and sat beside the desk, placing the jug carefully on the top.

"Sorry I didn't make Billy's funeral," he said. "From what I heard them cowboys say it was a beaut."

"It was that, Gunner," Dick Little said sadly. "You should have heard the fine things the minister said about Billy."

The Gunner waved his glass. "Sorry th' old son of a bitch won't be around anymore," he said. "I sort of liked th' bastard. Son of a bitch," he muttered. "Who the hell killed him?"

"El Gallo?"

"That pig's turd? Hell no! Gallo wouldn't have used a shotgun."

"Who then?"

The Gunner looked wise. "Someone who wanted Billy's piece of the map."

"What makes you think Billy had one?"

"I knew Billy, damn it! He got it somewhere off one of th' Mexes who got it from old Pancho. Billy got drunk one night an' sort of talked around it, he did. That's why I wanted to get him drunk enough to tell me about it. Cagey old fart. He caught on fast. Wouldn't let me."

"Suppose he did have one, would you like to see it?"

"You're goddamned right I would!" The Gunner exclaimed. His booming voice filled the room.

"Look in the desk drawer."

The Gunner opened the drawer. He saw the pistol and knife, holding them both up for closer inspection before replacing them. He reached into the drawer again, taking out the piece of the map. For a long time he studied it, turning it from side to side, upside down, even examining the back. He looked at Dick Little, puzzled. "What the hell is this?" he asked.

"I gather it's from the same map you have," Dick said, sipping from his glass. "Same paper, same ink, same hand holding the pen. I'd say it's another part of the map you're looking for."

"What's it say?"

Dick shrugged. "I haven't the slightest idea. An angle with a zero underneath it and a three on the side."

"Do you know what it means?"

"No more than I know what *your* piece means. But I have an idea."

"What idea?" The Gunner was sitting on the edge of the chair excitedly.

"I've just got the idea," Little said, "that every piece of the map means something. There're eight pieces. All eight have to be together to make sense. I've got another idea: it is a relatively simple map; drawn by someone who has, or had, a very clever mind, though not necessarily a devious one."

"What the hell do you mean by that?" The Gunner wanted to know.

"Just what I said," Little answered. "Look, Gunner. Suppose someone, anyone, wanted to draw a treasure map, but he wasn't up to drawing a treasure map?"

"I don't get you."

"Take a drink." The Gunner did. "Now," said Little, "take yourself: your mind is far from devious; it's too straightforward."

"Thanks," The Gunner said.

"You're welcome. Suppose you had a treasure to bury, say, somewhere around Deming. You bury it. Now, what sort of a map would you make so you could find it again?"

"I'd remember where it was." The Gunner said. He leaned back in his chair, thinking, interested.

"You'd remember where you buried it; but suppose you were burying it for someone else, and you wanted to tell that someone else where it was, and where it could be found? You'd have to draw a map. Else how could that someone else know where it was?"

"I'd've already told him."

"But suppose he couldn't dig it up right away. Suppose he'd have to wait for a while; say, years before he could get around to finding it? Do you think our someone could remember the instructions told him years before: that he could remember them exactly?"

The Gunner admitted defeat. "I suppose not."

"So you see the necessity for a map?"

"Yeah," he said. "Let me pour you another drink, Tiny." He got out of his chair and did so. Settling back, he said, "All right. I need a map."

"So you draw one. But you've never seen a treasure map before. You have to draw it simply, yet obscurely enough so that you will understand it, and so will the person you give it to. You switch things around on it; you put numbers on it no one but you and the other person would know what they meant. Do you get my point?"

"No," said The Gunner. "No."

"Very well, look at it this way: who do you figure drew the map?"

"Fierro."

"Good. Was Fierro devious?"

"What's that?"

Dick Little sighed. "How did Fierro think?"

"He was a bloody, murdering bastard!" The Gunner said vehemently.

"Besides that, how did he think?"

"He was a pretty good general, I'll say that for th' shit. I'll say that for him."

"Okay. Suppose Fierro drew the map, or had it drawn for him. He'd want the map to tell him certain things in case he forgot just where he put the treasure, wouldn't he?"

"I guess so."

"So, all he'd need was a reminder. Just by looking at it briefly. He gave a map to Villa. You said so. You were there."

"I was there," The Gunner nodded. "I was there."

"All he'd have to tell Villa was the vicinity of the treasure: one or two points on the map to hang the thing on, plus how he had scrambled up the code of the map, and what the code was. Now do you follow me?"

The Gunner shook his head. "I'm not sure."

Little laughed, taking a drink. "Then let's not talk about that part of it. Suppose we say Fierro did draw up the map. He was not an illiterate, but he was also not devious. Say he buried the treasure and wanted to tell one man in the world where it would be if that one man decided to come and dig it up. You understand me so far?"

The Gunner nodded. "I understand."

"Good. Because Fierro had a straightforward mind, he makes the map straightforward. He gives it to Villa. Villa understands the map because Fierro has told him the points of reference, has told him the code he used and how to use it. It's very plain. Except for one thing."

"What's that?"

"Pancho's tearing it up and giving away seven of the pieces. He scatters it among eight people, including himself, Fierro, yourself, and five others. Felipe Angeles gets one. A Captain Galinda gets another. Three others get the other parts. We know one was killed; we know, now, that Billy Thomas got that piece. What has happened to the other two who received pieces? We have no way of knowing."

"But you said all the pieces have to be put together to find the place where the treasure's buried."

Little nodded. "I'm afraid so. That's what makes your piece, and the piece in the desk, important and unimportant."

"I don't get you," The Gunner said, shaking his head.

Dick Little sipped from his glass. "These two pieces I'm talking about are unimportant until the other pieces are assembled. By themselves they mean nothing to anyone. But—they're important to the whole of the map. If someone, anyone, could get their hands on all of the pieces, and could figure out Fierro's code, they'd know where the treasure is buried."

The Gunner scratched his head. "I'm not sure. I'm not sure I follow you all the way," he said.

"Think it over," Little said.

"I'm going to. Shit!" he exclaimed, "I won't be able to think of nothing else." He grinned ruefully. "Nothing else," he added.

Dick Little held out his glass to be filled. The Gunner obliged, filling his own. "Here's to Fierro!" toasted Little.

The Gunner grumbled. "Here's to th' hell he's roasting his black soul in!"

They drank. The Gunner filled his glass from the jug. It was now less than half full. "Rodolfo Fierro," The Gunner said. "Rodolfo. You know, Tiny? Every time I think of that son of a bitch, it makes me happy I was with Angeles. There was a gentleman, by God! Let's drink to General Angeles. General Angeles!" He drained his glass; Dick Little sipped from his. "Do you know," The Gunner said, refilling his glass, "they wanted to make him president of Mexico once." He belched. "Fierro had guts, he did, but he wasn't half the man Angeles was. To Felipe. Felipe!" He drained his glass a second time. He was beginning to feel the effects of his mixture. He leaned back in his chair, a happy expression on his face. "We sure did have some times, didn't we, Tiny?"

"We sure did," Dick agreed. "Don't you think it's time for bed?"

"Bed?" The Gunner grinned. "Bed," he said. "Damned good idea. Okay, I'll go." He took a long careful time getting to his feet, his crippled legs not helping any. "Bed," he said. He made his way to the door slowly. "I'll make it," he announced. "I'll make it."

"Take care of yourself, Gunner," Dick said. "Take care of that piece of map of yours. I've got a hunch somebody wants it."

"Map? Oh yes, map. I'll take care of it, Tiny. I'll take care of it." He opened the door and was gone.

Dick Little grinned, looked at the remains in his glass, then gulped it down. He shuddered. Getting up from the bed he went to the desk, opening the drawer. He took out the pistol, letting his thoughts range back several years to another existence.

Fierro. How well he remembered him. How well he remembered the stories about the man called El Carnicero, "The Butcher."

Dick hefted the pistol. Rodolfo always wore a Colt .45 Single Action on his right side, high, under his jacket. He often carried another pistol, of a smaller caliber, in a shoulder holster under his left arm. He never left the Colt far from his hand at any time.

Dick Little put on his jacket. He needed a breath of fresh air. He put the pistol absently into an outside pocket, picked up his hat, smiling grimly at it. It was the same style and color as Fierro had worn. He put it on. Turning out the overhead light, he left the room, locking the door behind him.

There were no lights off the main street of Deming. They were dark and silent. Little walked along with long strides, passing dark, quiet houses, many of them empty. Deming had been a boomtown during the Big War. There had been an army training camp nearby, Camp Cody, and the town had grown into a city; but after the war, people had moved away leaving behind a depression and about fifteen hundred residents. Slowly the town recuperated until now nearly five thousand souls resided within its limits; but there were still traces of the boom in the empty houses, the empty stores, the empty lots with forlorn for sale signs weathering away.

As he passed two of the empty stores he heard a sound from the areaway between them. Before he could turn he was hit a stunning blow on his head. He fell to the ground unconscious.

He regained his senses slowly. He could feel his clothes disarranged. He'd been searched. He felt in his jacket pockets. The pistol was still there. A trouser pocket had been turned inside out. He felt on the ground for his change and penknife. He found the knife and some of the coins. He rose to his feet, feeling his head. The hat had saved him from a nasty wound. Taking it off, he felt his head again. There were no cuts, just a bump. He swore softly.

He had been pulled in an areaway between buildings. How long had he been unconscious? Five minutes? Ten? He couldn't tell. But it had been long enough for someone to search him thoroughly. What did he, or she, hope to find? Whatever it was he hadn't had it on him.

Brushing his clothes off as best he could, he tried to orient himself. He walked slowly to a street corner, looking around him in the moonlight. He recognized the corner. He was only a block or two from the house where Señorita Gutiérrez was staying. Perhaps he'd better call on her, he thought. Perhaps she might know something of this attack. Shaking his head, to clear it of the ache he was beginning to feel, he walked to her house. It was dark. He went up on the porch, knocking loudly on the door. No answer. He knocked again. Still no answer. He tried the doorknob. The door was open. Little smiled to himself. Very few people locked their doors at night in Deming. He knocked loudly again just to make sure. He entered the house quietly, closing the door behind him. For a moment he stood in the hallway. It was a two-story house with a peaked roof. His eyes became accustomed to the darkness, alleviated somewhat by the light of the moon. He began to make out details and masses where furniture was located. He saw the stairs, and went up them quickly, quietly. A board creaked under his foot. He stopped, pausing, listening for any sound. He heard nothing. Continuing up the stairs, he came to the landing, pausing again. A door was open. He went to it noiselessly, stopping. It was her room; he could smell her scent. He entered. The moon gave him seeing light. He went to her dresser. The top was neatly cluttered with the articles a woman uses: brushes, combs, bottles, a tray with hairpins, a silver-topped cut glass decanter. He opened it and smelled. Her perfume. He opened a drawer feeling its depth, his hands crossing soft cottons and softer silks. He felt a leather box. Taking it from the drawer, he opened the snap, feeling inside. Jewelry. And a wallet. He opened the wallet, going to the window to see better. Money and papers riffled under his fingers. They stopped. He took out a piece of paper, looking at it intently. He was breathing faster now. Taking a match from the breast pocket of his jacket, he struck it with his fingernail. It flared into flame as he narrowed his eyes. He held the match close to the paper, memorizing the lines upon it.

N   G   N   U   E

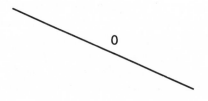

Quickly he blew out the match, returning the paper to the wallet and the wallet to the box. He placed the box back in the drawer, closing it. He left the house noiselessly, shutting the front door behind him. His long legs took him around the nearest corner where he stopped. He was breathing hard, his forehead covered with perspiration. He wiped his forehead with a sleeve and rested against the side of a building. His head was hurting, yet his thoughts were racing.

So, Señorita Gutiérrez was connected with the treasure after all! But how? And why? Just who was she? Whose side was she on? Did she have any connection with El Gallo? If so, what? He sighed. He realized he would have to question her as subtly as he could, but he had the feeling he wasn't going to get very far. She was too smart; too clever to let him penetrate that cool beauty which concealed a brain: a working, thoughtful brain.

He felt no remorse about his burglary. Everything was fair in love and war, he told himself, excusing himself. Besides, whatever part she was playing, she was playing for keeps; and there had been one death already, two assaults upon himself, plus all the mysterious goings-on he'd encountered since his arrival.

Well, he sighed, he was in it up to his *como se llama*. There was no doubting that. And all because of a story which was yet to be written.

He left the dark shadows of the house he'd leaned against, heading back to his hotel.

As he opened the door, turning on the light, he said, "Shit!"

His room had been ransacked again, but this time more neatly done. No one had used a knife to cut up the pillows and mattress, although they were thrown on the floor in a welter of covers, and clothes from the dresser. The drawers of the desk and dresser were on the floor. El Gallo's knife blade gleamed in the light. Whoever had searched was an amateur. From past experiences, Little knew that. His metal trunk was undisturbed as he knew it would be. The level of the liquid in the gallon jug had been lowered. Little smiled to himself. He needed some of that, too. But, first, he was going to straighten up the room and remake the bed.

If anything was missing he'd discover what it was in the morning. But, first, he was going to sit down, relax, and make use of his excellent memory.

As he was sipping some of The Gunner's concoction, he brought to mind the pieces of the map.

N G N U E V O M E X

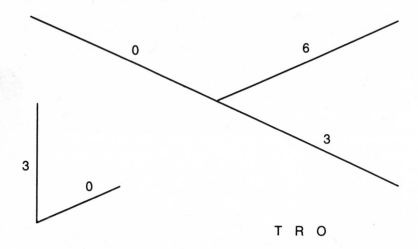

T R O

They didn't add up to much, but he was beginning to see a pattern in those he had seen. Dick Little realized he was working on the assumption there were two triangles involved: equilateral. He couldn't read or make any sense of the numbers. What had he told The Gunner earlier? The map had been made by a clever mind, not a devious one.

Well, then, since it had been torn into eight parts, the top left piece he'd call number ONE; the last on the right, number FOUR; bottom left, FIVE; and bottom right, EIGHT. He'd seen parts number two, three, five, and seven: The señorita's, Gallo's, Billy's, and The Gunner's. He'd include his later. He could guess what part of number one would tell him, because number two continued from it: D-E-M-I. Two with -N-G-N-U-E. The third with -V-O-M-E-X. And, obviously, the fourth with -I-C-O. D-E-M-I-N-G-N-U-E-V-O-M-E-X-I-C-O: *Deming, Nuevo Mexico; Deming, New Mexico!* The line slanting across numbers two and seven had two numbers above it: 0 and 3. 0-3 what? Piece number five was an angle with a 3 on the base and a 0 above the line, slanting up. Number six was missing, but obviously the upward slanting line cut through it to piece number seven. So, above the line, on number five was a 3, and on three, a 6. 3 something 6. On piece number seven, near the left torn edge and below the slanting line, were the letters T-R-O. What the hell did they all mean?

He'd been right in telling The Gunner it was necessary to have all the parts together before they made any sense. He thought over the parts once more, and gave up.

Dick Little finished his drink, turned off the light, then stretched catty-cornered out on the bed. As the gentle breeze from the overhead fan moved over him he had but one thought before falling into a deep and dreamless sleep.

It had all started with Villa's *compadre:* that fat, thieving son of a bitch, General Tomás Urbina!

CHARLIE WOKE HIM the next morning by knocking on the door. He opened it sleepily. "Telegram, Mr. Withers," Charlie said, holding out the yellow envelope. Dick Little took it, tearing it open. He read its brief message. "Thanks, Charlie," he said. "No answer."

Sitting on the bed he read it again. "Richard Withers, Baker Hotel, Deming, N.M. Thanks. John." He smiled to himself, putting the telegram on the night table. If anyone wanted to break in again and read it, they were welcome.

After bathing and dressing in clean clothes, Dick Little sauntered down the street to the Manhattan Café. He was almost finished with breakfast when he looked up to see Señorita Gutiérrez gazing down at him. He started to rise.

"Please, Señor Withers. May I join you?"

"Certainly," he said, settling himself again. "Breakfast? Coffee?"

"Coffee, if you please. I had breakfast early."

He noted her costume. "Riding early this morning?"

"Yes. I had to come by here and happened to see you through the window."

He signaled for the waitress. "What will it be?"

"Coffee, please," she said, smiling up at the waitress. She waited until the cup was in front of her. Reaching for the sugar, she said, "I want to apologize for the other day."

"Apologize?"

"Yes, for worrying you in Las Palomas."

He smiled. "If that's the least you'll ever do to me, I forgive you."

He reached for a slice of buttered toast as she was pouring cream into her cup. He spread jam on the toast. She tasted her coffee after stirring it. "Señorita Gutiérrez," he asked, "would you mind very much if I asked you a personal question?" He bit into the toast.

She looked at him steadily over the rim of her cup before she put it down slowly. "No," she said, "I do not mind your asking. The answer will depend on your question."

"Fair enough," he said, smiling slightly at the barb. He hesitated. "Why are you really in Deming?"

She started to laugh until she saw the calm, serious expression on his face. He took another bite out of the toast. "I believe I told you," she answered, "I'm visiting my uncle."

"No," he said seriously, "I mean your real reason for being here."

"Visiting my uncle," she repeated.

"This could get us nowhere," he said.

"Do you have reason to believe otherwise?"

"Yes," he said simply, "I do."

She smiled. "Suppose you tell me."

He took a swallow from his coffee cup before he answered. He set the cup down, wiped his hands on his napkin, then reached for his Bull Durham. He started to roll a cigarette. "Ever since I've come to this town," he began slowly, "people have been after me for a reason I can't figure. I've been shot at once by an ex-revolutionary called El Gallo, a brigade captain and one of Pancho Villa's Dorados. My room has been searched twice. I was knocked on the head last night." He felt the spot. "Unfortunately for them, I was not seriously injured." Her eyes opened wider. He continued, "I've had an old friend murdered, and," he added, "I have suspicions you are mixed up in it up to your beautiful—eyes."

She leaned back, looking at him levelly. "What makes you think so?"

A smile crossed his lips. "Because you did not indignantly start to leave just now. You want to hear more?"

"I certainly do," she snapped. "I haven't the slightest idea what you mean, or what you're talking about!"

"Day before yesterday we went to Las Palomas. You entered a house and mysteriously disappeared."

"I did not disappear. I was in the house."

"Were you? Not when I searched it for you. As you know, I was worried about you."

"You searched the house?" Her voice rose indignantly.

"Certainly," he said, matter-of-factly. "I was looking for you."

"You had no right!"

"Beside the point. You were not there. To make a long story short, it was in the cantina next door that I was attacked by El Gallo. Fortunately, I am a better man with my fists than he is. You've told me you didn't know El Gallo."

"No, I do not. I have seen him. I do not know him," she said emphatically.

"Then why did he attack me?"

"Mr. Withers," she said slowly, coldly, "I think you're getting some wrong impressions about me. I do not know any El Gallo. And as for your suspicions, I did not set him on you, if that is your impression. I do not now, or before, know the man. I only know *of* him."

He looked at her steadily. "I believe you," he said finally.

"Thank you. That is most kind of you." Her eyes flashed at him.

"What do you know of the treasure which is supposed to be buried around here?" he asked abruptly.

She was taken aback. "Treasure?"

He nodded over the rim of his coffee cup.

"I know of no treasure."

"Pardon me for saying so, but I do not believe you this time," he said.

"Are you calling me a liar?"

"Not at all," he said smoothly. "I'm merely saying I have reason to believe you know something of what is going on, or that you are mixed up in what is going on. There is a treasure; that much I know. I know where it came from. I suspect how it got here. I knew the people involved. I don't know where it is, except that it is buried somewhere in this area. I suspect, for some reason, people are congregating in Deming who are most anxious to find it. What the motives of these people are, aside from greed, I do not know. I suspect you are wrapped up in it as tightly as you can get. Why? I'm asking you now."

"Señor Withers," she said scornfully, "I think you are talking complete nonsense. I have never heard anything so preposterous as what you are telling me now. Why should I stay here and listen to the ramblings of a madman?" She started to move from the booth.

"So now I am a madman," he said laconically. "Am I so mad to tell you I have recently seen a piece of Fierro's map? And that it is here near Deming?"

"Oh no!" she gasped.

"Oh yes, *señorita*. Here, near Deming. Do you want me to draw it for you? I'd be most happy to."

Taking a pencil from his pocket, along with a notebook, he quickly sketched for her the line, figure, and word he had seen on The Gunner's piece. He tore the page from his notebook, handing it to her with a flourish. She couldn't avoid lowering her eyes to it, or taking it in her hand. For a long moment she studied it. "Keep it," he said airily. "It is yours."

She raised her eyes to his. "Where did you get this?"

"From Gunner Marks," he answered. "He runs an illegal bar here in town. The Gunner was an officer under Felipe Angeles at one time. I knew him back there when."

"Gunner Marks?"

"Yes. He was once in the U.S. Artillery. He joined Villa after Madero was murdered. Because of his experience with heavy guns, he served under Felipe Angeles and was one of his best and most trusted officers. Toward the end of '15, he was horribly wounded by a bursting shell which almost killed him. He's been here in Deming for some years now. I ran into him the other night. He showed me this part of, what he said, was a treasure map. If you know the story, he was at the dinner at Villa's headquarters when Pancho tore up the original and passed the pieces around. If you want, I'll introduce you to The Gunner. He'll be glad to show you his original piece. Since he can't make heads or tails of it, he figures he has nothing to gain by keeping it hidden. Would you like to meet him?"

"Not necessarily. May I keep this? As a souvenir of—of—" she hesitated, "of a most ridiculous accusation?"

"You can keep it; but I don't feel my accusation is so ridiculous."

She folded the paper, putting it into a pocket of her riding skirt. "I must go now," she said.

"You know, Señorita Gutiérrez," he said, stopping her with his words, "I've become involved in this treasure hunt, too, since I've been here. I know something of its history. I have been told, or hinted to, that the treasure is near here. What could be more exciting for a visitor than to take part in a search which could pay off in millions of dollars?"

"If there were a treasure," she said coolly, "and it is near here, as you say, wouldn't it be dangerous for you to participate in a search which has already taken one life?"

He glanced at her sharply. "One life?" he asked. "Whose?"

"That cowboy. Er—Thomas. The one who was killed only two days ago."

He appraised her with a long look. She wet her lips with her tongue. "What makes you think Billy Thomas was mixed up in the treasure hunt?" he asked abruptly. "What do you know about Billy that I don't?"

She stood up quickly to cover her confusion. "I—I don't know what you're talking about. Good day, Mr. Withers!" She strode purposefully from the café. He watched her depart. He reached for another piece of toast with one hand and for the jam with the other. He was smiling to himself.

THAT AFTERNOON, Richard Henry Little decided on another trip south. He went to Nordhau's store, buying a few things necessary for his journey. In his room he took other items from his metal trunk, putting them all together in a bedroll. He'd decided not to take the automobile because it was too conspicuous. His horse at O'Conner's was rested, well fed, and needed the exercise. First he told Charlie at the desk he'd be away for two or three days and to look out for his automobile. The clerk promised to see it was put into a garage. Dick Little gave him the key. Secondly, he informed O'Conner where he was going and approximately how long he thought he would be away. Tying his bedroll to the back of the saddle, he mounted and rode slowly out of town toward the south.

He took his time riding to Columbus, making several side trips. When night overtook him he was camped at the foot of the Floridas, cooking his supper over a small fire. This was the life which contented him most: out in the open, under the moon and the stars, a simple meal, and a thick enough blanket to keep the chill from him as he slept. The horse was hobbled nearby, chomping at the patches of grass growing among the rocks. Little had been careful in choosing his campsite. It was hidden behind boulders. His fire could be seen only if an observer was directly overhead looking straight down. Even then, his fire was small, throwing only enough heat to cook his beans and bacon, and to boil his coffee.

Little relaxed on the thin bed sheet, rolling cigarettes, smoking them, thinking over the events which had happened since his arrival in Deming. His thoughts turned to Stella. She was a pretty girl, well built, but wiry as women who lived on ranches often are. He imagined she could be very direct and very stubborn when she was so inclined; yet she was all woman, as desirable as many he had encountered on his travels. In fact, he could list her highly among the women who had crossed his path over the years and with whom he had had more than a passing acquaintance.

Then, of course, there was Señorita Gutiérrez. She possessed all of the fire certain attractive Spanish women had. She'd had good breeding, obviously. And she could also think for herself. He'd met women like her before in the Latin countries, and they had never ceased to excite him physically as well as mentally. He recalled vividly an affair he'd had with the wife of a Mexican colonel who had been imprisoned briefly during one of the many shifts in politics in Mexico City. He laughed aloud. That had been two weeks of high passion and satisfyingly tranquil hours. What a name she'd had: Concepción!

He fell into a deep sleep without knowing it.

The next morning he caught and saddled his horse. His breakfast consisted of fried eggs, bacon, and coffee. He completed his toilet behind a rock out of sight from his camp. He cleaned his frying pan and coffeepot, rolled up his bed sheet and blanket with the utensils inside, strapped it to the saddle and mounted. He headed for Columbus at the same lazy pace he had established the day before.

It was afternoon when he reached the remains of the town. He rode up and down the deserted streets looking at dilapidated houses, at the very few which weren't, and at the still visible signs of Villa's destructive raid when he had burned the town. Or most of it.

He found one woebegone café where he ate a late afternoon steak. It was tough but flavorful, fresh-killed meat from Las Palomas over in Mexico. He found some grain for his horse, leaving it in a stable after rubbing it down. The horse was frisky, showing no signs of the journey. It was ready to go again.

He'd asked questions of the Mexican boy serving as cook and headwaiter at the café. Long strides took him to a neat one-story house, where a casually dressed man with silvery hair, a long face, and the drooping eyes of a beagle was watering some plants from a sloshing bucket.

"Mr. Devereaux?" he asked politely.

"Yes. Can I help you?" He put the bucket down carefully beside a plant.

"Perhaps you can. I understand you used to be the stationmaster here in Columbus."

"I was," the man answered. "For many years."

"Mind if I ask you a few questions?"

"Not at all. Let's sit on the porch. It isn't often I see a strange face here in Columbus. What sort of questions, Mr.—? Mr.—?"

"Withers," Dick Little said without hesitation.

They sat on the floor of the small porch to the house, their feet on the ground. Devereaux took a pipe and tobacco from a pocket. He filled the pipe with deliberation, packed down the tobacco with his thumb, then lit it with a flaring wooden match. Little rolled a cigarette, taking a light from the offered match.

"What can I do for you, Mr. Withers?" Devereaux asked. His speech was slow, concise.

"I'm a newspaperman," Little told him, deciding a little truth was necessary for the occasion. "I'm tracking down a story concerning some Mexican nationals who unloaded a boxcar here several years ago."

Devereaux puffed on his pipe several times. "You're investigating the Fierro treasure?" he asked calmly.

Little was delighted at the directness of Devereaux's answer. "Yes," he admitted, "I am. I rode down from Deming to see if I could find someone here who could fill me in on different parts of the story."

"Do you believe there's a treasure buried near here?"

"Yes I do, sir," Little said. "I have heard the story from several sources over the years. I decided I'd come down and dig it out for a magazine article. The boy at the café told me you had been with the railroad here for a long time; so, here I am."

More puffs on the pipe. "I'm retired now, you know," Devereaux said calmly. "I was stationmaster here for a long, long time before the raid. We used to call the early morning train from El Paso The Drunkard's Express due to the number of hangovers who'd roll out of the cars to report for duty at Camp Furlong. Sunday and Monday mornings especially." More puffs on the pipe. "I recall the episode you're referring to." He knocked the burned tobacco from his pipe against the palm of his hand. His thumb pressed down the bowl. More puffs. "I believe in the treasure stories, too." Devereaux smiled. "I never looked for it. I guess I'm one of the few who isn't interested in a lot of money and the trouble it brings."

"How is that, sir?"

"I'm satisfied here. I worked for the railroad until they retired me. I have my house. My plants." He pointed his pipe stem at the places he had watered. "I have a small library of books. I have a few friends still here I can visit with. I lack nothing. I want very little." He puffed some more.

Dick Little decided to let the man ramble on.

"I guess it was sometime in '15; late summer, maybe. I received notice that a boxcar out of El Paso would be shunted to a siding here to wait for freight to be unloaded. One morning, there it was; a Mexican Central car on the siding. We'd had Mexican Central cars before, but this was different. There were six men with it. Soldiers. Mexican soldiers." The pipe had burned out. Devereaux knocked out the dottle and refilled the pipe from his pouch. A match flared.

He puffed, drawing the flame downward. "They were tough *hombres*, those soldiers." Puff. "Dressed in a sort of uniform." Puff. "They wore pistols." Puff. "Carried Mausers." Puff. "Had cartridge belts about their waists." Puff. "And slung over their shoulders." Puff. "Crossing over their chests." Puff. "They had on tight pants and wore big spurs on their boots." Puff. "They made music when they walked." Puff. Puff.

Devereaux took the pipe stem from his mouth. "They had hard faces. Big mustaches, most of them. They wore large sombreros, the kind with the wide brims. They didn't speak English, but they did talk among themselves, laughing and joking, looking at any of us who came by with hard eyes and guns handy. I remember those men."

He held the bowl of his pipe between his hands, his hands between his knees, hunched over. "The captain of the soldiers," he continued, "their leader, whatever he was, was a tall man with a pinched hat like our soldiers wear, only it was white. Just like yours, as a matter of fact," he added. "This *jefe* spoke some English. I can hear his voice now. He was used to command, and his voice carried without his having to raise it. He was all muscle, that man. I heard later he was General Rodolfo Fierro. He moved like a panther, smooth and quick. I'll never forget him to the day I die."

Devereaux paused, lost in his thoughts. "He told me he didn't want anybody coming near the car; that they'd be out of the siding in a couple or three days. As far as I was concerned, whatever he did was all right with me. I only worked for the railroad and did what they told me to do. I told him he could leave the car there as many days as he liked, as long as the railroad was satisfied and I knew about it. That was the only conversation I had with him." Devereaux straightened. He struck another match to light his pipe. "I don't recall how many days the car was on the siding." Puff. "I do know I got my orders about it one day, and the next it had been picked up by the east freight and, I presume, sent back to Mexico." Puff. Puff. There was no smoke.

Devereaux emptied his pipe again.

"How was the car unloaded?" Little asked. "Did you see what was taken from it?"

Devereaux shook his head. "No," he said slowly, "you'd have to ask Sonny Johns about that."

"Who?"

"Sonny Johns. He used to own a store here until it was burned down during the raid. Still lives here, as a matter of fact. Over there." With his pipe stem, he pointed to a house a quarter of a mile distant. "He could tell you about the unloading."

"Would he be home now?"

"Can't say. He might be in Las Palomas about this time. He owns cattle on both sides of the line."

"If he's not at home, where would he most likely be in Las Palomas?"

"Try the Palomita bar over there. He usually goes there to eat when he's across the border."

"Well, Mr. Devereaux," Dick Little said, standing up, extending his hand. "It has been a pleasure talking with you. And I thank you for taking the time."

Devereaux smiled. "That's all I've got left, Mr. Withers," he said, shaking hands. "If you come this way again, stop by. It's been nice meeting you."

"Thank you, sir."

Little left Mr. Devereaux picking up his bucket to water more of his plants.

He walked to the house Devereaux had pointed to. There was no one home. The door was locked. Dick Little walked back to the stable, saddled his horse, and rode south to the border. The same Mexican customs guard was on duty. He waved Little on. It did not take long for him to locate the bar called La Palomita. Tying his horse to the hitching rack in front, and casting a look along the street to note nothing had really changed since his last visit, he entered the bar through the swinging doors. He spotted Sonny Johns immediately.

Johns was the only Anglo in the place. He was seated at a table with a bottle of beer, a glass, and a plateful of steak in front of him. The man was round: round of body, head, arms, and fingers. Dressed in a business suit he looked to Little like many-sized balls somehow strung together and dressed. His eyes were small, his mouth round. He wheezed slightly as he breathed. Dick Little went up to him. "Mr. Johns?" he asked.

The man darted a look at him. "That's me, brother!" he boomed.

"Sit down!" His voice was amazingly deep and carrying. Dick Little pulled up a chair, sitting across the table from Johns.

"My name is Withers," he introduced himself. "I'm a newspaperman writing a story on the treasure which is supposed to be buried somewhere near here."

"Treasure!" Johns boomed. "I can tell you a story about treasure! Have something to eat. The food's pretty good here."

"I ate not long ago," Little admitted, "but I will join you in a beer."

"Cerveza!" Johns called to the back of the room. A man sauntered up to the table with a bottle and glass, setting them in front of Little. "What do you want to know, Mr. Withers?"

"I'm tracking down an event which took place in Columbus in the latter part of '15. I've just talked with Mr. Devereaux about the boxcar which came up from Mexico."

Johns chewed on his food. He looked levelly at Dick Little with steady round eyes. He grunted after he swallowed. "That one?"

"That one."

He grunted again. "Thought so."

"What happened, Mr. Johns?"

"Very mysterious, Mr. Withers. Very mysterious." He took another bite of food, chewed, then drank from his glass. "Mexican fellow; big man. He came to my store asking for me. He wanted to hire five wagons and double teams. I told him I had the wagons and horses; I told him I'd have to round up that many drivers: it would take a couple of days to get the men I wanted. He didn't want the men. He had men of his own, he said. I told him to go to hell. No drivers, no wagons. We settled for the wagons and teams."

"Did he threaten you?"

Sonny Johns laughed until his body shook. "I'll say he did," he chortled. "He threatened me with the full price of the whole shootin' match —in gold. He counted it out right there at my desk. I made a price. He paid it. U.S. gold pieces. You're damned right he threatened me!" He laughed again, booming good nature throughout the barroom. "I had to give in."

"Then what happened?"

Sonny Johns signaled to the bartender for another round of beer. "I got the wagons together, with the teams. He sent over five Mexicans to drive them off. I didn't see hide nor hair of them for the next five days." He cut into his steak. "Five days later the wagons and teams drifted back to my stable. At least, two of them did. I had to get some men and go out and look for the others. We found them. There wasn't a Mexican in sight."

"What do you think happened, Mr. Johns?"

Johns chewed reflectively on a mouthful of meat. "You really want my opinion?"

"Yes."

"I think those Mexicans filled those wagons with whatever they had in that boxcar they parked on the siding at the station. They loaded them at night and drove north somewheres. They buried whatever they took with them; then the big man killed every one of those poor dumb sons of bitches, that's what I think. After that, he just turned the wagons loose to let the horses find their way back. Of course, he covered his tracks pretty well."

"How do you mean?"

Sonny Johns' eyes glittered. "You don't think I didn't try to track down where he took those wagons, do you?" He laughed again. "Hell, I rode all over that country looking for what he took along with him. Never did find it. Never found a trace of where those wagons went. Oh, I could follow them for a piece after they turned off the road, but two things hid the tracks after that."

"What?"

"The ground. He chose well. The ground didn't hold tracks and, besides, a couple of days later, we had one of the goddamndest gully washers this part of the country had in years. Lucky for him. There was no way to trail them after that."

"Too bad."

Johns' laughter boomed again. "Yeah. I could have been rich, I figure."

"So you think it was a treasure that was moved?"

"You're damned right it was!"

"Know who the leader was, the man who contacted you?"

"Hell yes," he said, taking another bite of his steak. "It was Fierro."

"You recognized him?"

"Why not? Him and Pancho used to drop in to my store from time to time." He smiled. "I used to do a certain type of business with old Pancho. You understand?"

"I understand."

"That was when the United States was doing business with him also." He winked. "They used to drop in to order their merchandise. Sometimes they would go on up to Deming to sort of look around and meet

with their agents, I suppose. Anyway, I knew that bastard, Fierro, to
see him. Couldn't very likely forget a man like that. Drowned in Lake
Guzmán, I hear."

"Farther down. Nearer to Casas Grandes."

"Used to fish in Lake Guzmán." Johns poured himself a glass of beer,
draining it off. "Know Dr. Jim Smith in Deming?"

"No."

"Ask him about the dead man."

"Dead man?"

"An Anglo. Found him near the road about that time. Ask him about
it."

"Thanks, I will. So, you think Fierro buried a treasure somewhere up
north of here?"

Johns nodded, slipping the last bite of steak into his mouth. "Could
be anywhere. Those tracks leading off the road could have been a trick.
I figure it's anywhere between Cooke's Peak to the foot of the Floridas.
Never could find it."

"Ever see Fierro after that?"

"No, never. Then Pancho came in and burned me out in '16. Son of a
bitch! I was always fair with him, too. Never cheated him any more
than he expected to be cheated. I thought he was a friend of mine."

"Pancho is like that."

"Yeah."

"Well, Mr. Johns," Dick Little said, rising from the table, "many
thanks for your help. Dr. Smith, you said? In Deming?"

"Jim Smith."

"I'll look him up. Thanks again."

"Another beer?"

"Sorry, I've got a long ride back to Deming."

Sonny Johns' laughter filled the saloon. "I hope you ain't looking for
the treasure!"

Little shook his head. "Only writing an article about it."

"You'll probably make the most money that way. By the way, did
you know Fierro never came back for the difference?"

"Difference of what?"

"Of what he paid full price for the wagons and what I'd of returned
to him for hire. I came out all right, too."

"You were fortunate."

Dick Little went to the bar. He purchased two bottles of beer and
started out of the cantina.

"Say!" Johns boomed. "Somebody else was talking to me about those wagons not long ago!"

Little stopped, turned, facing the table. "Who was it?"

Johns shook his round head. "Don't know the name, but she sure was a pretty Mexican gal!"

Richard Henry Little set the pace back to Deming faster than the one coming down. He camped again at the foot of the Floridas, cooking his supper over a small fire, drinking his beer with relish and sleeping heavily through the night. The next morning, after he had cleaned the coffeepot and frying pan and packed, he mounted the skittish horse, let him buck a few times, then headed him back to the road. By noon he was in Deming eating lunch at the Manhattan Café, thinking of the two interviews he'd had and the one coming up. He asked the waitress where he could find Dr. Smith. She directed him up the street. He found the office on the second floor of a run-down building. Climbing the dark stairs, he knocked on the glass panel of the door which was lettered simply DR. JAMES SMITH, M.D. The doctor opened the door.

"Yes?" He peered into the gloom of the landing.

"Dr. Smith?"

"Yes."

"My name's Withers," Dick said. "I'd like to talk to you for a few minutes."

The door opened wide. "Come in! Come in!" The doctor stood aside as Little entered the anteroom. "Come into my office," said the doctor, leading him through another door, closing it behind them.

The office was small with filled bookshelves, from floor to ceiling, covering three walls. The furniture was scarce: a rolltop desk cluttered with papers; a rocking captain's chair; one deep leather-covered chair; one straight-backed wooden chair; a medicine and instrument case behind two glass doors; a couch and an examination table. The doctor seated himself in the chair in front of his desk, indicating to Dick Little to take the leather chair. He sank into it, his knees almost level with his chin.

The doctor was bald on top with a fringe of gray hair running around the back of his skull. His face was placid, but the eyes were alive. He wore a surgical white coat down to his knees, dark trousers, and shoes which could have used the services of a cobbler and a shoeshine boy. Dick noted his fingers were long, restless. The doctor's head was atop a long skinny neck and he held his head sideways like a bird.

"What can I do for you?" he asked in a soft voice. His accent was New Englandish.

"My name is Withers," Little announced. "I'm a newspaperman writing a story concerning a lost treasure in this vicinity. I understand, from Mr. Sonny Johns, that you know something about it."

The doctor sniffed through his lean nose. "Treasure? I know nothing about any treasure." He sniffed again. He pursed his thin lips, licking them with the tip of his tongue.

"Mr. Johns said something about a body found on the Columbus road."

The doctor thought a moment. "Ayah," he said. "Sometime back in '15, I recollect. I think there were rumors about a treasure then. Haven't heard much about it lately."

"What about the body?"

The doctor's eyes dimmed with thought. "Ayah. I was county coroner then. Someone found a body alongside the road and reported it to the sheriff. He was pretty far gone when I got there. He was dead all right. Shot through the back of the head with a large caliber bullet. We never did find the murderer." He brushed his fingertips across his lips. "Ayah. That was a long time ago."

"Was there anything strange about his death?"

The eyes came alive again. "Strange? The man had been murdered; that was strange. For no reason I could recollect."

"No reason?"

"None we could find. He was married; had one child, a boy. His wife was a sweet young thing. I delivered the boy, I recollect. Ayah. His name was Knight. Robert Knight. Found facedown in the ditch alongside the road. Tragic case. Left a young wife and a boy about two. Nobody knew why he was killed. Funny thing." He paused to sniff again.

"Yes?"

"His instruments were beside him. Nobody had touched his instruments, I recollect."

"Instruments?"

"Ayah. Knight had an assay office here. He also did surveying. Good at it, too." The doctor touched his lips with his fingertips. "His surveying instruments. That one you look through was in its box; the tripod was right beside it, I recollect. They were both beside the body. That was a long time ago."

"Eight years, sir."

"Ayah. After I was voted out as coroner, I retired. Only take care of my old patients now. Those who are left. Not many come to see me now." He sniffed.

"Was there anything else peculiar about the case that you remem— recollect?"

The doctor shook his head. "Ayah," he said quickly. "Peculiar. During the investigation, the inquest, it came out he'd been called out of his house in the middle of the night. Nobody saw who it was who waited for him. He just disappeared, I recollect. His body was found about five or six days later. They never found the person who murdered him." He fell silent as his eyes dimmed again with thought.

Dick Little unfolded his long frame from the depths of the chair. He stood, towering over the doctor. "You've been very helpful, sir," he said. "How much do I owe you for your time?"

The doctor looked up at him. He sniffed. "Owe? You owe me nothing. It has been my pleasure, your dropping in like this. I couldn't accept anything for a few words."

"Thank you," Dick said. "You've been a help. A big help." He shook the doctor's limp hand, leaving the office, closing both doors behind him as he passed. On the way down the dark stairs he was thinking of the young surveyor, a murdered man named Robert Knight, who, in all probability, had drawn the treasure map before Fierro killed him.

THE FIRST PERSON he ran into, on the street, was Stella Townsend.

"Oh," she said, startled. "I was looking for you, Mr. Withers." She smiled sweetly. "My father and I were wondering whether you could come to the ranch for supper tonight?"

Dick Little returned her smile, replacing his hat. "I'd be delighted, Miss Stella. At what time?"

"Say about seven?"

"I'll be there. Thank you for the invitation."

"You're quite welcome, Mr. Withers. We'll be expecting you." She smiled at him again, walking on down the street.

Little returned to his hotel. He told Charlie to have his automobile in front at about six, and to call him in his room when it was ready. He took his key and went upstairs. In a few minutes he was folded up in the bathtub at the end of the hall, half cursing, half singing. Back in his room, he shaved carefully, then took from his metal trunk a dark suit of clothes, white shirt, string tie, and a pair of dark dress shoes. He put them on carefully, polishing his shoes with the damp towel he'd used after his bath. He poured himself a drink from The Gunner's jug, looking at it a moment before taking a mouthful, swishing it about before swallowing. He shuddered slightly. He was sitting on the bed rolling a cigarette when the phone rang. It was Charlie telling him the automobile was ready.

Before he left, he opened the drawer of the desk and looked at the pistol he'd taken from El Gallo. Opening the loading gate, he spun the cylinder to see if it was still loaded. It was, all six chambers. He slid it under his coat, on the left side, and snugged it firmly in his belt. His reason for doing so was not clear, even to himself, but he began to feel better as he buttoned his coat, feeling the weight of the revolver at his waist.

The automobile started immediately. He shut it off at a thought, getting out with the measuring stick, taking off the top of the gas tank and inserting the stick to check the amount of gasoline he had. Martínez had filled it after the trip to Columbus. He got back in and started the automobile a second time.

The weather was perfect for the time of the year. The sun was still up and there was an easterly breeze which cooled the air. Dick Little had never lowered the top of the automobile. This offered further protection. He wore his Stetson still, tilted forward as an old cavalryman would do to shade his eyes until he turned off the road facing east, then he tilted it back, stopping the automobile long enough to roll and light a cigarette. The road didn't seem as rough as it had before, possibly due to the fact he was consciously paying attention to his driving, avoiding potholes as much as he could. He was tired in body, but with a healthy tiredness. After all, he had ridden several hours that morning to reach Deming and he hadn't rested much since. Driving the automobile relaxed him.

He was passing some hills on his left when suddenly the windshield shattered into a thousand pieces before his eyes. Before he could react, he heard a bullet zip past his ear. He ducked, letting the car run off the road into the ditch. Scrambling quickly along the seat, he opened the front door on the opposite side, sliding head first onto the ground beside the stalled automobile. He rolled, pulling his pistol, getting to his knees beside the auto. He peered over the radiator toward the hills. He saw a puff of smoke drifting away in the slight breeze. At the same time he saw another puff. The bullet hit the car in the door beside the steering wheel and zing-g-g-ed off into space. He was too far away to use the pistol effectively. He cursed aloud to himself. The man in the hills was using a rifle. He was taking careful aim to rake the automobile from one end to the other, concentrating on the doors and hitting them low enough to reach anyone who would be either lying on the seat, or on the floor. There was a pause for several minutes. Dick Little thought of raising his head when the rifle opened up again, firing rapidly and accurately. With a shoulder against the fender he could feel the car jump slightly each time a bullet impacted. Whoever was shooting, he was good with a rifle. The firing stopped. Dick Little waited as the silence grew deep and profound. Faintly he heard the sound of a horse galloping away from behind the hills.

Cautiously he stood up, holding his cocked pistol. There was nothing to be seen against the hills; no movement except for the grass and plants swaying gently in the breeze. The telegraph wires alongside the train tracks hummed slightly, giving an eerie sound to the almost dead silence.

Dick Little walked to the opposite side of the automobile. He fingered three bullet holes in the door where he had been sitting. They were spread out in a pattern so that if he had stayed in the car huddled up he would have been killed or seriously wounded. The back door had the same pattern of holes. There were others scattered about the frame of the car. He examined the hood. It was not as badly shot up as the body. It had one bullet hole in it. He opened the hood from the other side. The bullet had traveled through without touching the engine.

The car was merely stalled. The motor turned over easily when he stepped on the starter. He placed the revolver on the seat where he could reach it quickly, backed the automobile out of the ditch, and resumed his journey down the road. He turned into the ranch road at the mailbox, driving slowly, keeping his eyes open for further shots, his body tense in case he'd have to suddenly jump out of the automobile.

He pulled up in front of the S T ranch house without further incident. Sam Townsend was waiting for him at the gate. He came toward the car, hand outstretched in greeting. In the last rays of the sun coming over the hills in back of the house he saw the holes in the car and a few shreds of glass still in the windshield frame. His jaw dropped and his mouth opened. "What in hell happened to you?" he asked in amazement.

Dick Little got out of the automobile, carefully replacing the revolver in his belt. "I was shot at," he said simply.

"Were you hit?"

"No. Don't think so."

Sam looked him over. "You have a cut on your cheek. Come inside," he said. "Stella will fix you up."

Dick Little felt his cheek with his fingers and then looked at the blood on their tips. "Must be from flying glass," he said. "I'll need one more thing besides getting the cut fixed."

"You shall have it," Sam Townsend announced. "I have it ready on the table. Do you want it with, or without water?"

"Straight."

Sam chuckled, leading him into the house, calling for his daughter.

Stella efficiently cleaned the slight cut with stinging witch hazel. Little flinched. She laughed at him. She tore a piece of court plaster from a roll, spreading it over the cut, closing it. "There," she said, putting the cork back into the bottle. "You're all bandaged up now. It shouldn't bleed again. It's too shallow."

He laughed, finishing his drink. Sam Townsend poured him another, adding ice and a shot from the seltzer bottle. There was a worried look on his face. "Who could have done such a thing?" he asked.

"It certainly wasn't Indians," Little said. "This man was too good with a rifle."

"For what reason? Why was he after you?"

"I suppose," Little said slowly, "it's because of the treasure. I guess he thought I was dead and skedaddled."

"The treasure?"

He nodded. "I'm interested in the story. Yesterday I was in Columbus interviewing two men who saw Fierro bring it into the country: Mr. Devereaux and Mr. Johns. Today, I talked to Dr. Smith about the murder of Bob Knight. Did you know him?"

"I did," Stella said. "His wife was a friend of mine. Betty. She took care of me when Daddy had to go away on business. I can remember when he was killed. I was only fifteen then."

"What would Bob Knight have to do with Fierro's treasure?" Sam asked. "He wasn't a brigand, or outlaw, or anything like that. He was a personable young man making his own way in the world, building up a successful business for himself."

"It's my guess he was too successful," Dick said.

"What?" Sam Townsend was startled. "In what way? How?"

"Look, Sam, I've been able to pin down a few things. I know Fierro brought a boxcar full of something into Columbus in the late summer of

'15. He had five or six of Villa's Dorados with him, according to Mr. Devereaux. According to a Mr. Sonny Johns, Fierro unloaded what he had into five wagons and brought them up around here, possibly to Cooke's Peak where he buried it. He then killed the Dorados, turning the wagons loose for the teams to find their way back home. From what Mr. Johns told me, Fierro was familiar with Deming. He most probably hired Knight to draw up a map after surveying the treasure spot, then killed Knight to keep his mouth shut."

"Why," Stella gasped, "that's just like *Treasure Island!*"

Little nodded. "Captain Flint. Dead men tell no tales. That's about the size of it."

"How horrible!"

"Nevertheless, true. He took the map back to Villa; Villa tore it up, giving the pieces to trusted men. Now, it seems, all of a sudden, the treasure is important to a lot of people."

"But who?" she asked.

He shrugged. "Gunner Marks has a piece of it and makes no bones about having it. It's no good to him without the other pieces. All he wants is a percentage of the whole. He's not greedy. Not like some of the others."

Sam said, "I had no idea."

"Not many people have," Little commented. "It's all very complicated. I'm not sure anyone could ever dig out the truth, the whole truth."

"Well," Stella said, "I know nothing of treasures except what little I've heard and don't believe. Supper should be ready by now. Drink up and let's eat." She bustled off to the kitchen, taking the first aid kit with her.

Sam smiled thinly. "That's my girl."

"A very pretty one, Sam. You should be proud."

He nodded. "I am. Want to wash up before dinner?"

The dinner was excellent. Stella was a good cook. She saw to it that both of the men at the table were satisfied right down to the pie for dessert. While she cleaned the dishes, the two men sat in the front room, smoking. Dick rolled his cigarettes while Sam puffed on a black cigar. There was not much talk between them.

"Dick," Sam said after a while, "I haven't mentioned to anyone who you are. Are you working on a story about the treasure, or are you looking for it?"

Little laughed. "I'm writing about it."

"It could be dangerous if you were looking for it."

"I know. I value my hide. I'll let others find it if they can."

Sam seemed to relax. "Somehow," he said, "I'd rather have the good old days when murder was out in the open."

"In the open?"

"I can't help but think of Fierro. He's here, now, amongst us, doing his killing though he's been dead these eight years. Somehow, I prefer his old ways: direct and in the open as he killed Berlanga."

"David Berlanga? What do you know about that?" Little asked.

"I was in Mexico at the time. I heard about it. Berlanga was a pepper pot; always opening his mouth at the wrong time. I knew him and didn't particularly like him, but I was sorry about his death. Do you know the story, Dick?"

Little nodded. "I was told about it by one of my friends in the Ministry of War. Fierro was always self-assured and smiling: it was his habit. He appeared at the ministry to ask my friend for funds from the treasury. Not that they had many funds, but it was best to dole out several thousand pesos to him several times a week to keep him in a good frame of mind. It was a small price. Fierro told my friend he wanted to talk with him alone, so they went into the minister's bedroom, closing the door after them. Fierro sat on the bed, smoking a cigar, then announced calmly that he had killed David Berlanga, and that he regretted it. When asked why, he said his chief, Villa, had ordered it.

"My friend then narrated to me what Fierro had done.

"Berlanga was dining the previous night at a popular restaurant. In one of the private rooms, Villa's staff was having a party with some women. There was too much to eat; too much to drink; too much noise; and not enough money to pay the bill when it was presented. When the waiter brought the check, one of the officers signed it and added the tip. The waiter did not want to accept the signed check and went to Berlanga for advice. Berlanga was a steady and honored customer there. He was upset and became enraged. He began to raise his voice to the effect the officers of the Division of the North were only bandits and brought disgrace to the flag of the Revolution by doing nothing but stealing. The officers at the party heard Berlanga shouting. They heard him as he paid the waiter so the poor man would not lose a centavo, and so he, Berlanga, could keep the check for himself as proof of how Villa's staff behaved. Naturally the officers reported Berlanga's actions and statements to Villa the next morning. Villa was furious. He called Fierro aside, ordering him to get hold of Berlanga and shoot him.

"Fierro told my friend what else could he do but obey? Besides, he had done this for Villa before without regrets or bother. So, doing as Villa ordered, Fierro began to look for Berlanga with two automobiles full of Dorados. This was between midnight and one in the morning. They looked in several places without finding their man until Fierro went back to the restaurant of the night before. There Berlanga was. He had finished his late dinner and was smoking a cigar about halfway burned down, with the long ash still on the end.

"Fierro told him he had orders to take him to General Villa and that to resist was useless, as there were several Dorados along as an escort. Berlanga paid his bill, put on his hat and coat, all the time taking care the ash did not fall from his cigar.

"As they were driving through the gateway to the San Cosme barracks, Berlanga asked if that was the place they were going to lock him up. Fierro told him it was the place they were going to shoot him. When Berlanga asked when, Fierro told him right away. Berlanga did not ask any further questions.

"Fierro said Berlanga was as calm as when he had been picked up at the restaurant. Not even the color of his face had changed. He took off his coat with great deliberateness, went to a table in the guardhouse, and began to write in a notebook he'd taken from his pocket. He wrote at length without stopping. When he finished, he tore the papers from the notebook, took off his ring and articles from his pockets, handing them to Fierro, asking that they be given to his mother whose address was on the papers.

"Berlanga buttoned his coat on with deliberation, being careful not to disturb the ash on his cigar, it having grown longer and longer as the time had passed. In front of the wall, Fierro arranged a squad of Dorados, then told Berlanga all was ready. He replied that he wouldn't keep Fierro waiting. But he did, smoking his cigar almost to the end, contemplating the length of the ash. Finally, when there was almost no more cigar to smoke, Berlanga jerked his hand and the ash fell to the ground. Then, with a steady walk, he approached the wall, turning to face the soldiers. He refused a bandage over his eyes. He was shot.

"Fierro told my friend he had tried to smoke a cigar as Berlanga had, but was never able to, as his fingers would twitch and the ashes would fall. He had met his match: a man braver and stronger than he was." Dick Little finished his story.

Sam Townsend looked down at the ash on his cigar. Quietly and slowly he raised it to the tray and knocked it off. "Did Fierro kill just like that for Villa?" he asked softly.

"Frequently," Dick Little answered.

"And for no more valid reason than that?"

"Frequently."

Sam Townsend drew in a long breath. "There was so much I didn't realize," he said, half to himself. "I need a drink." He reached for the bottle on the table beside him, poured and drank his whiskey straight. He then poured another, adding seltzer. He reached for Dick Little's glass, filling it with the same mixture. "Here's to Colonel David Berlanga who was more of a man than his personality gave him credit for," Sam said, raising his glass. "I drink to his memory."

They toasted the departed.

Stella joined them. They sat talking about Deming, the country, and the impressions Dick Little had gathered during his visit. They were all careful to avoid Billy Thomas's death, and the ambush Dick had gone through on the way to the ranch. When it was time for him to leave, they bade him good-nights and come-agains as he started the automobile. He turned on its lights, heading for Deming far down the road.

He had been on the road but a short distance when his ear caught the pounding of several horses galloping. Before he could increase the speed of the automobile they were beside him, two mounted men on each side. He drew his pistol, and at the first shot from the riders, fired back, knocking one man from his horse. He fired at the horsemen on the other side. They turned their horses away. He fired at the remaining man on his side of the automobile, ducking as bullets whipped past his head. The second man dropped out of the saddle. He braked the automobile suddenly, jumping out, sending a lone shot after the two remaining horsemen who were riding into hilly shadows, sending strange cries to the starry heavens.

Dick Little waited a long time. He had two cartridges left in the pistol. No one came back. Turning off the automobile lights, he walked to where the second man lay quietly on the ground, unmoving. He knelt down and thumbed a match to light. He was Mexican; staring wide-eyed at the stars for the last time as he died. The first man he'd shot was also Mexican. He was already dead. In a match flame, Dick Little recognized him as the bartender of La Cucaracha, the cantina where he'd had his fight with El Gallo.

"Mr. Little, I'm asking you to get out of Deming; out of Luna County; out of New Mexico, if you will."

"And if I won't, Sheriff?"

Sheriff Chucho Armijo sighed. "I can make it hard on you."

"On what charge?"

"On any and all charges. Whatever I think up. Does it matter, señor?"

"Harassment?"

"If necessary. I want you away from here."

Dick Little laughed. "You'll have one hell of a time doing it," he said, suddenly serious. "What about those two attacks last night? Those two dead men? What are you going to do about them?"

The sheriff looked at him levelly. "How do I know," he asked slowly, "you killed them the way you say you did?"

"Oh hell!"

"Exactly. I could take you in on a charge of murder right now."

"And hold me until I prove myself innocent?"

"Exactly."

"I wouldn't try it."

"Why not?"

"I'd cause you too much trouble. You've evidently taken a look at my automobile; you've seen the bullet holes in it. Do you think I'd do that to myself?"

"You could have. Very easily."

"Yes, I could have; but what would be my motive in shooting up my own automobile?"

"To say someone attacked you."

"Why?"

The sheriff shrugged. "Why not? I don't know you, therefore, I do not know your motives. I do not know why you are here in Deming. You've been shot at, assaulted, your friend killed; now you've killed two men—what am I to think?"

Little shrugged. "Anything you want to, Sheriff. Anything but one: I'm not going to leave Deming, Luna County, or New Mexico simply because you say I have to. If anything, your order will keep me here longer. I'm a stubborn man, Sheriff. I come and go as I please, when I want to, and where I want to. Now, if you want to put pressure on me,

try it. You'll find it won't work. I'm minding my own business and will
continue to do so as long as I'm here. I won't force a fight with anyone,
but I sure as hell won't run away from it. Do I make myself clear to
you?"

The sheriff sighed. He stared at the glowing tip of his black cigar.
"You make yourself very clear, *señor*. I will have to watch you more
closely than I have been doing."

"You do that, Sheriff. You'll find I have nothing to hide. Now," he
paused, "who were those men who attacked me last night? And why?"

The sheriff shrugged. "They were from below the border. Two of
them were. I do not know the others who ran. I have been asking
around town this morning about them. They have been in Mextown
recently, but they kept to themselves and talked to no one. Yesterday,
when you drove to the S T Ranch, they followed you. That's all I
know."

"I know one was tending bar in a saloon in Las Palomas."

The sheriff's eyebrows rose slightly. "That is something. Which bar?"

"It is called La Cucaracha."

"Aha!"

"Bring to mind anything?"

"Only one thing," the sheriff said. "La Cucaracha is supposed to be a
hangout for ex-Villistas." He tapped the ash from his cigar into the tray.
"That is where you had your fight with El Gallo, no?"

"Yes."

"Now I understand a few things."

"What things?" Little asked.

"About why those men attacked you last night. Probably it was El
Gallo who wants you out of the way. Revenge, perhaps?"

"I don't think he'd go to all that trouble. Unless—?" Dick Little
thought of the knife and pistol.

"Unless, what?"

"Nothing," Little said. "Perhaps he did send those men after me
because of our fight, Sheriff. Why not try that angle and see what you
come up with."

The sheriff nodded. "It is possible. I will do so. In the meantime—"

"Yes?"

"Take care of yourself. Take *good* care of yourself."

In a moment the sheriff had left the hotel room, trailing cigar smoke
behind him.

So the sheriff is getting hard-nosed, Dick Little thought. He couldn't

exactly blame him with what was going on; but, at the same time, he
felt it would be nice if the sheriff would come up with something, or
someone else to blame. He was a little tired of being the clay pigeon.
The phone rang.

"Mr. Withers?" It was Charlie at the desk.

"Yes?"

"A gentleman to see you. Mr. Smith."

"Send him up, Charlie."

"Yes, sir."

In a few moments there was a knock on the door. Dick Little opened
it to a slender gentleman, nicely dressed in a light summer suit. He had
an open face, black hair, full mustache, and black eyes. The man removed his Panama, extending his hand to Little.

"Come in. Sit down. When did you arrive?" Dick asked in Spanish.

"This morning, not long ago." Mr. Smith sat in the chair beside the
desk. He crossed his legs, removing his gloves. "Having any trouble?"

Dick Little laughed. "Depends on what you describe as trouble," he
said. He recounted the events which had befallen him since his arrival.
"No trouble, really," he said. "The wolves are gathering and I'm not
sure why."

Mr. Smith smiled slightly. "Perhaps," he said, "I can tell you why.
Villa is trying to get the pieces of his map back. When you and I joined
forces I wasn't sure, but intelligence from Mexico tells me Villa would
like to have the treasure. There's rumor he might leave his ranch in
Canutillo and re-form his army in Chihuahua. The government, frankly,
is frightened he might do so. President Obregón is worried. For an army,
Villa needs capital: a great deal of it. He's regretting, now, his impul-
siveness in tearing the map apart and giving it away. You say El Gallo is
around? El Gallo is one of Villa's agents. A man the general can trust to
the last drop of blood."

Dick Little nodded. "I thought that, but I wasn't sure. Who else do
you know who is involved?"

Mr. Smith shrugged. "El Gallo, myself, you—"

"Señorita Gutiérrez," Little added.

"Of a certainty, Señorita Gutiérrez. Have you been able to locate
pieces of the map?"

"Several," Little said. "They don't add up to anything as yet, but I
think I'm on the right track. May I see yours?"

Mr. Smith smiled. "Certainly. The time has come, I believe, to put
the parts of the map on the table, so to speak." He reached into his

coat, took out a wallet, opened it, extracting from it a piece of paper. He handed it to Dick Little with the tips of his first and second fingers. Little walked to the window where the strong sunlight was flooding into the room. He stared at the new part of the map.

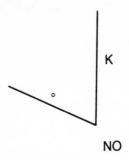

He handed it back to Mr. Smith without a word. The man watched him with bright eyes. "Well?"

Little shrugged. "It's an important part, but I don't know how important. The N-O, no. The other *O* on the line, the *K*." He shook his head. "They have no meaning for me."

Mr. Smith took back the piece of paper, inserting it carefully into his wallet. He sighed. "Then we are no nearer than we were before."

"Not quite," Little said. "I've seen other pieces since I've been here. If you'd like to see one, I'll have it brought over."

Mr. Smith straightened in his chair. "I would certainly like to see another of the pieces."

"Very well." Dick Little went to the phone. "Charlie," he said into the mouthpiece, "get me Gunner Marks. Yes." He waited a moment. "Gunner? Tiny. Come on by the hotel, will you, right now. There's a friend of yours here who wants to see you. Yes, an old friend. And, Gunner, bring along your wallet. Okay? Five minutes? We'll be waiting." He hung up.

Mr. Smith settled back in the chair, taking a gold cigarette case from the inside of his jacket. He opened it, extracting a black cigarette. Little held a match for him. Clouds of smoke were soon floating toward the ceiling. Little went to the window and looked out. There was silence in the room except for the soft hum of the ceiling fan. Through the open window Little felt the slight east breeze. He could hear faint sounds of the town, an automobile driving somewhere, the snort of a horse and the brake of a wagon. He saw The Gunner turning the corner, shuffling rapidly along in spite of his twisted body and legs. A knock at the door announced his arrival. Dick opened the door, letting The Gunner in. He came through the door. "Wha—?" he started to say, then his eyes seeing and his mind recognizing the man slowly rising from the chair, coming across the room to him with an outstretched hand. "Wha—?" he repeated, then, "I'll be a son of a bitch!" He grabbed the extended hand, pumping it enthusiastically. "Captain Galinda!" he exclaimed in his loud voice.

"How are you, Gunner?" "Mr. Smith" asked.

"Fine! Fine! I'll be damned, Tiny," he said, turning to Little, "where in hell did you find the captain?"

"Out of the blue."

"Goddamned! You look well," he said to the captain. "What brings you to Deming?"

Captain Galinda laughed. "Perhaps the same thing which brought you here," he said. "Fierro's treasure."

"Oh!" exclaimed The Gunner. "You, too?"

"I'm afraid so, Gunner," the captain replied. "Tiny has been telling me of his adventures since he came here; about you, and the map. I'd like to see what you have, if I may?"

"Sure, sure, Captain." He took his wallet out of his hip pocket, opening it and handing the captain his part of the map.

Galinda looked at it searchingly. He glanced up at Little, then back to the paper in his hand. Handing it back to The Gunner, he turned to Dick Little. He shrugged. Without a word he extracted his part of the map from his pocket, handing it to The Gunner.

"I'll be goddamned!" The Gunner breathed, looking intently at the piece of paper. "I'll be goddamned! This is the second piece I've seen besides mine. What do you know!" He handed the paper back to the captain. "Got a drink, Tiny?"

"Some of that stuff you left here. I'll get a glass."

Little found a glass and the gallon jug. He poured a drink for The Gunner who gulped half of it down thirstily. "I'll be goddamned!" he said again.

Captain Galinda had resumed his chair. "None of us," he said, "were allowed to see the whole map. Villa waved it about, but did not show it before he tore it up. The instant we received our parts, all of us looked at them before putting them in our pockets. We were afraid Villa would ask for them back. After dinner, we went our separate ways as quickly as we could. I wouldn't doubt each of us did what I did: I studied my piece until I could have drawn it while unconscious. I then put it in a safe place. You can believe the thought of all that money kept me awake many a night." He laughed. "Do you know," he said, letting cigarette smoke from his lungs, "after a while I actually forgot I had it?"

"Me too," The Gunner answered.

The captain stood up, putting on his gloves. "We will keep in touch, the three of us. I am registered at the Park Hotel. It is near the railway station on Silver Street. My name is still 'Smith.' " He smiled. "Tiny. Gunner. I'll see you both." He put on his Panama, nodded to the two men, and left.

"Now, there's a hell of a fellow," The Gunner remarked.

"Yes, he is."

"How did he know we were here?"

"I sent for him. After he got here, I told him about you."

"I haven't seen him since the night of Villa's supper." He remembered something. "Did I louse up anything by telling him I'd seen more than one piece of the map?"

Little shook his head. "I doubt it. It doesn't matter."

The Gunner swallowed some of his concoction. He lifted the jug from the desk, measuring its contents. "Two more," he said. "Two more." He poured his glass full, found Little's and poured that full. He looked at the jug again. "Empty," he said disgustedly. Setting the jug down, he handed Little his drink. "Captain Galinda. Cavalry. One of Fierro's men. Good officer. Where did you find him, Tiny?"

"In Guadalajara. I ran across him by accident not too long ago. I invited him to stay in my house in Santa Fe whenever he wanted to; so, he came to visit a few weeks ago."

The Gunner grunted. "I suppose he'll be looking for the treasure, too, won't he?" he asked.

"I suppose so, Gunner."

The Gunner shook his head. "I've got a feeling," he said seriously. "I've got a feeling about myself."

"What sort of a feeling?"

"I don't know," he answered. "I don't rightly know, Tiny. Had it once before. Just before that shell almost done me in. I got the same feeling." He drank half his drink. "You believe in fate, Tiny?"

Dick Little was surprised at the abrupt question. "To some extent," he answered. "We all have to die: that's fate."

"I mean about things goin' to happen?"

"Not really."

"I do. Something's gonna happen soon. Soon." He finished his drink.

"Who to, Gunner?"

The Gunner looked at Dick Little levelly. "Wish th' hell I knew, Tiny. Wish th' hell I knew." He put his glass down. "I gotta get back an' make me up another batch. Want me to send you some?"

"Be delighted."

"Okay. See you." He was out of the room.

Dick Little sat in the chair next to the desk. He set his glass down. Captain Galinda. Guadalajara. His thoughts turned back several months.

He'd been sitting at a table in a café when Galinda approached him with outstretched hand. They had never known each other well, but the comradeship of war brought them together. With his height, Richard Henry Little was never a man to be forgotten quickly; also helping was the fact he was a foreign correspondent of some renown. Captain Galinda, too, had been most pleasant to talk to. He was urbane, educated, quiet, and efficient. The fact he had served in Fierro's brigade of cavalry did not detract from his personableness, as he had taken on none of the characteristics of his commanding officer. Dick had shared meals with the captain on occasion, had always found him relaxing company. This was in the field.

Dick Little had forgotten the captain until they met in a café. The captain had changed little in appearance, not even a pound over the weight Little remembered. He was still hard in the stomach, ready to smile, and interesting to talk to. He owned a large ranch in the state of Jalisco and, therefore, was a man of leisure, more or less. The captain had introduced him around Guadalajara in the days following their meeting. They had visited from the top to the bottom, from *charradas* to bullfights, from dives to the best, their acquaintanceship growing with the passage of days. Finally it was time to part. Little had invited the captain to visit with him in Santa Fe, where he had purchased a small house in which to settle for a while and work on a book or two he felt like writing. The captain had accepted. Several months later he was Dick Little's houseguest: an idol of the town, a man known to all for his background, his manners, his pleasant character.

On several occasions, the captain would meet with fellow countrymen for a night of cards, or of wine. Little had been invited along and had accepted three or four times. The evenings had been delightful. On one occasion, the captain had excused himself to converse with a new arrival from Mexico. He came back to the party with an inner pocket bulging. Later, Little had seen him take a large and well-stuffed envelope from that pocket. It was done absently and while they were enjoying a nightcap before going to their separate rooms. Dick Little had wondered about that envelope, but it was none of his business.

Later the captain had brought up the subject of Fierro's treasure very subtly. Little had announced his intention of going to Deming to see that part of New Mexico he'd never visited before. The captain was quite interested in Dick's travels and had professed much interest in that area. Very quietly he had brought up the subject of the possibility of Fierro having buried a treasure near there and had learned that Dick knew of the treasure, or at least stories about it. They had talked about the possibilities of where it might be; had even brought out a map of New Mexico to locate points of interest to the story. The captain seemed to have had more direct knowledge of Fierro's activities than Little had. He could talk as if he knew the facts of the matter, whereas Little's knowledge consisted of some events he knew, and others he had heard from one source or another. Gradually they had reached the conclusion that Dick Little was to go to Deming to discover what he could regarding the treasure. They had arranged a code to communicate by telegraph; if a telegram mentioned the word *target*, the captain was to come to Little's aid.

All this had been done.

But, Little thought, there was one flaw. A minute one, to be sure. It had passed almost unnoticed that afternoon: the captain had not raised a question as to who Señorita Gutiérrez was when her name had been mentioned. Little had the feeling it had not been necessary to pursue the matter further because Galinda knew who she was and what she was doing in Deming.

Dick's thoughts turned to the señorita and her part in the scheme of things. It was during their second meeting she had warned him there were dangerous forces at work around Deming; she had warned him to get out while he could, and she had merely hinted trouble would follow in his footsteps, and would catch up with him if he stayed. It certainly had. In spades.

Dick Little finished his drink. He decided to stir things up a little more.

He left the hotel to look for a surveyor.

E. THOMAS MILLS, read the sign hanging over the door, SURVEYOR. Dick Little entered the shop.

Maps of the county and city covered the walls and one of the two tables in the office; one was a drafting table with a high stool in front of it. There was a desk and chair which were also covered with papers. Seated on the stool was a large hulk of a man, leaning over the drawing board doing things with a pencil. As Dick Little closed the door behind him, the man turned. He was red-haired with a bushy beard to match. Metal-rimmed glasses covered his eyes leaving the nose to jut from his face like a button. He wore an open-necked shirt with the sleeves rolled up revealing red hairy arms of considerable muscular strength.

"Yes, sir?" he asked politely.

Dick Little looked around the office before returning his gaze to the man. "Your name is Mills?" he asked.

"Yes, it is," the man answered with a full voice.

"Are you for hire?"

Mills grinned. "Depends on what you want me to do."

Little smiled back. "Some surveying."

"How much?"

"Depends on how upset some people get."

Mills pushed his glasses up from his eyes leaving them in his hair above his forehead. His brown eyes expressed interest.

"Would you mind explaining that to me, sir?"

Little laughed. "A joke on some people," he said. "I want to hire you to do some surveying for me. It will be an unusual type of job, but I'll pay you well until I feel the job is over."

"For example?"

"I want to know how far it is from the tip of Cooke's Peak to the highest point of the Floridas. I want to know the exact equidistance between the two. When you finish that, I want you to do the same between the highest point of the Floridas to the highest point of the Three Sisters. I want you to take your time, stretch out the job for several days, if possible, and tell no one I hired you to do the work. How about it?"

E. Thomas Mills scratched his head with blunt fingers. "What's this all about? I can give you those figures in five minutes and calculate the equidistances in another ten." He cast his eyes around the small office. "I'd have to find a couple of maps first."

"That won't do," Little said. "I want you out in the field, working where people can see you."

"What is your name, sir, if I may be so bold to ask?"

"Withers."

"Oh, the guy who's getting himself shot at and knocked on the head?"

"The same."

"And the purpose of my work?"

Little smiled. "Frankly, Mr. Mills, it is to get some people upset. You know, of course, the story of Fierro's treasure?"

Mills nodded. "Who doesn't in this damned town."

"There are people who are now here looking for that treasure. I want them to suspect someone knows where it is buried and to observe their reactions."

"Wouldn't that be sort of dangerous for me?"

"Why? You'd be out in the open doing a job. If anyone asks, all you'd have to answer is that you received your instructions by mail, along with a check for the work; aside from that, you know nothing. I'll give you a name and an address you can let out so they can check up on you. How about it?"

Mills scratched his head again. "Sounds intriguing," he said, "to pun a mite." He smiled. "I charge twenty-five dollars a day: for a full day, sunup to sundown."

"Agreed. I'll pay you for ten days in advance." He reached into his pocket, taking out a fistful of gold coins. He counted five of the coins, placing them into E. Thomas Mills' outstretched hand.

The surveyor laughed. "When do you want me to start?"

"Tomorrow morning?"

"Suits me fine, sir. I'll give you a receipt."

"Don't bother."

"Thanks for trusting me. Where do you want me to start, sir?"

"In the Cooke's Peak area. Make sure people can see you. You, undoubtedly, will be approached for information. Let them bribe you, if you can. Tell them exactly what you're doing, and who for. Understood?"

Mills nodded. "What will I do with the bribe money, if I may ask?"

"Keep it, but let me know who gives it to you." He looked around the office. "Do you have paper and pencil? Never mind, I have." He took his notebook from a breast pocket of his jacket, accepted the pencil Mills held out to him, writing down a name and address. Handing the pencil and paper back to Mills, he said, "There's the name of the person who hired you and his address. Mail reports there from day to day. A blank paper will suffice. All I want is the appearance. Let them know Ollie hired you, but not me. Okay?"

"Okay."

They shook hands to seal the bargain. Little asked where the telephone office was located and went there after leaving E. Thomas Mills, Surveyor.

At the telephone office he placed a long distance call to Oliver Lang in Santa Fe. "Hello! Ollie!" he half shouted into the phone.

"Tiny!" the voice came back. "What the hell are you doing down there?"

"What do you mean?"

"The New Mexican had a story about your being in an ambush. Did you get hurt?"

"No. I'm fine. Look, I need a favor."

"Name it, old boy."

"Some people might contact you to ask why you're hiring a surveyor here by the name of E. Thomas Mills. Got that?"

"E. Thomas Mills. Got it. What do I tell them?"

"First, try to find out who's asking, and why. Secondly, as to why you hired him, tell them it's none of their bloody business. Keep it mysterious."

"Mysterious? Sounds like fun. What else?"

"You'll be getting envelopes from Mills. He's supposedly reporting his work to you."

"What'll I do with them?"

"Burn them, for all I care. There'll be nothing in them anyway."

"Right. Anything else?"

"That's it."

"How's the captain?"

"Fine. He got in this morning."

"Give him my regards. Say, Tiny?"

"Yes?"

"Take care of yourself, you old son of a bitch."

"Same to you. See you."

He hung up, asked the operator for time and charges, paid the bill, and left the telephone office.

As he approached the Baker Hotel he decided to take a ride in his automobile. It was still parked on the street where he'd left it the night before. He got in, started it, and headed south on the Columbus road.

He had no idea where he was going, or why; he just wanted to drive somewhere and enjoy the breeze created by the moving automobile. A few miles out of town, he stopped and parked in the shade of a clump of cottonwoods beside the road. Searching around, he was fortunate to find a couple of bottles of beer Martínez had hidden from the eyes of the customs inspector. In a moment he had knocked the top off one of them, let the foam of the hot beer squirt out of the bottle, then tilted the bottle to his mouth letting the liquid flow down his throat. He got out of the automobile, and sat on a front fender. He was facing the Floridas, letting his eyes drink in the rugged scenery. He did not hear her ride up, as he was absorbed in his thoughts, cutting out the world around him.

"Señor Withers?"

He was startled at her husky voice. He stood up, turning, looking up at her on her horse. "Señorita Gutiérrez," he said lightly. "Would you like a drink of warm beer?"

She laughed, dismounting. He held out his hand to her, taking her by the elbow. She tied the reins to the radiator cap, then walked to the edge of the clump of trees, looking at the mountains. "They're beautiful," she said softly. "So strong, so mysterious, so quiet, so massive."

He was standing beside her, looking down at her face. "It is beautiful," he said. "It is mysterious."

She turned her head to look up at him, realizing suddenly he was not talking about the Floridas at all. She blushed, turning her head away. "I was speaking of the mountains."

"I was speaking of you," he said quietly. "You're a beautiful woman, Señorita Gutiérrez."

"Please," she protested.

"Anyone would be either blind or a fool not to recognize how beautiful you really are."

She turned to face him, head tilted up, her eyes flashing under the brim of her riding hat. "I will not let you speak to me in this way, Señor Withers!" she said angrily.

"Why not?" he smiled. "It's true."

She started to walk rapidly toward the car. He caught up with her, taking her by the arm, stopping her. She whirled to face him, arm upraised, her hand tight around her quirt. He grabbed her wrist, holding it firmly so she could not move. They stared eye to eye. He relaxed his hand allowing her to lower her arm. She turned away from him, standing still. "I'm sorry," she said, her voice low and husky. "I should not have tried to strike you."

"No offense, señorita. No need to be sorry. Come. Let's sit in the automobile and talk a while."

Leading her by an elbow they walked toward the automobile. She stopped suddenly and gasped. She whirled on him, looking up at his face, frowning, then turned back to the automobile. "Why!" she said, "those are bullet holes!"

"I'm afraid so," he said mildly. "It's a wonder you haven't already heard about the little scrap I had last night. All of Deming knows everything about everyone as soon as it happens, I'm told."

She looked at him strangely. "Who did this?"

"I don't know. Later I was attacked by four men. One happened to be the bartender in the cantina next door to the house of your friends, the Valencias."

Her eyes opened wide. "Are you sure?"

"Very. I had to kill him to prove it."

She gasped. "You—you had to—to kill him?"

"And one other. Do you know why they attacked me, señorita?"

"I?"

"Yes, you."

She turned away. "Why should I know who they were?"

"Because you know lots of things you're not telling."

"That's ridiculous."

"Is it?" He turned her toward him. "Do you remember the conversation we had on this very road only a few days ago? I do. Quote: Perhaps he wasn't shooting at you. Perhaps he wanted to warn you. Unquote. We were talking about El Gallo then. What the hell did you mean by that? You also said, quote: I saw him in Deming a few days ago, riding out of town. He passed very close to me, but did not see me. It gave me a cold feeling to know he had been so near me. He is a cruel man who would stop at nothing, even killing if he felt like it. Unquote. Do you remember saying that?"

"No—I—yes, I remember."

"You were speaking of El Gallo?"

"Yes, I was."

"Whom I last saw in La Cucaracha, next to the Valencias' house, in Las Palomas."

"So you say."

"A Villista bar?"

"Who told you such a thing?"

"Does it matter? I'm more interested in you right now."

"Me?"

"Yes, and what connection you have to this treasure hunt which seems to be going on at this moment. I might even accuse you of having a part of Villa's map. Surely you have heard that story? And what of your questioning a man named Sonny Johns recently?"

She stepped back from him. "Señor Withers—" she began.

He held up his hands, palms out to her. "I didn't say you had a part of it. I said I could accuse you of having one. Accusation and proof are two different things. But if you do, *señorita*, and you are trying to find the treasure yourself, you are in very dangerous waters, too. You could easily become the target yourself. In cases like these, people get very greedy and are apt to hurt anyone standing in their way. All I want to do is warn *you* of the possibility of danger. Though, I daresay, anything I tell you will just go in one ear and out the other. You are a very stubborn woman, Maria Luisa Isabel Gutiérrez y Velasco." He smiled at her.

"You're impossible!" she snapped at him.

"All too true," he nodded, the lines about his mouth deepening. "Still, I see things. Still, I hear things. And I have a mind which can calculate. The sum of my experiences is, you are likely to be badly hurt. You're going to have to tell me sooner or later; why not now?"

"As you say, Señor Withers, I am a very stubborn woman. I will tell you nothing because I know nothing of what you're saying."

He sighed. "All right," he said, giving up. "You win. Now, how about sharing a warm beer with me? I have another bottle."

Her mood changed instantly. She smiled. "Not today," she said. "Perhaps some other time."

She untied her horse and mounted. He walked up beside her, looking up at her. "You might say to yourself I've been talking utter nonsense," he told her, "but you know I speak the truth. Especially about one thing."

"What is that, Señor Withers?"

"You are a very beautiful woman, *señorita.*"

She gave him a fleeting smile, turned her horse, and galloped up the road toward Deming. He watched her until she became lost in the dust raised by her horse's hooves. He sighed. Taking the second bottle of beer from the front seat of the automobile, he knocked off the top and poured the contents of the bottle down his throat.

WHEN DICK LITTLE RETURNED to his hotel, Stella Townsend was waiting for him in the lobby.

"I've brought you Billy's things," she said, indicating a small trunk. A Winchester carbine stood upright against it.

"Thank you," he said. "I'll take them up right away."

"Could—?" she started to say. "Could I come up with you? I'd like to talk to you in private."

"Certainly." He picked up the trunk easily in one hand and the rifle in the other. They crossed the lobby under the watchful eye of Charlie behind the desk and climbed the stairs to the second floor. "Been waiting long?" he asked, opening the door, standing aside to let her enter.

"About half an hour. I didn't mind. Charles Elliott is an old friend. We talked."

"Would you like a chair?" he asked, indicating the most popular one beside the desk. She thanked him as she seated herself, sitting demurely with knees together, hands clasped in her lap. He noticed she was dressed in a long dark skirt and white blouse. She wore no hat. Her blond hair was fixed differently than he'd ever seen it, flowing rather than tied back with a ribbon as she wore it on the ranch. He seated himself on the bed, facing her.

"What can I do for you, Miss Stella?" he asked pleasantly.

She stared at her hands. "I don't know where to begin," she said. "I came here to ask for your help—your advice rather."

"About what?"

She hesitated. "My father," she said finally.

"What about Sam?"

She looked up at him, her eyes pleading, her forehead creased with worry. She fluttered her hands. "I don't know. Since yesterday—since you came to supper with us, he's changed so much. This morning, when I served him breakfast, he scarcely touched his food. Until I left the ranch to come to town to see you, he's been moody, hardly saying a word to me. There's something on his mind I don't understand. How could he change so much in so few hours? I've never seen him like this before. It worries me."

"You say he has something on his mind?"

"Yes."

"And you don't know what it is?"

She shook her head, her eyes lowered. "No."

He sighed. "He knows what happened to me last night after I left you?"

Looking down, she nodded without speaking.

"Who told you?"

"Sheriff Armijo."

He grunted. "Last night?"

She nodded, still not looking up from her hands. "He came very late. He told us you had contacted him about the shooting. We thought he meant the one on the way to the ranch, but when Sheriff Armijo told us about the second on your way back, my father became very agitated. After the sheriff left, he did something I've only seen him do once before, when my mother died."

"What was that?"

"He drank a lot of whiskey. So much he was practically drunk."

"Did he say anything about why he was doing this?"

She shook her head. "No. Nothing I could understand. Once I heard him say something about so much blood. He said that twice. But I don't understand. It made no sense to me."

"Probably it was about those two men I killed."

"I thought of that, but what would he know about them?"

Dick Little had to shrug. "Did he know either of them?"

"I'm sure he didn't. The sheriff mentioned only that two men had been killed not far down the road from the ranch. The sheriff said he didn't know who they were."

"Perhaps he meant Billy?"

She looked up at him. "Why was Billy killed—murdered?" she asked slowly.

Little shook his head. "I don't know. I don't know why Billy was killed."

"Mr. Little," she pleaded, looking across the room at him, "what can I do about my father? This morning he looked so—so old."

"I wouldn't take it to heart," he said. "Men are inclined to worry now and then."

"What do you think it is?"

"Billy's death perhaps. The two men. No one knows why they died exactly. Why did they attack me? Who attacked Billy? Perhaps your father is more sensitive than you realize. I'd worry if I were he."

"I don't understand at all. Everything has happened so suddenly."

"Why not wait a day or two more. If your father is still worried, I'll come out and talk with him. Sometimes an outsider can help more than you realize."

"Would you?"

"Certainly."

For the first time since he had met her in the lobby, she relaxed. She sat back in the chair, unclasping her hands. "I feel better for what you've said. I feel I can trust you." She opened her purse, taking from it a package of Sweet Caporal cigarettes. She extracted one from the package, holding it between her fingers. "Do you have a light?"

Dick Little was surprised. North of the border, he'd seldom seen a woman smoke. Below the border, it was not unusual, especially those *soldaderas* who followed their men in the army. He dug out a match from his jacket pocket, thumbing it to light. He crossed the room with it, touching the end of her cigarette with the flame. She puffed until the cigarette was lighted, blowing the smoke from her mouth without inhaling. Her movements with the tobacco were awkward; her smoking amateurish, as if she were just learning how. She looked up at him, smiling. "Do I startle you?" she asked.

He returned to the bed, sitting on its edge. "Yes," he said directly, "you do." He watched her puffing on the cigarette, taking in mouthfuls of smoke, blowing them out in a cloud with an occasional tendril coming from her nose. "Would you like a drink?" he asked.

"Certainly," she said defiantly.

He went to the sink, taking two tumblers off the glass shelf under the mirror. He came back to the bed, picked up the bottle of Bourbon from the table, returning to the sink to pour the drinks. In one glass he scarcely covered the bottom; he poured two fingers into the other. Adding water, he crossed over to her, handing her the weak drink. She took it warily. *"Salud!"* He held up his glass to her. She held hers out, clinking the rims. He took a large swallow from his. She followed his example. She choked, started coughing, bent over, fist to her mouth. She looked up at him, tears streaming from her eyes.

"That—" she gasped, "that—wasn't fair!"

He smiled, taking another swallow from his glass. "How many drinks have you ever had in your life?" he asked kindly.

She shook her head quickly from side to side.

"I thought so." He reached out taking the glass from her hand, putting it on the desk beside her. "There wasn't enough liquor in that to make a fly drunk."

"You're cruel," she said, wiping her eyes with a handkerchief she had taken from her purse.

He laughed. "Why did you ask for one then?"

She shook her head again. Suddenly she smiled. "I had to try it sometime," she said. She stubbed out her cigarette in the ashtray beside her. "I have smoked before," she announced. "It certainly is much easier than drinking."

"Not as many aftereffects either," he said. "Why were you showing off in front of me?"

She laughed. "I thought you might like a woman more if she's emancipated," she said.

"You've been reading," he said.

"Sometimes there's nothing else to do at the ranch. I've been reading about the women back East who are beginning to drink and smoke. It seems the thing to do now."

"Are you so lonely at the ranch?"

"Sometimes. We're so far out from town. It's often difficult for me to get back and forth. We do have a Ford, but Father doesn't like me to drive it alone. He thinks I'll have an accident or something. Once I drove it into town all by myself. On the way back, I ran out of gas and had to walk miles to get home. Father knows I can be irresponsible at times. He had told me it needed gas, but I forgot." She giggled. "Oh, I drive it around the ranch some, but not much. I drove it into town today," she said proudly.

"Why?"

"I wanted to see you," she said. "I wanted to bring you Billy's things, as I'd promised," she added hastily.

"And you wanted to talk to me, is that it?"

"Yes."

"What will the town say about your being here in my room alone?"

"They won't find out—unless you tell."

He shook his head. "I don't tell," he said. "I'm thinking of the way gossip gets started in a small town."

"But I brought you Billy's things," she protested. She paused a moment. "Who killed him?" she asked again worriedly.

"I don't know. Really I don't."

"Do you know why?"

"I think so," he said seriously.

She looked deep into his eyes for a long moment. "You know why?"

He nodded.

"Tell me, please, tell me."

He drew in a deep breath. "Well, Miss Townsend—Miss Stella," he said, "Billy was killed because he had a part of the map everyone seems to be looking for."

"That treasure thing?"

"I'm afraid so."

"How can you be sure?"

"Three reasons. First, that time I talked with him, he hinted to me he had one. Second, he was killed for it. Third, his room was thoroughly searched for it. Are those reasons enough?"

She nodded.

"I could add a fourth," he said.

She looked up at him with wide eyes.

"I've picked up enough hints here and there to feel that much activity is taking place around Deming to find it. I can't figure out just exactly why it's taking place now, but I think too many people are involved, each fighting for position, so to speak, and each is trying their damndest to find out what the others are doing. Most especially, what they know. It's a dangerous game any way you look at it."

"Is my father involved in this treasure hunt? Is that why he's worried?"

"I couldn't say. Probably he's worried because of Billy's death and the other two men last night. After all, Miss Stella, one of those deaths took place on his ranch, and the other two nearby."

"I wish I could help him," she said wistfully.

"Have you asked what's worrying him?"

"Of course I have," she said crossly. "He wouldn't tell me. He said it was nothing. That he'd be all right in a couple of days."

"Well?"

She shrugged. "I wish I knew what it was." She got up from the chair. "I'd better go now." She smiled up at him as he stood before her. "The town just might get the wrong idea. Although," she added, "I'm not sure I wouldn't like it."

He escorted her to the door. As he was holding it open for her, she turned quickly, stood on tiptoes, kissing him on the mouth. He felt the warmth of her body and the coolness of her lips. Her tongue darted into his mouth for a second. He was too stunned to move. She was gone. He watched her to the head of the stairs. She stopped, turned, waved her fingers at him before disappearing.

He closed the door quickly, walking across the room to his glass. A frown was on his face as he thought of Stella and what she had revealed of herself. He sat down slowly, thinking.

The vagaries of women! The ranch girl who wanted to be on the same level with women in the East. What would happen next? Desirable? Yes. Clean-cut, wholesome as far as others were concerned, yet touched with a restlessness hidden beneath a pretty exterior.

Someone had touched her. A kiss like that wasn't learned by oneself. It had to be learned, taught to her by someone who knew the art of love. You can't fool an old fooler, especially one who has been around for years and has seen things and done things all over the world. He had never been celibate in his life, nor would he ever be. He enjoyed himself too much. He took things as they came, women included, treated them with respect, and had never been deeply hurt. Or not hurt enough to let scars form on old wounds. This, then, was something unusual. What was she up to? Or was it hidden desires coming to the surface because he had often found himself to be attractive to women? On the other hand, who really knew about women except women themselves? The question was as old as Eve.

Dick Little suddenly laughed. Stella Townsend would be one woman to keep at arm's length, as he had the feeling he could easily be entrapped by that one before he knew it.

He finished off his drink, washed the two glasses, then opened Billy Thomas's trunk. It was half filled with clothes worn with usage, clean, some repaired meticulously with needle and thread. Other items were a pair of worn boots, an envelope with a newspaper clipping of a rodeo in Hot Springs which listed Billy as having won the bucking contest and the first prize money of fifty dollars. Another clipping, yellow with age, told of the death from typhoid of a Miss Mazie Breen and of her funeral. Nothing more: no date, no identification of the newspaper, or where Miss Breen had died. There was a battered book with the imprint of a secondhand bookstore stamped on the title page. It was one of Dick's own, written years before, when he was in Central America. The book had been severely used, with fingerprints on many of its pages. Dick Little felt very sad as he riffled through it before he put it down. His hand encountered a brown paper sack with several pouches of Bull Durham and several packets of cigarette papers. There was also a full box of wooden matches in the sack. Also in the trunk were a holster and belt with the loops filled with shells. He next took out two full boxes of .44 cartridges. Wrapped in a cloth, a .44 Colt Single Action with most of the bluing worn off. He was surprised to find a well-worn Bible. The final item was a buckskin pouch with the drawstring looped around the top and tied. Dick Little hefted the pouch first, hearing the clink of coins. He untied the drawstring, pouring the contents into his palm; ten fifty-dollar gold pieces, some gold nuggets, a woman's wedding band. Such were all of Billy's earthly possessions.

He packed everything back into the trunk except the buckskin pouch and the pistol. He unloaded the gun, thumbing the action, feeling the ease with which the hammer came back to full cock. He loaded it again, slipping it into the holster and hanging the belt over the back of a chair. Next he picked up the rifle, checking to see if it was loaded. It was. He levered the cartridges from it until it was empty. The mechanism worked smoothly in spite of its age. The stock was scarred and battered. He sighted the rifle out of the window for a moment, swinging it from side to side, working the lever, pulling the trigger, snapping the hammer. He loaded it again, noting it used the same .44 cartridges the pistol used. When he'd finished, he closed the trunk, carried it to the closet, putting it on the floor. The rifle he leaned against the wall, out of sight around the door. The paper sack of tobacco, papers, and matches he emptied into the desk drawer. The buckskin pouch he put into a breast pocket of his jacket. There was no evidence of Billy Thomas left to be seen in the room except the belt, holster, and pistol hanging on the back of a chair.

He opened the door to leave. The Señorita Gutiérrez was standing before him, her hand raised to knock, a startled look on her face. He stepped aside. "Come in," he invited, bowing politely and sweeping his hat from his head. "I was just going to look for you."

"Oh?" she asked. She smiled at him, entering the room. She was still in her riding clothes although she was without her quirt. She took off her gloves as she examined the room with her eyes. She noted the pistol for a moment, then the bottle of Bourbon on the night table. "Aren't you going to offer a lady a drink?" she asked.

"How do you like it?"

"Two fingers, a little water."

"No ice?"

"No ice."

"Good," he smiled. "I haven't any." He mixed two equal drinks, handing her one. She sipped it.

"Just right," she commented, seating herself in the chair beside the desk. The most popular chair in the room, Dick thought to himself.

"You're probably wondering why I'm here," she stated directly. Before he could answer, she continued, "I came to apologize—again."

"Apologize? Again? For what, this time?"

"My behavior this morning." She laughed. "I was thirsty, but I was too proud to accept your offer of the beer. Before I returned to Deming, I was suffering for my pride. It made me think."

"About what, *señorita?*"

"About what you told me this morning. You are right, of course." She sipped her drink.

"Thank you."

"But what I'm curious about is your connection with the treasure. You have been as vague with me as I have been with you."

Dick Little paused for a moment. "You're willing to lay your cards on the table?"

She shrugged. "Why not? Why work at cross purposes? I suspect we are both after the same thing."

He raised his glass to her. "Here's to an equal partnership."

She frowned. "I wasn't thinking of equality," she said. "Something else."

"What, for instance?"

She paused before she answered. "Ten percent for your share."

He laughed loudly. She looked at him steadily. "I'm sorry," he said, "I didn't mean to laugh."

"Fifteen percent?"

He shook his head, smiling. "Sorry."

Her eyes flashed. She sat up straight. "I suppose you've had a better offer?" she snapped.

His face grew serious. "What do you mean by that?"

"I saw her come out of this hotel."

"Who did you see come out of this hotel?"

"Stella Townsend!"

"What about it?" he asked. "This is a public place."

"Is your room a public place also?"

"Now wait just a minute, Señorita Gutiérrez!" he said slowly, approaching her until she had to bend her head backward to look up into his face. "Who I have in my room, and at what time, is of no concern of yours," he said, his voice taking on a hard tone she'd never heard him use before. "If someone comes here who wants to see me, and whom I want to see, that is strictly my business. If you are here to question my morals, or to check on my visitors, you'll have to leave. Do you understand what I am saying?"

Her face drained of color. She made an effort to control herself. "I apologize," she said slowly, every syllable an effort for her to say.

He relaxed. "That's better." He backed away from her, seating himself on the bed. "Why are you so interested in Miss Townsend?"

She thought before answering. "I'm not interested. I'm suspicious."

"Of her?"

"Yes."

"Tell me why, if you please."

She took a gulp of her drink without making a face. Little gave a fleeting thought to how she could pack it away. "I don't like her," she said finally.

"Why not? You hardly know her."

"That's right. I hardly know her. But I know her type."

"And what type is she?"

The señorita smiled devilishly. "I would say," she said slowly, "that Miss Stella Townsend is a thoroughbred bitch. She is the type of woman who would sell her body first for what she wants, then her soul. I'll wager she knows how to sell, too."

"Those are very strong words, don't you think?"

"What was she doing up here?" Señorita Gutiérrez asked abruptly, changing the subject.

"If you really want to know, she's worried about her father. Seems he has taken the death of an old friend to heart."

"What friend? Billy Thomas?"

"You knew him?" Dick Little asked, amazed.

"Of course I knew him. This isn't my first trip to Deming, you know. I'm not exactly a stranger here. My uncle lives here. I've visited often. I've met the Townsends socially, if that's what's bothering you."

Dick spread his hands. "Amazing."

"You haven't done your homework, have you?"

"I guess not."

"Very well," she said, sipping from her glass, "let's get down to business. I'll go as high as 20 percent."

He chuckled. "I like that," he said. "The treasure hasn't been found, and already you're offering me 20 percent."

"You know where it is, Mr. Withers."

He looked at her incredulously. "Are you out of your mind?"

"Of course not!"

"Then how in hell can you sit there drinking my Bourbon and calmly state I know where the treasure is?"

"Because I think you do know."

"Agh!"

"What did you say?"

"I merely made a sound of disgust, *señorita,*" he answered. "I'm beginning to think you're fantastic. You haven't the slightest idea who I am, where I've come from, yet you accuse me of knowing something many others would like to know. Right out of your hat as a magician pulls out cards and rabbits. I wish you'd let me know how you figured that one out."

"I will," she said, holding out her empty glass, "if I may have another drink."

He took the glass from her, pouring whiskey from the bottle, adding water from the sink. He went through the same process with his own drink. Sitting again on the bed, he said, "Now, tell me."

She sat up straighter. "Good," she said. "First, I don't trust your looks."

"That's a fine start," he interjected.

"Silence, please," she snapped. "I don't trust your looks. You're too good looking. The strong, silent type I read about. Yes, you're a gentleman, all right, but you're steel, too. You kill two men and think nothing of it."

"They were trying to kill me, remember? Should I lose sleep over that?"

"That's just it. You knew how to take care of yourself in a most direct manner. Without hesitation."

He sighed.

"Secondly," she went on, "you're not upset about the treasure. It doesn't bother you at all. You laugh at it. At me. At everyone. You pay no attention to it; yet you know more about it than other people."

He sipped from his drink, watching her face as she talked. Her expressions changed, one after the other. He was fascinated. "Thirdly," she continued, "if you didn't know so much, why are people always attacking you? You've been assaulted once, shot at twice, in a fight once, and God knows what else since you've been here. You're a magnet for trouble. Why? Because the others think you know more than you're telling, and they've got to find out what it is." She stopped, took a swallow of her drink, leaned back and stared at him. "That's why I know you know where the treasure is."

He shook his head slowly. "You're better than I ever gave you credit for."

"Do you have a cigarette?" she asked suddenly.

"In the drawer beside you," he said, pointing to the desk with his glass.

She opened the drawer, saw Billy's Bull Durham and papers. Without hesitation she soon had rolled herself a cigarette, lighting it with a wooden match she scraped on the bottom of the desk drawer. She inhaled deeply, letting the smoke out slowly through her mouth and nose.

"You did that well," he said admiringly.

"I was raised with *vaqueros*," she said. "I am not a simpering infant."

"God forbid!" he said under his breath.

She leaned forward in the chair. "Well?"

He scratched his head, then rubbed his chin. "I really don't know where all your information comes from, *señorita*," he said slowly, "but most of it is wrong."

She made a husky noise.

"I am here on a vacation, so to speak. Yes, I do know about the treasure—have known about it for years; but only as story, legend, myth. Since I've come to this part of the country, I've become convinced it was buried somewhere near here. But I have no way of knowing where. If I did, do you think I wouldn't have uncovered it by now, and been on my way long ago?"

"You have reasons not to."

"Ha! Spoken like an idiot."

"Don't you call me an idiot!" she spat at him angrily.

"Then don't talk like one! You can use that brain of yours when you want to! Use it!" His tone of voice slammed her back in the chair. She glared at him over the rim of her glass. He was finishing off his drink. "Want another?"

"Yes!" Her Spanish blood was boiling.

He mixed two more. "I know no more as to where the damned treasure is than you do," he said coldly as he handed her the glass. "I've seen pieces of the map, yes. I showed you one. Can you tell me what it means? I can't tell you because I haven't the slightest idea. I will tell you this," he went on, "I've seen more of the pieces than you have and I still can't make heads or tails of them. I have to see all of it before I can start to figure out what they mean. Do you understand?"

"*Mierda!*"

"The word suits your temper!" he said directly.

She began to laugh. "You had better watch out," she told him when her laughter subsided, "I might bring you more trouble than that Stella Townsend ever will."

"WHAT DO YOU KNOW of Tomás Urbina?" she asked.

"I never liked him, if that's what you mean," he answered. "He was a thief from the word go. I've met him, talked to him; walked away from him once. I know Fierro killed him, and I know why."

She rolled her glass between the palms of her hands.

"Pancho Villa," he continued, "killed the son of a *hacendado* for raping his sister. Anyway, that is the way the story goes. He had to hide out for his life. He joined a band of bandits in the mountains of Chihuahua, changing his name to Francisco Villa from Doroteo Arango. Among the bandit gang was a dark, chubby man named Tomás Urbina. He and Pancho became fast friends. Villa was a born leader; soon he headed the gang of bandits with Urbina as his right hand. He saved Urbina from the Rurales one time, carrying the little man for almost two days. They were, as you say, blood brothers.

"When Villa became powerful, Urbina was his second in command. When Díaz was ousted, Villa joined the Revolution. So did Urbina. When Madero was murdered, and Villa again took to the field, Urbina was with him. Villa made Urbina a general. They fought side by side through many battles. When Fierro joined them, Urbina was Fierro's friend; but he was also Villa's right hand. Fierro became Villa's bodyguard and railroad transportation expert. You follow me so far?"

"Very clearly," she said. "When did you know Urbina?"

"In Mexico City when Villa was there. I first saw him during the *entrada* when he was riding at Zapata's right hand. Urbina was a man wearing a tan pith helmet. He looked ridiculous and very dangerous."

"He was also a thief," she interjected.

"I know that. The Revolutionists had little money, or claimed they had none. Urbina was given the right to collect so-called taxes for the occupation army. He had many devious ways of raising money. He was very good at it, having the soldiers and Villa's power behind him. He was a real *chingadero.*"

"Do you know what happened after that?"

"He deserted Villa, after Celaya."

"What else?" she asked.

"He robbed Villa's Division of the North of its pay chest and all of its money."

"That's true," she said. "He did. He also robbed many rich churches and haciendas. Do you know where he went after that?"

"No," Little said.

"He came to San Luis Potosí, he and his brigade of men. They robbed, looted, raped all along the way. It wasn't an army, it was a mob with Urbina at its head." She paused. "They came to San Luis Potosí," she said in a far-off voice. She gulped her drink to the bottom of the glass. She held out her hand for more. Dick Little fixed her another. She only nodded, when he handed it to her; her thoughts were elsewhere, her mind's eye seeing things she could not describe.

"My family owns a bank in San Luis," she began again, slowly, her voice low and huskier than usual. "Urbina's men robbed that bank. The general, himself, shot my father dead, in front of the vault. Then he rode out afterward to our ranch to make it his headquarters. I knew Tomás Urbina and I knew him well.

"His men were animals, drunken beasts most of the time. They shot our *vaqueros* for the fun of it. One of my many uncles was tortured before my eyes until he died a horrible death. They thought we were hiding more gold and jewels at the ranch even after one of our servants had already betrayed our hiding place. They were insatiable. Once they had something, they wanted more and more, and couldn't understand when there wasn't any more. They thought torture and rape and death would open up other vaults to them. They saved me for Tomás Urbina himself."

She drank half of her drink.

"They burned most of our ranch; killed our livestock for food; broke into our cellar for drink; raped and killed our servants for fun. But I was saved for General Tomás Urbina, himself!" She spat on the rug of the room. "I was sixteen. I was a gentlewoman because I was the daughter of the *hacendado*, the *estanciero*. I was locked in my room awaiting his pleasure. He took his time, overseeing the gathering of the loot his men had robbed throughout the city and country. Oh, Tomás would never let pleasure affect his business, especially where loot and money were involved! It had to be packed most carefully in special wagons, drawn by special mules, driven by special, trusted men. And, of course, guarded most carefully. After taking care of the details, he had time for me."

She finished off the other half of her drink. Dick Little silently gave her a refill. She swallowed more of the liquor before she resumed.

"He came to my room as if he owned me, my ranch, my world." Her voice was almost a whisper. "He was wearing that silly hat of his, that helmet, you called it. He took it off with a flourish and a bow. I almost laughed. Next he put aside his sword and pistol; he unbuttoned his jacket, taking it off, placing it carefully over the back of a chair. He was most deliberate. I could see his dirty shirt and smell his sweat. He smiled at me. He smoothed down his big mustache. All the time I was backing away from him. Backing away until I was against the wall, and I could go no farther. He reached for me with both hands, grabbing me by the arms. He leaned forward to kiss me on the mouth. Then, for the first time, I was no longer frightened." She paused to take another swallow of her drink.

"Then what did you do?"

"I gave him my knee—in the *cajones!*"

Dick Little laughed. He couldn't help himself. She looked at him, then began to smile. In a moment she was laughing, too.

"Oh, you should have seen Tomás Urbina!" she laughed. "All doubled over in pain. Holding his balls, trying to call someone to help him, but not having any voice to do it with. Do you know what I did then?"

"No, what?"

"I took him by the hair, held his head up and spat in his face. I slapped him on both sides of his face as hard as I could. After that I picked up a bottle of wine he had sent to my room, and I hit him as hard as I could on his head. He fell so heavily I thought I had killed him, but that little son of a whore had too hard a head. One of our servants told me later they found him the next morning still unconscious. And all through the night, his men thought he was enjoying me. He enjoyed, all right!"

"How did you get away?"

"By disguising myself as one of my own maids. Changing my dress for hers, doing my hair differently. Later I was able to waylay a *soldadera* and steal her clothes. By that time I was so dirty and smelly I could pass for one. Then I stole away from the army after they left San Luis and went back to what was left of our ranch, to weep for my father and my uncle."

She stopped talking. She gave a deep sigh. "Yes," she said, "I knew Tomás Urbina. I knew him well."

"Do you know what happened after that?"

She nodded slowly. Her voice took on more timbre. "Urbina's brigade began to disintegrate. By the time he reached the hacienda he had appropriated, he had only a few men left. He hid the treasure he had collected, on his property, murdering the men who buried the loot. He thought he could settle down to a quiet life for the rest of his days." She paused to drink. "I—I don't know the story after that. Only that Urbina was killed."

"I can tell you the rest, señorita, from what I have read and been told." Dick thought a moment. "When Villa heard Urbina was at his rancho, in the state of Durango, at Las Nieves, a few miles south of Hidalgo del Parral, in Chihuahua, he went there as fast as he could. With him were Fierro and some of the Dorados. They surrounded the ranch house, making noise; possibly a gun went off. Urbina came out to see what was causing the commotion and was fired on. He was hit, falling, holding himself. Instantly, Villa was all compassion for his old friend and *compadre*. He called a cease-fire, running to Urbina, taking him in his arms. 'Don't worry, old friend,' he said, 'I'll take care of you. I'll see you get to a doctor. You'll be all right!' And other words to that effect. Then Fierro spoke up. 'My general,' he said, 'do you remember your order to shoot all men who have been traitors to you?' 'Yes,' replied Villa, 'kill him, Rodolfo.' Then Villa walked to his horse and rode from the ranch."

Dick Little paused to reflect. He sipped his drink. "I can only imagine what happened afterward," he said. "They had come to take from Urbina the treasure he had stolen, not only from the Division of the North, but from other places and people he had robbed, such as your father. The Dorados had searched the ranch without finding anything. Fierro talked to Urbina alone in the ranch house. My conjecture is, Fierro found out where Urbina buried his loot; found it, then calmly shot Urbina to death."

"What happened then?"

"The ranch was not too far from a railroad. Fierro had the treasure transferred to a boxcar, then reported to Villa he had killed Urbina as ordered. Perhaps the two of them decided to get the treasure into the United States, away from the Revolutionists and Constitutionalists where it would be safe. Fierro, who had been raised on the railroads, had the car moved to Juárez. I do not think it was too difficult for him to arrange its passage across the border, through customs; not with his railroad connections and the power of Villa behind him. Then, too, there were thousands of Villa's sympathizers north of the border. I

believe he had no trouble having the car moved to Columbus. He had
been in this area many times before. He knew its proximity to the
border and to Las Palomas. He knew the ruggedness of the mountains
here. He knew the terrain of the country. After all, he was one of Villa's
generals, a cavalryman above all, one who moved about scouting for the
enemy primarily. He was mentally equipped to assimilate all this knowledge and decide that here was the best place, and the closest to Mexico,
to hide the treasure. There were not many people living here then, in
the city or in the country. It would be easy to move the treasure from
the railroad to wherever he wanted to hide it. Besides, Villa also knew
this part of the country from his incognito and frequent visits here.

"So, the scene was set. The car is on the siding in Columbus, along
with the Dorados acting as guards. Fierro buys, or rents, five wagons
and double teams. The treasure is loaded onto the wagons. They head
north. At one point they turn off the road, but their tracks are wiped
out in a flash flood. They may have returned to the road somewhere
else. All we can be sure of is the empty wagons and teams were turned
loose. None of the Dorados were ever seen again. The empty boxcar was
returned to Mexico. A surveyor from Deming was found in a ditch, shot
in the back of the head. Fierro was also among the missing.

"But he wasn't dead. He turned up at Villa's headquarters with a
map which the general tears into eight parts. Villa keeps one. The rest
are passed around to Fierro, Felipe Angeles, Gunner Marks, Captain
Galinda, and three others. That group never met again. They scattered
all over Mexico. Some died, some still live. The living are trying to put
the pieces of the map together again and find the treasure." He stopped
for long moments. "That is the way I see it," he concluded.

She sighed, took a drink, leaned back in the chair, arms outstretched.
"That's quite a story," she said.

"So is yours."

"How can you be so sure?"

"We know Urbina took the money from the Division of the North.
That's history. We know no one ever found it. That's history. We know
Fierro killed Urbina. That's history. There is a time between the killing
of Urbina and Fierro's next appearance in Juárez. That's history. There
was a Mexican Central boxcar on the Columbus siding during the time
Fierro had disappeared. That I know. It was Fierro who hired the wagons. That I know. Fierro was several times in the Columbus and Deming areas. That I know. The story of the map. That's history. Several
people, who have parts of the map, are now in Deming. That I know. I

know, also, you're one of them." He paused to watch her reaction. She merely shrugged slightly, watching his face intently. "What I don't know is who has them all. Or if all of the parts are here. I'm also not sure why this sudden activity and rushing about to find it."

"I can tell you that," she said. "Villa is anxious to recover the treasure. For what reason I don't know, except that he has always liked money. Lots of it. It is rumored he wants to form his army again and fight Obregón. It is rumored he wants to make his ranch at Canutillo a showplace. It is rumored he just wants the money. These rumors have been spreading around Mexico for some months now. If Villa is anxious to find the money after all these years, other people are just as anxious he doesn't."

"What are your motives?"

"My family," she said simply. "I want to return to my family all the money Urbina stole from it."

"And the rest?"

She shrugged again. "We'll see when we find it."

"And I'm to get 20 percent?"

"Yes."

He sighed. "Señorita Gutiérrez, you are still incredible."

"Perhaps. What have you done, Señor Withers, to find the treasure?"

"I have seen many pieces of the map. From them I know it is near this room. Within a few miles."

"But you don't know where it is exactly?"

"No, I do not."

"This mountain—this Cooke's Peak, has been suggested as the hiding place. What do you think of it being there?"

He shook his head. "I'm not sure, but I'll go on record it is somewhere else. Not Cooke's Peak."

"Why do you think not?"

"A feeling. A hunch, as we say. How much of the map have you seen?"

"I have a piece."

"What do you think of it?"

"I cannot read maps."

"But you must have some impression? Draw me your part." He took out his notebook and pencil, handing them to her.

She put down her glass, thought a moment, sketched hurriedly, then handed the notebook back to him. He glanced at it. She had put a four above the slanting line, instead of the O he'd memorized. She was still playing games with him. He accepted that fact and immediately thought of a fitting punishment.

He went to the desk, opening the drawer, taking out Billy's part. He handed it to her in silence. She looked at it a long time with deep interest. "Billy sent me that just before he was killed," he said. "Now you've seen two parts. Tell me where you got yours."

"It is too simple. One of the officers Villa gave a part to is another of my uncles—on my mother's side. It has been in our family since then. Major Humberto Valencia still lives in San Luis Potosí. His first cousin now lives in Las Palomas. If you must know, I was visiting my distant cousin when you took me there. I was reporting to him what I had learned since coming here this time. He wrote my uncle everything I told him. Even the things about you."

"About me?"

"Yes. How you turned up here. The attacks on you. Why I thought you were mixed up with the treasure. Everything. I know all about you."

"I'm flattered." He crossed the room to take her glass for another refill. The bottle was getting low, but it was still a third full. He put less water in her glass, but the same amount of whiskey. She accepted it eagerly, taking two quick swallows. A slight shudder crossed her face. "Captain Galinda is in town," he announced casually. She choked on her drink. "Know him?"

She was coughing. "Yes," she gasped. She wiped her mouth with her handkerchief. "I met him in Guadalajara once. I was attempting to get him to come in with us."

"But he wouldn't?"

"No."

"Why not?"

"He didn't give me any reason. He was very charming, but he wanted nothing to do with us."

"Who's us?"

"My family. Of course, he had other plans for me, if I agreed with him."

"That's not so strange. Typical, I'd say."

She laughed. "Are they the same as yours?"

"I wouldn't know what his were, but I know what mine would be," he said, smiling at her.

"You're just like all the rest of the men."

"Oh, I wouldn't say that. After all, you don't know what my plans are."

"I can guess."

He changed the subject abruptly. "Who were the other two men who received parts of the map?"

She hiccuped gently. "One was named Gurule, the other Treviño. Gurule was killed shortly afterward."

"He must have been the one Billy tried to help."

"Billy? Help?" she asked.

"He wrote me he'd taken his piece from a general who was dying. Obviously not a general, but to Billy most of the commissioned officers were all alike. The officer asked Billy to take his part back to Fierro. By then, Fierro was already dead, so Billy kept the piece. Somebody killed him for it."

"Who would do a thing like that?" She pushed her hat to the back of her head.

"One of the treasure hunters," he said. "I told you, this is a dangerous game you're playing. Who is Treviño?"

"I don't know. He disappeared about three years ago."

"You have good information. How do you know so many things?" he asked.

"We made it a point to find out."

"Then where is Fierro's piece? It wasn't on him when they pulled him out of the lake."

"Don't know." She took another swallow.

"Maybe it was lost in the water?"

"Perhaps."

"Then, again, he could have given it to someone. I understand Angeles gave his part away." He watched her closely. No reaction.

"He did? Who to?"

Dick Little shook his head. "Drink up," he said, "I'll fix you another."

"Good idea." She gulped down her drink. He mixed another for her.

"You're pretty good at this," he observed, handing her the drink.

"Raised on tequila. On the ranch. This stuff's weak."

"I can see that," he said. "Don't leave any."

She drank again. Her head began to weave. She had trouble finding her mouth with the glass. She giggled.

"What?" he asked.

"Th—the room—it's moving."

"You're at sea."

"Liar," she said. "I—I'll show you what I do to liars." She staggered to her feet, dropping the glass on the rug. "Come here."

He moved toward her, catching her as she stumbled into his arms. She put both of her arms over his shoulders and around his neck. She kissed him full on the lips, a long, lingering kiss with open mouth. Her tongue met his. They were one, for minutes.

She drew her head back, looked into his eyes and murmured, "Liar!" She collapsed.

He picked up her dead weight, carrying her to the bed. He unbuttoned the neck of her blouse after removing her hat. He unlaced her boots, taking them off, placing them carefully by the bed. He began to smile. He undressed her completely, folding and putting her clothes carefully on a chair. When she was entirely naked, he rolled her over, pulled down the covers of the bed and rolled her back. For a long time he gazed at her nude body before arranging her comfortably with a pillow under her head, her arms at her sides. He pulled the sheet up to her chin, tucking it in. Finished, he went to his ruined Gladstone in the closet, taking from it folded papers of seltzer powders. He placed these on the night table, along with a glass of water. He put a sack of Bull Durham, papers, and matches where she could reach them. He made sure the windows were darkened. Picking up his hat, and Billy Thomas's gun, he surveyed the room, noting the fan was turning gently. He leaned over and kissed her on the mouth. She moaned softly, moving her body under the sheets. He stood up, putting on his hat. He looked at her face on the pillow once more before he left the room, locking the door behind him.

FOR THREE DAYS Dick Little thought it best to stay out of town.

He bought supplies, picked up the horse at O'Conner's, and headed northeast. It didn't take him long to locate his surveyor. "How has it been?" he asked E. Thomas Mills, noting the sun had already burned his skin almost as red as his hair.

The man grinned up at him. "One day on the job and already several people have 'just passed by' to see how I'm getting along, sir."

"Anyone we know?"

"The Townsends rode by not long ago. The sheriff asked me what I was doing. I've had one Mexican keeping an eye on me for a while. He's ridden away." Mills shook his head, grinning. "How the news does travel!"

"Good," Little said. "Keep at it around here for the rest of the day and until noon tomorrow. I want you to move down south and start shooting the Floridas and Las Tres Hermanas. Make it look good. I'm heading down that way and will probably see you around there somewhere."

"As you say, boss," Mills said happily. "I'll mail that report just as soon as I finish here today."

"Excellent. See you south of here."

They waved to each other as Dick Little turned his horse toward the Floridas, riding far enough east to circle the town.

There was no place he was headed in particular, just as long as he stayed away from Deming for a while. He couldn't help smiling as he thought of the Señorita Gutiérrez waking up in a strange room with a colossal hangover, nude, in a strange bed, and wondering what the hell had happened to her. He could almost visualize her temper as she realized she would have to call the desk clerk to come up and unlock the door for her. He laughed aloud.

In the late afternoon he had pitched camp at the foot of the tallest peak of the Floridas, hidden so that anyone would have to come very close to even know he was there. He had enough supplies to keep him well fed for four or five days, and he'd picked up a couple of books before he left town. He had missed reading all the time he had spent in Deming.

The following morning, he decided to climb up the face of the Floridas as far as he was able. He made it quite a ways until the abrupt face of the rock stopped him from going further. He carefully sat on a rock so he could look to the west at the terrain. It was flat except for the jutting up of several mountainettes. He could see more easily the range to the west, and even mountains in Mexico. The Three Sisters were clear to him. He studied them thoughtfully. There were caves in those mountains. This he had learned by asking questions of some of the old-timers in Deming. They had been mined for bat guano off and on for years. He was too far south and west to see Cooke's Peak; it was around the north end of the Floridas. But he could see north where another range of mountains began, or ended.

The view was breathtaking. He stayed on his perch until the sun began to lower, then he climbed down and went back to his camp. After his small supper, he stretched out on his ground sheet with his blanket half pulled up, and opened one of his books.

When the moon passed over the crest of the Floridas, he had been asleep for hours.

The following morning he climbed up the face of the mountain again, as high as he could. Again he surveyed the countryside, but this time with his field glasses, bringing points of interest closer to his eyes. He sighted three dust trails traveling the road to Columbus. Spotting the source with the binoculars, he recognized Martínez's Model T taxi heading south. The second dust trail was a horse and wagon heading north; the third was a horse and a covered wagon heading south. Climbing down, he fixed some sandwiches at his camp, saddled his horse, and began riding southward, angling toward the road. He caught up with E. Thomas Mills several miles away.

The surveyor had tied his horse to a bush and was busily setting up his instruments. "Well," he said when Dick Little rode up. "We do meet in the strangest places, don't we?" He grinned.

Little observed Mills' covered wagon, outfitted for slow traveling. "Looks as if you're planning to stay a while?"

"Always good to get out into the open air. I plan to stay two or three days. Anything special you want done, or should we just play the game?"

Dick Little dismounted, hunkering down beside the surveyor's tripod. "Been thinking," he said slowly. "Make sure you shoot from the highest peak back there"—he gestured with his thumb toward the Floridas— "to the three peaks there." He indicated the Three Sisters. "I want to know how far it is from the highest of the Sisters to the highest point of those mountains."

Mills looked at the points Little indicated. "That over there would be Florida Peak," he said. He grinned. "Can do easily. Anything else, sir?"

Little shook his head. "Not that I can think of, except to stay in sight so people can see you. After you've played around with that, just play some more at whatever you want. I still am interested in who comes to watch and ask questions."

"I'll work here for an hour or so before heading south, sir. Okay?"

"Okay."

Dick Little mounted his horse and rode back toward the mountains. Fierro, he thought, you're a son of a bitch, a clever son of a bitch. If I could only read your mind!

He had brought one of his books along with him. Taking it from his jacket pocket, he began to read, slouching in the saddle, letting the horse have his own head. They covered ground slowly but consistently. He was unconscious of where he was when the horse stopped. Dick raised his eyes from the book. They were almost to the foot of the Floridas. The horse lowered his head and snorted. Dick Little looked around. He raised his head high to look up the mass of rock in front of him, then twisted it to look back over his shoulder at the plains falling away from the mountain. He looked to the north and then to the south. Suddenly he was aware he was looking at something he hadn't recognized. Almost at his horse's front hooves was unmistakably a wagon trail. For a time he sat on the horse, following the trail with his eyes. He could make it out for some distance on either side as it snaked along around boulders and contours into the distance. He decided to turn the horse north.

He followed the trail for several miles until it turned into a canyon. He followed it. Within several hundred yards he was in a box canyon covered with grass and brush, with sheer rock walls rising from the floor.

Dick Little could see where it had been used to hold cattle. There was an old fence across the mouth, the gate being poles pulled across the entrance from one post to another. The droppings of animals were much in evidence. He rode around the bottom of the canyon, closely scanning the faces of the cliffs, occasionally focusing his glasses on spots which caught his interest. Once he saw a cave. He dismounted, climbing among heavy rock to reach the entrance. It went back into the mountain only a short distance. He kicked at the small rocks and dirt on the floor of the cave, then left. After casting one last look around, he left the box canyon to ride north toward his camp. He'd eaten his sandwiches at the mouth of the canyon. Saving supper until dark, he again climbed the face of the mountain, taking along his glasses and book. He settled comfortably in a niche where he could read and watch the road. He saw several more plumes of dust from the road, observing each through his glasses; all were heading south. All were automobiles. As the sun was sinking, they came back, heading north, not in a group, but spread apart at intervals of fifteen to twenty minutes. All were speeding back faster than they had headed south. Dick Little chuckled to himself as he climbed down the mountain back to his camp.

When he had finished supper, and was stretched out reading by the firelight, his interest began to wander from the book. More and more his thoughts turned to his adventures since his arrival. He reviewed in his mind what had happened to him, who he had spoken to, what they said, where he had been, and what he had picked up casually. He began to sift the facts in his head, arranging them in some logical order since the day Urbina had been killed at Las Nieves, the hacienda in Durango. Naturally, his thoughts turned again to Fierro.

It was said of Fierro, when he was frowning and grouchy, the time to approach him was propitious. When Fierro smiled constantly, and was in good humor—look out! He was dangerous!

John Reed had told Dick of a time when both he and Fierro were in Ciudad Chihuahua for a spell. Fierro had killed fifteen citizens out of hand, for no reason; but Fierro was Villa's closest friend and was always forgiven little pecadillos such as offhand murder. There was also the Benton murder which caused Villa no end of trouble internationally, and almost caused him to lose the friendship of the United States, which was very strong at the time.

William Benton was a feisty Englishman who owned ranches and mines in the state of Chihuahua. He got drunk one afternoon and went to see Villa to protest the rustling of cattle from his ranches. Villa listened to him in his house in Juárez until Benton became more than abusive, which raised Villa's hackles. He did not like to be talked to as a peon. Benton began to curse Villa, to pound on his desk; he reached into his pocket for a handkerchief, but Villa interpreted the movement as reaching for a gun. He threw Benton out of the tent, turned to Fierro, telling him to kill Benton. Fierro took him from Juárez and had a grave dug for him. But, instead of shooting Benton, he killed him by hitting him over the head with the butt of his revolver. Villa reported Benton had been shot for cause. When the English consul in El Paso insisted on Benton's body being dug up to be buried in a cemetery, or shipped home, all hell broke loose. Benton had been bludgeoned to death; Villa had said he was shot. So, when the corpse was raised, Fierro calmly put several bullets into the body. Later, on examination, it was discovered Benton had been dead some time before the bullets hit him. The English protested; the United States protested; but, in the long run, nothing came of the protests. Villa was able to ride out the storm, and Benton was soon forgotten for other, more important international incidents.

Dick Little fell into an uncomfortable sleep, as his mind recalled Fierro's modulated low voice and those half-slitted obsidian eyes. In his dreams he heard Fierro talking to him, protesting he was a gentle man; his words chosen carefully, no profanity, one gentleman talking to another. Little started from his sleep, recognized where he was and fell back. His dream was broken. He slept well the rest of the night until early dawn.

The third day was quieter. He let his horse graze, hobbled, while he sat in the niche, reading and watching the road. More automobiles headed south and later returned north. He recognized Martínez's taxi, in the late afternoon, headed for Deming. He couldn't make out the passenger clearly, but he could guess who it was. That night was the same as the ones before—uneventful. And in the morning, feeling refreshed, he saddled his horse, broke camp, riding to town and the fury of Señorita Gutiérrez.

Sam Townsend was seated in a booth at the Manhattan Café when Dick Little entered. He was waved over to sit with the rancher. He chose the seat across the table.

Sam had aged. His gray face was deeply lined. His eyes had lost their sparkle, their aliveness. His shoulders sloped more than ever. Sam took out a tobacco pouch, filled his pipe and lighted it slowly. Dick ordered coffee from the waitress. "How've you been?" he asked Sam, rolling a cigarette.

"Not good, Dick. Not good. I haven't slept well these last few nights."

"Something on your mind?"

Sam Townsend sighed. "You might say that."

"Anything I can do?"

"Maybe." He paused. "Dick, why was Billy Thomas murdered?"

Dick Little shrugged, keeping his voice level, emotionless. "Because he had a piece of Fierro's map."

Sam looked as if he had been slapped in the face. "He what?"

"Had a piece of Fierro's map."

"But—but surely that story is only a myth? I can't believe it." But his voice betrayed his feelings. He did believe. He was concerned. "Even so, what did Billy know of the treasure?"

"Not much, Sam," Dick Little admitted. "Billy was given part of the map to return to Fierro by an officer named Gurule. Gurule had been mortally wounded. Anyway, Billy couldn't take it to Fierro because Fierro had drowned. He kept it, and somebody found out he had it."

"Who?"

"The person who killed him. Someone he knew who could walk right up to him, unsuspected, and blast him with a shotgun."

"I don't know," Sam said, shaking his head. "It's all so confusing."

"Yes, it is; but it is also so real."

"What I don't understand, really, is why you were ambushed twice on the same evening."

"By two different ambushers. They could have thought I had a part of the map. The first was a man who's pretty good with a rifle. Unknown. The Mexicans, I think I know who set them on to me, but that's immaterial. I'll get to him later. Incidentally, Sam," he asked, "how is it you're not interested in the treasure?"

"I'm a rancher, Dick. I've got no time to traipse all over this country on a wild goose chase. I suppose, if I stumble on it by accident, I'd be interested. But not to look for it. It would be nice to find it, though."

Dick Little agreed. He looked at Sam closely. Here, he thought, is a man with more on his mind than he's letting on.

"Dick," Sam said uneasily, "I might not be as unbiased as I've said."

"Yes?"

"Yesterday," he sat up straighter, "Stella and I heard there was a surveyor working around the country. Tom Mills from Deming. We drove down to see him."

"Yes?"

Sam Townsend was looking down at his plate. "He talks as if he's on to something."

"What do you mean?"

"Well, he's shooting the high peaks all around. He hinted it was a very hush-hush sort of job he's doing. He did mention a man named Oliver Lang who lives in Santa Fe as having hired him."

"Interesting," Dick allowed.

Sam smiled slightly. "He seems to have kicked up a cloud of dust. There were others on the road who stopped to talk with Mills, too, I suspect."

"Know any of them?"

"Miss Gutiérrez was one who passed us. There was a man who was driving to Columbus who stopped by. Mills mentioned him. My guess is they were both interested in what Mills was doing. Aren't you?"

"Not particularly. As I've told you, I'm not interested in the treasure, except as a story. It looks as if it will be a good one."

"With what's been going on around here, I can believe that." Sam sighed deeply. "I hope all will be well."

Dick Little stood up. "I'm going over to The Gunner's. Buy you a drink?"

Sam shook his head. "Thanks anyway, Dick."

With a "See you," Dick Little left the café.

He was walking the hot streets of Deming, passing an areaway, when he heard himself called. He stopped, turning slowly, suspicious. El Gallo was standing in the shadows between the two buildings. He was holding up his hands, palms outward. "I come in peace, *señor*," El Gallo said in Spanish. He had a broad piece of white court plaster stuck across the bridge of his nose and under his eyes.

"What do you want?" Dick Little unbuttoned his jacket letting El Gallo see he was wearing a gun belt about his waist. The Mexican glanced at it briefly. He managed a sickly smile.

"I wish my gun and knife back," he said. "They are my old friends."

"I have them at the hotel."

"I will go with you in peace, *señor*, if you will be so kind as to give them back to me."

Dick Little stared at the Mexican for several moments. "All right," he said. "Come along."

They walked together to the hotel, Dick managing to convince El Gallo to lead the way. In the lobby, he told El Gallo to wait while he went to his room. In five minutes he was back handing the articles to the Mexican. El Gallo checked the gun slowly to make sure it was loaded. He stuck it into his belt under his coat. The knife he held casually, but Dick could see he was testing the handle. Evidently he was satisfied because he slipped it into the sheath at his back. He straightened his coat. "Many thanks," he murmured. He started to turn to leave.

"One moment," Dick said, stopping him.

"Yes, *señor?*"

"Why did you send those men after me the other night?"

El Gallo smiled. "I am sorry they did not kill you," he said regretfully, "but I feel you are getting in my way."

"Do you still feel I'm getting in your way?"

El Gallo shrugged. "Perhaps."

"Then let me tell you this, Gallo," Dick Little said evenly, looking directly into El Gallo's eyes, "if you send men again to kill me, or try anything funny with me, I'll come after you as certain as the sun rises. And you will not see the sun set. Do you understand me?"

"Perfectly, *señor*."

"So you're after the treasure also," Dick said casually. He noted that El Gallo blinked quickly.

"Treasure? I do not know what you mean, *señor.*"

"You needn't lie to me, Gallo. Everybody and his grandmother in this town would like to find Fierro's treasure. You included. Who are you working for? Villa?" Again El Gallo blinked. "Who is your contact here?" he continued. "You're not smart enough to read the map, even if you had all the pieces."

"I do not understand you, *señor,*" El Gallo shrugged. "You are talking to me of nothing."

"Bullshit!"

El Gallo looked Dick Little directly in the eyes. "All right, Señor Leetle," he said. "For many years I am a foreman on the general's ranch at Canutillo. One day Colonel Trillo talks with me about the treasure. He tells me my general would like to have all the money. Colonel Trillo gives me a part of the map and tells me to come here and find it for the general. I am here. I cannot find it."

"Why are you telling me this all of a sudden? You don't like me in the least."

Again El Gallo shrugged. "I don't like you, that is true, *señor,* but I trust you. I know you from the old days. We do not agree on many things, true, but if you are here to find the treasure, I will be not far behind."

"With your knife?"

"Most probably, *señor.*"

"Then I will be watching for you."

The Mexican smiled. "I would expect you to, *señor.*"

Dick Little laughed. "If I find it—if I find it," he repeated, "I'll make sure you're not around when I do."

"That is the game, *señor.*"

"You won't tell me who is your contact here?"

The Mexican shrugged, saying nothing, his black eyes expressionless.

"Go with God," Dick said, turning from him toward the stairs, leaving the Mexican standing alone in the center of the lobby.

So, THOUGHT RICHARD HENRY LITTLE, the part of the map he'd found in El Gallo's knife handle was Pancho Villa's. At least that mystery was cleared up. Colonel Trillo was Villa's aide, secretary, and what have you; had been for years. If he told El Gallo to find the treasure, one could bet a bottom dollar the original idea had emanated from the general himself.

He stretched out on his bed, deep in thought. There were still parts of the map to be accounted for, but he knew where another one was and wasn't worried about it. His memory had captured it years before and it was available to him whenever he needed it. He recalled the pieces he'd seen in Deming: The Gunner's, Señorita Gutiérrez's, El Gallo's, Billy Thomas's, and Captain Galinda's. Six, actually, what with the one other he'd seen. Now, what had happened to Fierro's piece? Had it, indeed, been lost in the lake near Casas Grandes when Rodolfo drowned? Very possible.

Pancho had ordered Fierro from Villa Ahumada to Agua Prieta to take command of his troops there and conclude a stalemate with the Constitutionalists. Fierro had headed for Casas Grandes first, with the idea of turning north as the shortest and quickest way to Agua Prieta. But, near Casas Grandes, he had to cross the neck of a lake the Mormon colony there had built for irrigation purposes. It was in the crossing he lost his life.

Dick had heard at least three different stories about Fierro's death, all supposedly told to him by eyewitnesses. Fierro and his men had reached the crossing. Several of his men had attempted to cross the water, but had turned back. Fierro, impatient, told them he'd go first, and had forced his horse into the water. One witness said the ground was marshy; another told of the horse stepping into an underwater hole. In any event, the horse floundered and sank. Fierro, who could not swim, went down with the horse two times, the horse coming up a third time without him. Another witness said Fierro had stood on the saddle while the horse sank into the marsh under him, until he slipped and fell off the saddle, the horse rising to swim to the other side. Another factor in Fierro's death was his *banderolas* crossed over his chest, and his belt, which were full of gold coins, their weight adding to Fierro's death by drowning.

The third eyewitness he'd spoken to told essentially the same story as the others with minor variations. They all added up to the one fact: Fierro was dead.

Men searched the lake for five days before the body was found. One man said there were two Japanese who were in Fierro's party and who dove time and again into the water, searching. Villa appeared on the scene the day the body was found by a peon. It was caught in a clump of bushes along the edge of the lake. Villa awarded the peon with a handful of gold coins from Fierro's belt. Fierro's diamond ring, his good luck charm, was missing from his finger. It was said one of the Japanese divers got it.

They took the body to the railroad station in Casas Grandes, wrapped in a sheet, laid out on a door, Fierro's white hat placed on his head so it shaded the dead eyes. The body stank so much, and was in such a state of decomposition, creosote was poured over it to cut the stench and keep the flesh together. There was no embalmer in Casas Grandes. Pictures were taken of the corpse. The final end of Rodolfo Fierro—he was buried in Cuidad Chihuahua.

Villa had lost his best and most loyal friend.

Those were the stories Dick Little had heard. But he had his own opinion: he was a newspaperman and had dug through the different stories until he had come close to the truth.

Fierro had indeed forced his horse into the waters of the lake. The horse had floundered in quicksand. When Fierro had called for help, his men had thrown him a rope, which Fierro had caught. But, instead of pulling El General Matón, "The Killer General," out of the quicksand, his men had allowed him to sink to his horrible death—so suited to the man. It was slow, and Fierro had time for rapid thoughts before he suffocated.

In time, his men pulled the body from the quicksand and brought it to the railway station at Casas Grandes. There the corpse had been photographed—perhaps to make sure there would be no untrue rumors Fierro had actually survived. The photos showed the body of Fierro could not have been in the water a long time: there was no bloating or other evidence of deterioration. The ring on his right hand showed clearly in the photos.

Eight days later, on October 21, 1915, Fierro was buried in the National Cemetery in Ciudad Chihuahua.

As there was very little embalming in Mexico, especially in outlying towns like Casas Grandes, Fierro's body had been put in a plain box to be taken to Chihuahua. Without preservation, and in the hot days of late October, no wonder the corpse stank and had deteriorated before he was placed in his grave.

So much for the legends of Fierro's death.

Dick Little had checked the civil archives in Chihuahua just to make sure. He'd read the burial record in the large book, written in flowing Spanish by someone who was an artist with a pen.

Dick had wanted to make sure Fierro was dead. The way Rodolfo had died was a simple matter of putting two and two together after he had seen the photographs.

Fierro, The Butcher, was really, unlamentedly, finally and thoroughly dead.

Of that Richard Henry Little was convinced beyond doubt.

Dick Little's thoughts changed. The map. The damnable map. Say Fierro's piece had been lost with him. He'd seen six: he needed one more if he was to crack Fierro's code. He pictured all of the pieces he'd seen.

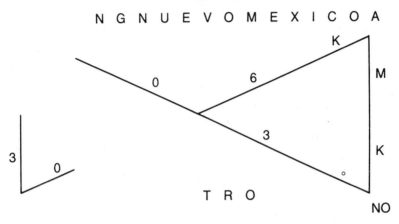

N. North? O? Remember, the surveyor probably wasn't too familiar with Spanish. O could stand for *Oriente:* East. He might have anglicized the words, Northeast, as N-O, easily, instead of *Nordeste,* Northeast. What was northeast? Of course, a line through the Three Sisters would point northeast!

What about the *A* after *Mexico? A? A,* what? *A?* What would be there? No! What would be *here?* Here? *Aquí!* Here! What here? How about the base point for all of the calculations? Otherwise, why stress that point?

He thought of figures 0-3-0 again. There was something different about the final number. What was it? Aha! It was an *O,* but not a big *O.* It was a little *o.* Little *o?* 0-3-o. Move the little *o* up a bit. 0-3-°. Why not 0-3°? Three degrees of an angle. If the angle of a line at the point of the southernmost peak of the Three Sisters was correct, he had another part of the map solved. The zeros meant nothing: they were blinds.

Now, he almost had it. The highest point of the Three Sisters to the highest point of the Floridas. That would be blank six kilometers. One

line. The northernmost Sister to the southernmost Sister was another
line three miles long. If a third line, on an angle of three degrees was
drawn from the southernmost Sister, A, to the Floridas, wouldn't its
point on the baseline be three miles from the tallest point of those
mountains?

What would the two triangles look like then?

Dick Little moved quickly to the desk after taking his notebook from
the pocket of his jacket, which hung over a chair. Pulling up the chair,
he sat at the desk and began to draw a crude map in the notebook.

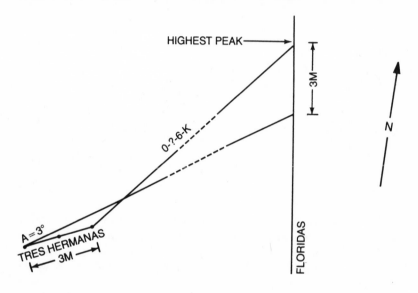

With the addition of his piece, he might be able to figure out the
whole: after all, he'd studied the country, and the map was now nearly
complete.

He concentrated.

Piece number one, probably Fierro's—missing; yet, undoubtedly the
letters D-E-M-I had been across the top of it. The legend across the top
of the map would then read (D-E-M-I)-N-G-N-U-E-V-O-M-E-X-I-
C-O-A. Deming, New Mexico, A. There was no doubt this was the area
the treasure was buried. Whether Fierro had wanted to be that specific
in locating the area, there would never be a way of telling. The surveyor
had written it on the map, and there it was.

The triangle sides running from the upper left, and missing angle, to the bottom right, piece number eight: 0-3-0.

The triangle sides from lower left, piece number five to piece number four, upper right: 0-blank-6-K.

The angle in piece number four, baseline: M; at point of angle: A; triangle side: K.

The angle in piece number five, baseline: 3; angle line: 0.

M-A-K. The *K* is written twice, the *A* once, the *M* once. Try M-K. M-K? m-k? K-M. What relationship would they have? Distances? The map deals with measurements and distances. Therefore, wouldn't *K* stand for Kilometers and *M* for Miles? Why not? Try it.

The baseline figures. Three on one to M-K on the other. What would be three Kilometers, or three Miles? Wouldn't three Miles be most likely against blank Kilometers: a criss-cross? Now, what is three miles long? Save that for later.

Piece five is missing. Who has it? No matter.

Piece number six: triangle side with a 3; plus the letters T-R-O near the bottom. T-R-O. What word would end in T-R-O which would most likely be used on a map to indicate a position? Why not (C-E-N)-T-R-O? *Centro*, Center. Center of what?

Piece number eight, lower right: an angle. Triangle side: O; baseline: K. Then what in hell is the N-O, no, for at the bottom of the map? Try a direction.

Oh, that Fierro! he thought. Clever! Clever! Clever!

Centro? Center? The second of the Three Sisters, or the center point from the peak of the highest north to the peak of the southernmost? He would get Mills to shoot the Three Sisters from peak to peak to get those measurements. He would calculate the Floridas for himself, using trigonometry, the mile and a half south of the tallest peak. And, since Fierro was not a mountain climber, he would look at the base of the mountain where the treasure would most likely be. If, of course, someone hadn't stumbled onto it long before, and had moved it.

Dick Little was elated. He poured himself a drink, turned in water from the tap, and drank a toast to himself and the treasure. He drank another toast to the memory of Robert Knight, who had obviously been murdered after calculating and drawing the map for Fierro.

Dick returned to the notebook on the desk. He looked at his drawing on the page, then ripped it out, placed it in an ashtray, and lit a match to it.

When the paper had been reduced to ashes, he sat down and began to

list the supplies he would need. He then broke the list down into three
parts, listing each part on a different page. Putting on his jacket and
hat, he left his room, heading for The Gunner's place.

The Gunner set up a beer as Dick Little entered the back room.
"Something's happened, Tiny," he said. "You look excited."

Dick poured the beer into a glass and drank. "Something has happened, Gunner," he said finally, licking his lips of the foam. "I want you
to do a job for me."

"Anytime, Tiny. Anytime. What is it?"

Dick reached into his jacket pocket, took out a folded paper, handing
it to Gunner Marks. "Buy these supplies for me. Wait until the last half
hour to go to Torrea's grocery store. Bring the stuff here. I'll pick it up
from you after dark. Do you have a back door?"

"Through my bedroom," he said, thumbing over his shoulder.
"There's a door there leading into the alley."

"Good." He laid a fifty-dollar gold piece on the bar. "Change that
and use paper money at the store. I don't want anyone to know you're
buying so much stuff. Got it?"

"Got it," The Gunner answered.

"Can you take off from here for a few days?"

"Anytime! Anytime!"

"Good. I'll talk to you more about it this evening. Got a phone?"

"In the pool hall, Tiny."

Dick excused himself, found the phone near the front window of the
pool hall. He gave a number to the operator. In a moment he heard
Martínez's voice. "This is Dick Withers," he said. "Can you pick me up
at The Gunner's place?"

"Five minutes, *señor.*"

"I'll be waiting."

He was absently knocking a few balls around on one of the pool
tables when the Model T pulled up in front of the building. Racking his
cue stick, he left the building, climbed into the taxi, and drove off with
Martínez. They drove west of town to a quiet place under some cottonwoods.

"Here, *amigo,*" Dick said to Martínez, giving him a page from the
notebook and some folding money. "Get these supplies. Try Jack
Tidmore's store first. If anyone asks what you're going to do with them,
say you're helping a cousin to build a house. Or tell them anything you
want, but not that you're buying them for me. Understand?"

"Very clearly, *señor.* "

"Bring them to The Gunner's back door tonight after dark. Okay?"

"Okay," Martínez answered simply.

"Think you'll have enough money?"

Martínez read the list without expression. He glanced at the bills in his hand. "Okay," he said.

"Good. Take me back downtown."

Both men had left their supplies in The Gunner's bedroom. Dick Little checked them out against the lists. He'd added several things he'd purchased at Nordhau's after Martínez had let him out downtown. He was satisfied. The Gunner hovered about, grunting and making noises as he shifted the supplies so they wouldn't be in the way in his room. It was plainly furnished with a sorry dresser and chair, and a bed whose springs had seen much use. A soiled sheet was spread over it. From the ceiling an unshaded light dropped on a wire. It glared brightly in the small room.

"That's it," Dick said finally.

"Need any dynamite?"

Little was surprised. "Hadn't thought of it," he said. "Got any?"

"About ten sticks, Tiny."

"Caps and fuse?"

The Gunner grinned. "Got those too," he said.

"Might as well bring them along," Dick said.

"I'm going with you?"

"Counting on it, Gunner."

"When?"

"Late tonight."

"I'll be damned," The Gunner breathed. "I'll be damned!"

Dick Little loaded more supplies he'd bought at Nordhau's into the automobile, covering them with a tarpaulin to hide them from any inquiring eyes that might be interested in what he was doing. He was driving down a street when he saw Señorita Gutiérrez walking along the sidewalk, her back straight, her head high. He pulled up beside her, raising his hat. "Good afternoon," he called to her cheerily. "May I drive you somewhere?"

She stopped and looked at him coolly. She walked to the automobile. He opened the door for her. When she closed it, after seating herself next to him, he asked, "Where to, *señorita?*"

"You may take me for a drive," she said, not turning her head, staring straight through the new windshield.

"Certainly, *madame*," he said in his best chauffeur voice. He shifted the gears, turning the car down the road toward the east.

He drove a long time, concentrating on the road, before she said anything. "I did not appreciate what you did to me the other afternoon."

"Didn't think you would," he said.

"You made a fool of me."

"No," he shook his head, "you did that yourself. If you can't handle your liquor, stop drinking."

"I wasn't talking about that."

"Oh?"

"What you did after I became drunk."

"You mean putting you to bed?"

"Yes."

He smiled. "That was the best part."

"You might think so. It was very embarrassing to me when I woke up to discover what you had done to me."

"I didn't rape you."

"I know that, but you did undress me."

"That I did."

"You enjoyed it," she said, as a statement.

"I did."

"I don't suppose it mattered to you I had to leave the hotel alone after I dressed."

"I thought of that."

"Now the whole town thinks I spent the night with you."

"You couldn't have done better."

"You're insufferable!"

He grinned at her. "I recall a story," he said, turning to look at her. "There was this handyman around a town. He wheeled all his tools from one place to another in a wheelbarrow. At night he had the habit of visiting a girlfriend of his, a widow. They had a nice little romance going for themselves until one time one of the town busybodies complained to the mayor about his wheelbarrow always being outside the widow's house at night. She thought it highly immoral and undignified for the town. The mayor told the handyman he'd have to stop leaving his wheelbarrow in front of the widow's house at night where everybody could see it and figure what was going on. So, the handyman started leaving his wheelbarrow in front of the busybody's house at night."

When he stopped she asked, "What is that supposed to mean?"

"You were acting like a busybody." He glanced at her out of the corner of his eye. She had her head bowed, her hand covering her face. She was trying to suppress her laughter. He turned his head, smiling at her. "Not mad?"

She shook her head, taking her hand down. "You're such a fool," she said, turning to him smiling. "You had the opportunity and lost it."

He shook his head. "That wasn't an opportunity. Besides, I could never take advantage of a helpless human being. With you, I want you to be wide awake."

"Are you propositioning me?"

"Not exactly a proposition. Say, a wish; or, to be more specific, a thing to come."

"What are your intentions, Señor Withers?"

"The same as any man who is free and who thinks of the future."

She looked at him silently, her face serious. "You are a very unpredictable man, *señor,*" she said. "Most men I meet are not serious. They want me to go to bed with them, or they want to marry me for my money."

He laughed. "I never knew you to have any."

"I own a very large ranch near San Luis. I thought you knew that."

He shot a glance at her. "I know only you are a very beautiful and desirable woman, *señorita.* I know, also, you were nearly raped once. I know you would like the treasure for your family. Beyond that, Señorita Gutiérrez, I know nothing about you."

"Then you should know," she said, "that I do not play games with my life, or my future. When I choose a man, it will be my choice, not one forced upon me."

He shook his head. "Still, you are not disturbed about the other afternoon?"

"Why should I be?" she shrugged. "I am not a child. I am not going to be upset by something I deserved. I am a woman, *señor,* but I am not a puppet for any one, or any man, to pull my strings when they feel like it. Do I make myself clear?"

"Very." He swung the automobile in a U-turn. "I will take you back home, *señorita.* Perhaps we will talk of this later."

"Perhaps," she said, lapsing into silence.

He drove her home before returning to his hotel, a very disturbed man.

Dick Little opened his metal trunk, taking from it a highly polished wooden box with a handle on it, and a light folding tripod. He removed the boxes of cartridges from Billy Thomas's trunk, checked the rifle and the pistol at his side. He poured himself a drink. He sat down with a book to wait until dark before going to The Gunner's place. He found, however, he couldn't concentrate on the pages before his eyes. His thoughts were straying to Señorita Gutiérrez and the conversation they'd had that afternoon. He knew it was no use to try to analyze a woman—any woman for that matter—as they were more changeable than a chameleon on a plaid jacket. And for less reason. But here was a woman who was not afraid of life and the living of it; nor was she afraid of circumstances, or worried about those things of the past which were past worrying. She lived in the present, and hoped for the future. A way of life so few followed.

He thought also of General Felipe Angeles who had been a high-ranking officer in the Mexican Army before the second part of the Revolution. He had been a friend of Madero; was with him in captivity just before Madero's murder by Huerta. Hating the self-styled president of the country, Angeles had joined with Villa to oppose Huerta and, eventually, to drive him into exile. But Angeles had been more than just a high-ranking professional officer. He was an intellect, a student of war, a gentleman, a good friend, a respected man wherever he went. He was a superb artillerist and strategist of the kind who won battles for his superior: Villa.

When Villa did not take his advice, Villa had lost and Angeles crossed the border into the United States to live for a time. But he had made one mistake: he returned to Mexico, was captured, was shot by a firing squad in Ciudad Chihuahua. Too bad Obregón hadn't seen fit to take him into his government and make use of Angeles's talents for the betterment of Mexico. Felipe Angeles had been his friend, Dick Little recalled; a good friend. It was Felipe's part of the map Dick had memorized years ago. The general had given it to him with the comment he wasn't interested in the treasure unless it could be used for the betterment of his country; and since he was then in exile, with little possibility of ever returning, Dick might find a way to look for it at some future date. For Richard Henry Little, his search for Rodolfo Fierro's treasure had begun at that moment.

The sun sank ever so slowly that afternoon. Dick Little was nervous. His palms sweated, and he wiped his face several times with a towel. He paced his room, feeling as confined as a prisoner in a cell. But eventually it grew dark enough for him to begin his expedition.

Strapping the pistol about his waist, he buttoned his jacket, put the cartridges in a pocket, picked up the wooden box and the rifle. He glanced about the room, then left. He crossed the lobby quickly to his automobile. He drove off without a backward look. In a few moments he was parked in the alleyway next to The Gunner's back door.

Gunner Marks opened the door at Dick's knock. He was dressed in old clothes with a disreputable hat on his head. Quickly they loaded the rest of his supplies, those Martínez had brought, and those The Gunner had purchased. As a second thought, The Gunner added two gallon jugs of his lethal brew to the cargo. Re-covering the backseat of the car with the tarpaulin, they started out, heading on the road south. Within a few miles, The Gunner fell asleep, rocking his twisted body with the lurches of the car. It was much like riding on an artillery caisson as of old at which The Gunner was a practiced hand.

Somewhere near the Three Sisters, Dick saw a small campfire alongside the road. It was Mills' camp. He guided the automobile as close as he could, stopped, turning out the lights. The Gunner slept on. Dick approached the fire, hunkering down, accepting a cup of steaming coffee. "How has it been?" he asked.

"Interesting, sir," Mills replied, pushing his glasses to the top of his head. "Sam and Stella Townsend paid me a visit; so did a dandy Mexican who was on his way back from Las Palomas in Martínez's taxi. The sheriff also stopped briefly, asking questions. That Mexican woman, Gutiérrez, wanted to know what I was up to. Another Mexican, an ugly brute, threatened me, but I told him I was just doing my job and he went away after a while."

"Anybody bribe you?"

"The Mexican in the cab did. I told him just what you said to. I don't think he was satisfied, Mr. Withers."

"Doesn't make any difference, Mr. Mills. Pack up tomorrow and return to Deming. Mail out the report, then relax. The job is finished."

"Suits me. It is a little lonely here, sir," he said with a grin.

"Do I owe you anything more?"

"Not a penny, Mr. Withers. Not a cent, sir. It's been nice working for you."

Dick Little sipped on his coffee. "Did you shoot the distance from the tallest of the Three Sisters to the highest point of the Floridas?"

"This afternoon."

"What is the distance?"

E. Thomas Mills took a notebook from his hip pocket. He flipped open the cover, turned a few pages, then studied some of his figures. "Sixteen miles."

Dick Little nodded. "About twenty-six kilometers," he observed.

"About that," Mills said.

A feeling of elation ran through Dick Little. The map was right! At least one of the figures came through: the 6-K. Then the O's were blind: meaning nothing. The number two piece was missing. Therefore, the 0-3, the señorita's and The Gunner's pieces, plus the small o of Galinda's, meant just three degrees! For the first time since the afternoon, he felt himself relax. He took another sip of the hot coffee, enjoying it. He wondered a moment who had the missing pieces; the part which had the 2 of the twenty-six kilometers, the sixth part; and who had the first piece with probably another O and the letters D-E-M-I across the top? No matter. His calculations had been confirmed. He finished his cup of coffee.

After shaking hands with the red-headed, hulking surveyor, he climbed back into the automobile, and headed south. The moon was giving enough illumination for him to see the road without headlights, so he turned them off. He was surprised at the amount of light being reflected from the moon. Just as he was reaching the southernmost point of the Floridas, he turned the automobile to the left, off the road, onto the plains. There was no track. He guided the machine automatically through the brush and around those rocks he could see, until he came to the foot of the mountain. All the time The Gunner slept, snoring slightly. Finally, he came to the trail he'd found two days previous. He turned north on it, driving slowly to avoid any accident this late in the game. Time passed. The car rocked forward slowly, its low gears grinding in the night, providing the only sound aside from The Gunner's snores.

At last they reached the blind canyon. Dick Little guided the automobile through the cattle gate to the back wall. He turned it around until the hood pointed to the entrance. He turned off the motor.

The silence awakened The Gunner.

"What?" he said with a start. "What happened?"

Dick Little laughed. "We're here, Gunner," he said. "Let's unpack and set up camp."

"We're where?"

"Come on, old timer," Little said, getting out of the car and stretching. "You set up the camp while I do some work. There's a flashlight somewhere in back. Make a small fire behind some of these rocks. I'll be back when I've finished."

"Okay, Tiny."

As The Gunner climbed slowly out of the automobile, Dick reached into the back for his wooden box and tripod. He hefted them in both hands and started walking to the mouth of the canyon, leaving The Gunner yawning and stretching. In a minute he was busily unloading the automobile.

THEY CAME BACK TO TOWN the same way they'd left it: at night. They drove the automobile to The Gunner's back door, unloading it directly into his back room. "Well," Dick Little said, his voice tired, "What do you think now, Gunner?"

"I think I need a drink," Gunner answered. "Those skeletons got to me." He scuttled into the bar, returning with a bottle and two glasses. "Good Bourbon," he announced loudly, holding the bottle high, then pouring two stiff libations. He handed one to Dick. "Here's to you, Tiny. You pulled it off!" A big grin crossed his seamed and unshaven face. They clinked glasses and drank. The Gunner sighed. "That was a lot of work." He drank again. "What next?"

"I'm going to the bank tomorrow, Gunner," Little answered. "Then I'm going to continue my visit here as if nothing had happened. I advise you to do the same."

"Oh, I will. I will. Good God Almighty, Tiny! Wasn't that something!"

Little nodded. "Indeed it was, Gunner. It was really something." He finished his drink, handing the glass back to The Gunner. "First, I'm going to the hotel and take a bath and shave. Next, I'm going to hit the bed for a long night's sleep. It's been nearly a week since I've slept in a bed, and I'm bone tired."

He bade The Gunner good night, and drove to the hotel. He made two trips from his automobile to his room; the first, carrying his wooden box, tripod, and rifle; the second, two heavy canvas bags. The bags and wooden box he placed in his metal trunk. Next he shaved at the sink after stripping off all his dirty clothes. He laughed at the result he saw in the mirror. His face was clean where the soap and razor had been applied, the rest was brown with dirt and dust. Not much later he was soaking in the tub, filling and emptying it several times, letting the dark water swirl down the drain. He washed his hair twice to make sure it was thoroughly clean. Finally, he returned to his room, taking clean clothes from his dresser, laying them out for the morning. He climbed between the clean sheets of the bed. In an instant he was fast asleep.

"Ahem! Yes, Mr. Little, we'd be most happy to open an account for you." The banker's eyes behind his steel-rimmed glasses glittered. He was dressed in a black suit, white shirt with a stiff detachable collar, and a tightly knotted tie. His skin was unusually white and his hands moved restlessly among the papers on his desk. His hair was dark, parted in the middle, combed back. As for the face, it was average, with a mouth held tight until the lips thinned. In spite of the heat within the bank building he did not sweat, but he had a habit of taking a linen handkerchief from his inside coat pocket, patting his forehead with it, and replacing it in his pocket. "Ahem! How much did you wish to open your account with?"

Dick Little raised one of the canvas bags to the desktop, opened it, spilling gold coins from its mouth until they formed a gleaming pile on the desk. He ignored, for the moment, those which had rolled on the floor. The banker's eyes bugged. He reached out a nervous hand, picking up one of the coins to examine it closely. "Ahem! Yes," he said in a worshipful whisper. "Gold! Yes. Ahem!"

The tall man smiled at him. "There are a thousand coins there," he said, "all U.S., all fifty dollars, all gold, fifty thousand total. Can you handle it here at this First National Bank?"

The banker couldn't take his eyes from the pile of gold. "Ahem! Yes, yes, yes, we can—er—handle it for you, Mr. Little. Ahem! Er—yes. Let me find the forms for you, sir. Ahem! Yes." He turned his attention reluctantly from the coins to papers in a desk drawer. "Ahem! If you would be so kind as to fill out these forms and sign here, here, and here. Ahem! I think we can take care of it for you immediately."

Dick read the forms, signed them, listing his address as the Baker Hotel. "I will probably be transferring this account to another bank rather soon," he said. "There will be no trouble, will there?"

"Ahem! Er—no, no, no, not at all. We are solvent here, sir, with a considerable reserve. Ahem! We can transfer any funds you deposit with us without delay. Ahem! How soon will you be making your transfer?" Worried lines had appeared on his forehead.

Dick Little shrugged. "I don't know. A week perhaps. A month. I'm not sure as yet."

"Ahem! Yes." The banker reached to the coins. "Ahem! Shall we count them?" He smiled thinly as if he were afraid Dick would remove them from his desk into the bag and leave his office.

"By all means," Dick said.

They both had to get on their hands and knees to search the floor for a few of the coins which had not stayed on the desktop. The banker counted the coins twice to make absolutely certain the full fifty thousand was there. He examined the forms Dick had signed. He made out a deposit slip with a trembling hand, botching the first two tries until he finally had one which looked almost like his regular handwriting. He handed it to the tall man.

"Now," Dick said, "if you will write me a short note, on your stationery, stating I've made this deposit, I'd appreciate it."

"Ahem! Yes." The banker complied with Dick's request, blotting the signature nervously.

"I would appreciate it, sir, if you would not say anything about our transaction."

"Ahem! Yes, yes, yes! I mean, no, no, no! To no one, sir! This bank prides itself on its confidences."

"Very well." He stood up, holding out his hand to the banker. "Thank you." The other's hand was sweaty. As he left the office, Dick glanced back. The banker was patting his forehead with his handkerchief, staring at the coins, which had been arranged in neat piles, as if he couldn't believe his eyes.

The negotiations at the Bank of Deming produced much the same results, except that the banker there was very dignified: the only emotion shown was by the twitching of his large white mustache. "Yes, Mr. Little," he said sonorously, "we can comply with your request for silence. It is not our policy to reveal our clients' business with us."

"I just wanted to make sure," Dick said. "I would like a bank draft. It will be for half the amount I've deposited. It will probably take several weeks to clear, I take it?"

"Where will it be deposited?"

"In Virginia."

"We could clear it by telegraph, if you will have the recipient so inform their bank. Matters will be expedited here, I can assure you."

"Thank you, sir."

At the post office, he sent the draft to his sister by special delivery, registered mail. She would certainly be surprised and bowled over, he thought to himself, to receive a check from him in the amount of twenty-five thousand dollars. He enclosed a short note to explain about the telegraph service between banks.

He was feeling good. The summer sun was shining as brightly as ever, the heat was as hot. He decided to take a horseback ride. He didn't want to stay in town where he was beginning to feel confined. He picked up the horse at O'Conner's and rode west of town along the road to Lordsburg. At one point he lashed the horse into a full gallop, crying at the top of his lungs the rebel yell he'd learned as a boy from his father.

Both he and the horse felt better when he rode back into town. He tied the animal in front of the pool hall, entering for a bottle of cold beer. He felt like celebrating and talking with The Gunner about their experiences in the mountains.

As he pushed open the door to the bar he was suddenly alert. Someone had fired a gun in the room recently. There was the acrid smell of gunpowder in the air.

"Gunner!" There was no answer. "Gunner!" he called again.

He crossed the barroom to the door to Gunner's bedroom. It resisted his push. He leaned against the door, shoving harder. Slowly it opened, resistingly. The Gunner was on the floor, face down, his back covered with blood. The room was ripped apart. Dick knelt beside his friend, turning him over slowly. He felt for a pulse at the neck. Faint. His training told him he had little time to lose. He ran to the front of the pool hall, picked up the phone, and asked the operator to connect him with Dr. Smith immediately. It was an emergency! The Gunner's feeling of something going to happen had come to pass with a vengeance.

When the ambulance drove away, taking The Gunner to the Deming Hospital, the doctor sighed. He brushed his lips with his fingertips. "Gunshot wound," he said. "In the old days I worked on many of those, but not these days."

"How will he be?"

"He's tough, Mr. Withers. Ayah, very tough," the doctor answered, gathering instruments and bandages, placing them in his black bag. His white smock was stained with blood. "The bullet went through. They'll

clean the wound at the hospital and rebandage him. They may have to
operate. But, I'd say he has a good chance of survival."

Dick Little sighed with relief. He waved his hand toward the bar.
"Drink?"

The doctor gave him a thin smile. "Thank you, no. I prescribe one for
you, however. You're as pale as a sheet."

"Thanks, Doctor."

Little poured a generous libation from a bottle of Bourbon he found
behind the bar. He drank it down straight, shuddering, color returning
to his face.

"Well," Dr. Smith said, "I must return to the office. I'll keep in touch
with you if there's any change. He'll be in good hands at the hospital."
He left Dick Little in the barroom, walked through the deserted pool
hall, and out the front door.

When the doctor had gone, Dick searched The Gunner's room. The
bag of coins had disappeared, as he expected. So, the motive *had* been
robbery. The thief had made himself rich by shooting an old and crippled man in the back. He returned to the barroom, seating himself at a
table with the bottle and glass in front of him. Fierro's influence for
death was still working.

Fierro.

Ambrose Bierce had referred to him as El Matador Fierro, "The
Killer" Fierro. Villa and his Division of the North had retaken a city.
They had captured over five hundred of the enemy, three hundred of
Pascual Orozco's Colorados and two hundred Federalistas. Villa hated
Orozco, decided to make an example of his men: the federal prisoners
were to be allowed to join his division. Fierro was to execute the others.

A small village, late in the afternoon: the Colorados were herded into
a stable yard guarded by some of Villa's men. Fierro rode up, tied his
horse, and examined the yard. There were three cattle pens under a
shed, which opened into a narrow passage which, in turn, led into the
yard. At the end of the yard was an adobe wall about six feet high and
about a hundred yards away. The other two sides were faced with the
backs of low adobe buildings whose roofs sloped into the corral. Fierro
consulted with the officer in charge of the prisoners. They were herded
into the cattle pens. Fierro's orderly spread out a blanket on the
ground, pouring cartridges on it from boxes he'd brought along. There
were two pistols on the blanket along with the bullets. The orderly
loaded the pistols nervously, setting them aside. The officer in charge of
the prisoners yelled for silence, then explained to them they would be

let out of the narrow passageway ten at a time. Anyone making it over the wall at the end of the corral was a free man.

Fierro stood where the men could see him as they came out into the light; the guards were behind the prisoners, or on the roofs of the houses where they could see and still be out of danger. The first batch of ten prisoners were forced out of the passage. Fierro, twenty paces away, called to them, "Come on, *muchachos!* I'm only going to shoot, and I'm a bad shot!"

They started to run toward the wall, screaming, twisting and turning, each trying to shield himself behind the others. Fierro fired, a gun in each hand. One, two, three, four, five—one man reached the wall—he was almost over when Fierro's bullet caught him in the back. He fell, screaming. Ten men fell; the wounded were finished off with rifle fire from the guards on top of the buildings. Another ten. And another. Each ten being forced from the narrow passage into the arena of death. Fierro firing methodically as they appeared. He was accurate, deadly, a machine of death, shooting at moving targets that twisted, leaped, dodged, slipped in pools of blood, jumped over writhing wounded, and contorted dead; the soldiers on the roofs joining in the fun, shooting the wounded and those still moving.

For over two hours Fierro killed. When the twelve bullets were emptied from the two guns, there were two more pistols handed him by the orderly, fully loaded. The last batch was of twelve men Fierro killed as they panicked their way across the corral. The last man swung over the wall—free.

Fierro was tired. His shoulders drooped. He rubbed his trigger fingers in opposite palms to reduce the swelling. He told his orderly to pick up the spent cartridges and bring them along in the blanket to the last pen for reloading. It was now dark. The orderly found Fierro sitting on a rock in the pen, smoking. "I'm so tired I can't stand up," he said to the orderly. "Make up my bed."

In a few minutes the orderly had spread out a blanket over straw. Fierro lay down, rolling himself in the blanket. In moments he was asleep. Hours later he woke up in the moonlight. He could hear a faint groan from among the bodies in the corral. The groaning continued. "Water—please—water!" Fierro shook his orderly awake. "Hear that?" he asked. The orderly answered, "Yes, Chief." Fierro said disgustedly, "Shoot the son of a bitch so we can get some sleep." The orderly slowly got up from his bed of straw. Shortly after came the sound of a shot.

Then another. By the time the orderly returned to the last pen under the shed, Fierro was sound asleep again.

Dick Little smacked the top of the table hard with an open palm. The pain broke his thoughts of Rodolfo Fierro. Eight years drowned. Eight years roasting in hell. Fierro. *El Carnicero:* The Butcher. *El Matador:* The Killer.

He went into The Gunner's room, and locked the back door. He found a lock back of the bar, closed the door to the room leading into the pool hall, snapped the lock on the hasp. He shut the front door to the hall, standing on the sidewalk, drinking in the sudden brilliance of the sunlight after the twilight of the bar, realizing, suddenly, it was just after noon.

"There is nothing I can do, Señor Little," Sheriff Armijo protested. "He was found, as you say unconscious, and there is doubt he will live. I have talked to Dr. Smith and to the hospital. They do not know when I will be able to question him."

Dick Little rolled a cigarette. He looked around the sheriff's office, a small room with a couple of wooden file cabinets, a rolltop desk, two chairs; the wall covered with postcards from law enforcement officers with the descriptions, and sometimes, the photographs, of wanted men. "In other words," he said, "you will do nothing?"

The sheriff shrugged. "What can I do? I have nothing to go on." He looked at Little curiously from his chair in front of the desk. "Perhaps you can tell me a few things, *señor*, that I should know."

"Like what?"

Again the sheriff shrugged. "Like," he said slowly, "what the motive is for anybody to shoot Gunny Marks."

"Robbery perhaps," Little offered.

"Robbery of what?" the sheriff asked smiling. "I have never known him to have more than a few dollars around his place. Why would one man shoot another for a few dollars?"

"I've seen a man killed because a woman looked at him and smiled."

"That is different, *señor.*"

"I doubt it."

"What were you doing these last few days, *señor?* Perhaps that will tell me something of the shooting."

"The Gunner and I were on a camping trip."

"Perhaps you were looking for the treasure?"

"Why would we be doing that?"

"Gunny Marks had a part of a map which is supposed to tell where the treasure is buried."

"You've seen it, of course?"

The sheriff smiled. "Of course, many times."

"Do you think that piece could tell you where the treasure is—if there's any treasure?"

The sheriff laughed. He lighted one of his cigars. "I could not find it from what Gunny showed me." He blew smoke at the ceiling, smiling. "If the two of you did find the treasure, that would be a good motive for his shooting."

"What motive?"

"He could have brought some of it back with him. Then robbery would be worthwhile. Perhaps the burglar wanted information about where the treasure was. Have you thought of that, Señor Withers?"

"I've thought of it," Dick answered. "It's valid, except for one thing."

"And that is, *señor?*"

"The treasure itself. Where is it?"

The sheriff sighed. "You are a stubborn man, Señor Withers." He pointed a finger at the tall man. "I have a feeling you found what you went after, *señor,* " he said seriously. "You brought some of it back with you. The man who shot Gunny stole Gunny's share. He shot him because Gunny would not talk about finding the money, and where the rest of it is. That is the way I see it."

"You're so certain," Dick said straightforwardly. "You're so certain we found something while we were out camping, aren't you?"

"I am certain."

"Why?"

"Because of the deposits you've made at the banks. A man doesn't deposit a hundred thousand dollars in gold coin just like that." He snapped his fingers. "That is why I am certain."

"Who told you about the deposits?"

The sheriff shrugged. "The story is all over town by now."

Dick Little shook his head. "It had to be, I guess," he said ruefully. "One of the bankers couldn't resist telling his wife, telling of the deposit with a great deal of satisfaction. Naturally, he asked her not to say anything. Naturally, also, she couldn't help but tell her best friend. It always happens in towns of this size. All right, Sheriff," he said, looking straight into Armijo's dark eyes, "suppose I did find the treasure? What about it?"

Again the sheriff shrugged. "Perhaps you will have trouble keeping it."

"How so?"

"Every time you move out of the hotel there will be people watching you—following you every step you take. If you go out to get more of it —and I know there is much more—you'll be followed."

Dick nodded. "People are greedy, aren't they?"

"They are of a certainty, *señor.*"

"Then, I'll have to be careful, won't I?"

"Very careful," the sheriff nodded.

"You will protect me, of course?"

"As well as I am able to, Señor Little."

"Thanks," Dick said drily. "Well, if that's all, I'd better be going."

"*Hasta la vista!*" the sheriff called to his back as he was leaving the office.

Dick Little walked to the small hospital. He stopped a nurse in the corridor and asked about The Gunner. She told him to wait a moment while she called the doctor. In a few minutes, a young man with a harried look on his thin face, and a shock of disheveled hair covering his head, approached. "Can I help you?" he said, removing his badge of office, his stethoscope about his neck. He rolled it up, putting it into a pocket of his white medical coat. He clasped his hands behind his back.

"Gunner Marks," Dick said.

"Oh yes, our estimable local dispenser of illegal spirits," the doctor said, a slight smile playing about his lips. "A very tough individual that. You a friend of his?"

Dick nodded. "A very good one."

"Good. Good." The doctor smiled.

"Will he be all right?"

"Amazing, but true. Do you know, when I operated to stop the internal hemorraging, I found pieces of metal, shrapnel, I think, still in his body. He's full of it." The doctor shook his head. "From the wounds that man has suffered, it's amazing he's still alive. Where did he get it?"

"In Mexico. During the Revolution."

"Ah, one of those. I sometimes wonder how any of the wounded survived during those times."

"As you say, Doctor, they were tough. Besides, they did have doctors in Mexico during those days. Good ones."

The doctor sighed. "What an opportunity to learn surgery well," he said, half to himself. "Now, sir," he continued, looking at Dick Little, "about your friend The Gunner: he will survive. It will be a long time before he is up and about, but he will survive. Amazing."

"What is?"

"That he's still alive. The wound. Blood loss. His condition." The doctor smiled. "I suppose if he weren't almost embalmed on that mixture of his—that juice and alcohol—he'd be dead by now, what with his other wounds and physical condition."

Dick couldn't help smiling. "I see you're familiar with his specialty."

The doctor laughed. "I have partaken upon occasion," he said. "So has half the town—the drinking half. I wouldn't doubt if his prescription and dosage of that stuff is better than most of the drugs we give the sick here. At least, it certainly would make them more lively. It's too bad he won't be able to serve any for a long time."

"I have some in my room at the hotel if you'd like a glass or two," Dick invited.

"Very kind of you, sir. Most kind. I just might take you up on your offer."

"Do that, Doctor." He paused. "About the bill here, and yours, of course. There will be no worry. I'll see they are taken care of."

"Splendid, Mr. —?"

"Little, Doctor, Richard Henry Little."

"Ah, the correspondent. I've read many of your books. It is nice meeting you, sir."

"Thank you. Will you tell The Gunner I dropped by?"

"Most certainly, Mr. Little. If you'd like to see him, I'll allow you to. I must admit, however, he's heavily sedated and wouldn't recognize you."

"In that case, I'll return tomorrow, or the next day."

"He'll be awake and aware by then, I assure you," the doctor said confidently.

Dick took his leave, walking back to the hotel.

As he entered the lobby he saw Señorita Gutiérrez rise from a deep chair. He noted she was dressed in her riding habit. She approached him swiftly, her face contorted.

"Traitor!" she hissed at him, raising her arm and slashing him suddenly across the side of the face with her quirt. In spite of the quick and awful pain, he laughed. He grabbed her by the shoulders, pulling her to him. He kissed her full on the lips, then released her. She strode from the hotel, back straight, head high, cheeks flaming with color.

As Dick Little turned, he saw Charlie behind the desk looking at him, his eyes bulging.

IT HAD BEEN a very busy morning and here it was just past noon. Already the story of his finding the treasure was out. There was no hiding it any longer. What now? When Charlie recovered his composure, he handed Dick a message. Would he please call the editor of *The Graphic* for an appointment for an interview? Not at the moment, Dick thought. The sheriff had been right. Everyone would be watching his every move from now on. Well, let them. He decided to drive out to Sam Townsend's ranch for a little talk. There were a few things bothering him in his mind that, perhaps, Sam could clear up for him.

To think was to act.

He drove the automobile to the garage and had the man fill the tank with gasoline. It was almost empty. From the way the man looked at him, Dick knew he was not only an object of curiosity, but he had suddenly attained the status of the town's celebrity. When he drove away from the garage, and down the main street, he saw faces turned in his direction; once someone pointed him out to another person. He waved as he passed. Surprisingly, both men waved back.

On the road to the S T Ranch, his mind began to churn as he once again thought over the events of the last two weeks: the murders especially. The more he thought, the more he became aware of some inconsistencies he'd never bothered to think of before. For instance, who, when he had first arrived, knew who he was? Sam Townsend, for one. El Gallo, for another. The Gunner. Who else? Yet Sheriff Armijo had called him Mr. Little once before. An unconscious slip, perhaps, but how had Armijo learned his real name? One point to ponder.

Another point was the position of Captain Galinda. He had not seen him in Deming since that visit in his hotel room. Just how did he fit in the overall picture? And why his visit to Las Palomas?

Of Señorita Gutiérrez, he was sure. There was nothing hidden in her motives: they were as straightforward as arrows. He rubbed his cheek, and felt again the lash of her quirt. He smiled to himself. Now, there was a woman! In all of his forty-some-odd years, she was the best he'd

met anywhere. He let his mind pursue thoughts in her direction. They
were pleasant. They made his journey enjoyable.

He found Sam Townsend in the barn, examining the hooves of a
horse. "Will have to shoe him soon, Dick," the rancher greeted him.
"Welcome. Like a drink?"

"No thanks, Sam," Dick replied. He noted Townsend looked much
better than the last time he'd seen him in the café.

"Hear you had some good luck lately," Sam commented.

"How so?"

"The treasure."

"Yes, Sam. I found it." He paused to roll a cigarette. "How about
telling me your connection with it now?"

Sam Townsend straightened up suddenly. His face became drawn; his
skin took on a faded look underneath the tan of the outdoorsman.
"Wha—what do you mean, Dick?"

"I want to know your connection with the treasure, Sam. I've been
thinking over a few things which have happened these past weeks and I
want some answers. Like why you visited the surveyor twice at two
different locations."

The rancher ran the palms of his hands nervously down his trouser
legs. He gazed steadily at Dick for some moments, watching the tall
man lick his cigarette and light it. He made up his mind, with a sigh.
"Okay," he said. "It will be a relief to get it off my mind. Let's go
outside."

They left the barn. Sam led Dick to the corral rail. They climbed up,
and sat on the top rail looking out toward Cooke's Peak. Dick handed
Sam the makings. Sam built his cigarette slowly, thinking. He accepted
a light from Dick, took a deep lungful of smoke, letting it out slowly.
Pushing his hat back, he began to talk in a low voice.

"It all started in the early nineties when I first went south of the
border," he began. "I made a lot of money in Mexico, working for
American interests there. I invested it in this ranch, the S T: Sam
Townsend. It also stands for my wife, Sarah, and my daughter, Stella.
You know how it was in those days, Dick. You were there. We Ameri-
cans rode high, wide, and handsome; did as we pleased, and didn't give a
damn for the Mexican people. I guess I was just another gringo in that
respect, because that was the way I was. I was paid well for my work
and I did it well, if I do say so. Then came the Revolution in 1910.
Madero wasn't too bad for me, because he kept the old guard around
him after Díaz went into exile. I could still deal with those fellows as if

nothing had happened. That was Madero's mistake. When Huerta had him assassinated, nothing changed, really. It was the same business at the same old stand; only a little more difficult. The greatest difference was the *mordida*, the bribe, was bigger. Well, as you know only too well, Huerta's takeover opened the box. The Revolution was on in earnest. That stubborn old bastard, Carranza, proclaimed himself the first chief and stuck to his guns until everything came his way, in spite of hell or high water. The worst part of the Revolution was because of him. He could have settled it if he'd dealt with Villa, Zapata, and others on an equal basis. No, he had to have his own way."

Sam puffed on his cigarette, knocking off the ash with the nail of his little finger. "Alvaro Obregón was the man to watch. Zapata was insular: all he wanted was to stay as close to his land in Morelos as he could until he got what he wanted—land for his people. Villa was different. He wanted to fight Carranza at any time, or anywhere, just as long as he could drive the old son of a bitch out of the country. But Villa was mercurial. He couldn't be trusted from one day to the next. I lined up with Obregón. When things got too difficult for people like me in Mexico, I came here, but as an agent against Carranza and for the general. I still am. I'm his direct contact from this part of the United States to the Presidential Palace. Agents send me information from the western part of this country, and I pass it on. I pay agents; I recruit agents; I am still paid by the Mexican government as an agent. Nothing violent, you understand; cloak and dagger is not my meat. I just work quietly, doing my job, and getting well paid for it."

Sam flipped away his cigarette butt. "Then, this treasure thing came up. I was instructed to keep my eyes and ears open regarding the treasure. The Mexican government would like to lay their hands on it in the worst way. Naturally they would. It's worth—what? Twenty million dollars, U.S.? I don't know. I was even sent a piece of Villa's map, but I couldn't make heads nor tails of it. All it was was a slanting line with a 2 above it and, on the bottom, three letters: *C, E,* and *N.* From that I was supposed to find where Fierro had hidden millions. I tramped all over Cooke's Peak looking for it until I came to the conclusion it wasn't this far north. In the Floridas, probably. I searched there as much as I could, without success: or even the hope of success.

"I knew Gunner Marks had a part because he never denied it. Anyone who wanted to see Gunner's piece could. I've seen it many times. I knew it tied on to the right edge of mine because of the way it was originally torn, and the word underneath was C E N T R O. But, what the hell, a slanting line, like mine; a 3 above the line? I sure as hell wasn't going to find Fierro's treasure with that little information. Not with the other pieces out somewhere." He sighed. "So I just sat tight, doing my regular work for Obregón."

He took off his hat, wiped his forehead on his sleeve, and replaced it on the back of his head. "I was waiting for something to happen. Like, for instance, your turning up here in Deming. Of course, I recognized you the minute I laid eyes on you; I'd seen you often enough in Mexico City during those days when Villa and Zapata met there. Naturally, I was curious why you used the name Withers instead of your own and came to the conclusion you had something to do with the treasure. Lord knows you've traveled about enough to find out things I couldn't know. In your profession as a correspondent you could ask questions and get away with it. Stella asked about you after you left that night. I explained to her who you were. I didn't say anything about why I thought you were here." He gave a little laugh. "I don't tell her everything I do and think."

Dick Little started to roll another cigarette. He said nothing while his fingers manipulated the paper and tobacco.

Sam Townsend continued. "I realize, now, that Billy Thomas must have been mixed up in the treasure somehow. Right under my nose, and he never so much as let on he had any interest in it. I believed you knew him back there when. I began to put things together, and worry when he was murdered. I still cannot figure out why, or by whom. It hit me like a ton of bricks when I realized the possible motive: he must have had a part of the map, or knew something about the treasure the murderer wanted. Then, that attack on you when you were coming here at my invitation. And the attack by those Mexicans as you were leaving. It suddenly became too much, and too complicated for me. I guess I nearly broke down completely."

Dick Little nodded. "I guessed as much."

Sam Townsend held out his hand for the makings. He rolled another cigarette more slowly than the first. "My big worry, now, is what I'm going to tell *El Presidente,*" he said. "My second worry is who killed Billy, then tried to kill you."

"Tell Obregón," Dick Little said slowly, "the treasure has been found. Tell him I'm taking 25 percent of the whole, and that I'm also going to make restitution to one bank, which was robbed. The rest he can have. But," he paused, "he'll get it only when I say when, how, and where. Is that understood?"

"*Seguro,*" Sam said. "How about the murderer?"

"I know who he is," Dick said, his voice low. "I know him, and I'm going to get him."

On the way back to Deming, Dick drove off the road into the foothills. He parked the automobile, and unpacked it of the remainder of the supplies he'd brought back from his trip to the Floridas. Sorting them quickly, he cached those he wouldn't be needing again. After eradicating all traces of his digging, and replacing rock, he sat on the running board of the automobile, and proceeded to clean Billy's rifle and make sure it was loaded with a live cartridge under the hammer. He next cleaned and reloaded Billy's six-shooter, filling the chambers full. He replaced the pistol in the holster on his side. He started up the automobile, backing it slowly away from his hiding place, turning it to face the highway, and stopped. He walked back to his cache, examined it closely, made a few adjustments, and left. Within an hour, he was back in Deming and in his hotel room. It was beginning to get dark as twilight settled over the town.

He took a long bath, dressing in clean clothes from the skin out, remembering afterward he had taken one the night before. He poured and drank a good slug of Bourbon. Before he left the room, he strapped the gun belt about his waist, making sure the pistol was loose in the holster. He left for the café.

After eating, he walked to the house where Señorita Gutiérrez was staying. He knocked on the door loudly. There was no answer. He knocked again. He heard movement behind the door, and knocked loudly a third time. The door opened a crack.

"Go away," she said through the crack. "I don't want to see you!"

He pushed open the door, caught her by the wrist, and pulled her onto the porch. Her long black hair was streaming down her back almost to her waist. She tried to scratch his face with her free hand, making small noises in her throat. He caught the raking hand in his, holding her so she couldn't move. "Stop that!" The sudden insistent tone of his voice startled her. She looked up at him with wide eyes. Her arms relaxed. "That's better," he said, his voice softening. "We're going to take a walk."

"No!" Her voice cracked at him.

"Very well," he said, "I'll carry you." He bent down to pick her up.

"No." Her voice was softer. "I'll go. I'll get my hat." She started to turn from him to the door.

"You'll go as you are. Come along."

Never relinquishing his grip, he took her by the elbow, forcing her to come with him, side by side. They descended the porch steps and walked to the street, turning away from town, from the lights.

She brushed against him. "You're armed," she said. "You're wearing a gun."

"I am," he said. He changed sides so his gun was on the outside, away from her. "I want to talk to you."

She gave a silvery laugh. "By kidnapping me?"

"Why not?" he shrugged. "You wouldn't have come if I'd asked you politely. Now, would you?"

"I suppose not."

"Then, I've kidnapped you."

They strode quickly along until she protested he was walking too fast for her. He shortened his strides. Soon he relaxed his grip on her arm until he was no longer holding her. She kept up with him.

"Where are you taking me?"

"Where it is dark and where no one can hear us. And," he added, "where no one can come upon us without my knowing it."

A half hour later, they were past the outskirts of town. He led her to a clump of cottonwoods, and stopped. "Here," he said. "We'll do our talking here. Cigarette?"

"Yes, please."

He took from his pocket a package of Piedmonts he'd purchased earlier from the café. Shielding the match in his cupped hands, he lighted hers, then his. "Sit here," he said, letting his long frame fold downward until he was on the ground, a tree bole at his back. He removed his hat. He could hear the rustle of her clothes as she sat beside him.

"Well," she said finally, after a long silence, "what do you want to talk with me about?"

"The treasure," he answered her simply.

She drew in her breath sharply.

"You must have heard by now that I found it."

"I heard."

"How much did Urbina steal from your father's bank?"

"Why do you want to know?"

"Would you mind just answering my question first? How much?"

"One million, three hundred thousand, six hundred and forty-one pesos—in gold."

"You're very precise."

"How could I forget?"

He smoked in silence for a moment. "I propose to repay the money to your bank," he said simply.

"When?"

He laughed. "Just like a woman. Not how; but when? As soon as I can. There will have to be arrangements made, of course. Probably through one of the Deming banks. Perhaps through a bank in El Paso. I don't know yet. I'll have to find out first."

He could feel her eyes looking at him in the dim light of the waning moon. "Why are you doing this? For me?"

"Yes."

"Why?"

"Because I like you, *señorita,*" he said, staring out into the distance. "Actually, it's more than liking."

She laughed her husky laugh. "Love?"

"Some people call it that."

"I'm sorry," she said. "I didn't mean to laugh." She paused. "What if I do not love you in return?"

She saw his shoulders rise in a shrug. "I won't press my intentions if that's the way you feel. We'll just forget the whole thing. I'll go my way, and you yours. No one is hurt."

"You will be hurt."

"I've lived a long time," he said. "I don't doubt I'll get over it."

"You're a damned fool!" she said sharply. "A damned, damned fool!" She rose to her feet quickly, looking down at him in the shadows. He could not see her face clearly, but he had the impression it was flaming with temper. "Why the hell haven't you made love to me?" she asked angrily. "You cold gringo fish! Don't you think I have feelings, too? You play with me, Señor Little! You make fun of me; you don't think I have any thoughts, or feelings; then you very coldly tell me you love me! Ha!" She turned away from him.

He rose to his feet, spun her to him, and took her in his arms. With a finger, he raised her chin, then bent down and kissed her firmly on the lips. He could feel the rigidity leave her body as she pressed herself against him. Her arms raised, encircling his neck. She gave him pressure against his lips. He felt emotion rising in both of them, holding her closer as he tightened his arms about her. For a long time they stood molded together, body feeling body, their heat rising so that each felt the other's passion. Suddenly she broke away, stepping back from him a step.

"Well," she said in a strange voice, "you're not such a cold fish after all, gringo!"

"Shall we try that again?"

"Yes," she said simply.

As they kissed, they sank to the ground under the trees. They were one in the shadows, moving compulsively. There were faint throaty noises, and a quiet rustling on the ground. When they separated at last, she sat up, brushing and straightening her clothes. "We will have to save something," she said, her voice deep in her throat.

"For what?" he wanted to know.

"For our marriage," she answered. "You don't think I'll let you go after you've compromised me, do you?"

He laughed. "Shall I compromise you some more?"

There was a pause. "Yes," she said, and sank down beside him again.

It was another hot, cloudless day in Deming. Dick Little rose early, dressed, found himself humming under his breath. He strapped on his gun before putting on his jacket. He left the room in good spirits, ate a hearty breakfast at the café, and went to the nearest bank to make some inquiries. From the bank, he called the hospital to ask of The Gunner's condition. The Gunner was, in spite of protests, sitting up, eating, and raising all kinds of hell to be released. Dick laughed. He picked up an El Paso newspaper at the drugstore, which had arrived by train early that morning, scanned the headlines, read the lead story, and felt a great sadness. He returned to the hotel for his automobile, started it, heading out of town toward the Floridas. The automobile bounced along the road, keeping a steady speed, sending up a cloud of dust behind it.

He saw a man standing in the middle of the road, waving him down. As the automobile came closer, he recognized Captain Galinda. The captain was dressed as if he had stepped out of his home in Guadalajara on his way to pay a visit to his friends. Even his shoes were shined, in spite of his standing in the center of a dusty road. Dick stopped the automobile, its radiator just a few feet from the captain. He opened the door and got out.

"Well, Captain," he said evenly, "imagine meeting you way out here."

"Good morning, Tiny," the captain greeted, keeping his hands in his jacket pockets. He was smiling. "I had the feeling you'd be out this way this morning, so I waited for you."

"Oh? What sort of feeling?"

"That you were going to the treasure again."

Dick laughed. He unbuttoned his jacket casually. "That's strange," he said, "I have no idea of going to the treasure today. I'm just out for a drive."

"Just the same, *amigo,*" the captain said casually, "I'd rather you drove to the treasure." He took a hand out of his pocket. He pointed an automatic at Dick. The captain was no longer smiling. "My friends and I insist you take us where you found the treasure."

Dick grinned, shaking his head. "It would take all day from here; and, as you can see," he said, indicating the backseat of the car, "I have no supplies, no extra gasoline."

"Where is it?"

"Over there somewhere in the Floridas." He waved his left hand in the direction of the mountains.

"You'll take us there, of course." The captain's voice was growing harsh in a military commanding way.

Dick hesitated. "Us?"

Seeming to rise from the ground, El Gallo stood on one side of the road and Sheriff Chucho Armijo on the other. Both were smiling broadly, both pointing pistols at Dick.

"Yes, Señor Little." The sheriff smiled at him a little crookedly. "Us!"

Dick nodded. "So, you're all in this together?"

"A surprise to you?" the captain asked.

"Not much. I knew there had to be a contact man here in Deming," he answered. "You're it, eh, Chucho?"

"*Si, señor,*" Armijo answered, with a mock bow.

"Figures. Gallo had to know my movements from someone. Who better than the man who openly professed he'd keep an eye on me. I suppose you were the one who ripped up my room?"

The sheriff nodded. "But of course. Señor Galinda informed me of your coming before you arrived here."

"Well," Dick Little asked, "what now?"

"The treasure, please." The captain was becoming impatient.

Dick shook his head. "I'm afraid not."

"Then we shall have to kill you," Armijo said pleasantly.

"Obviously." Dick watched the three men closely, his eyes shifting from one to the other. The smile never left his face. "Where's your shotgun, Chucho?"

"Shotgun?"

"The one you killed Billy Thomas with," Dick stated. He was pleased to see the sheriff's expression change drastically. He was no longer smiling. A look of hatred crossed his face. The sheriff took a step forward, raising his gun.

"How did you know that?" he spat.

"Who else could it have been?" Dick asked. "In your capacity as sheriff you probably rode up to Billy, the shotgun hidden from his sight on the side of your horse away from him. I figure you started to ask him about the map, and when he began to get suspicious of you, you shot him out of his saddle. After that, you rode back to the bunkhouse to search his room."

"A regular detective, eh, *señor?*"

"Wasn't hard to figure. The same person who searched Billy's room had searched mine—the first time. Very thorough, Sheriff, but no good to you." Dick reached into a breast pocket of his jacket with his left hand. Immediately three guns were raised to ready. Dick heard El Gallo's pistol click twice to full cock. He smiled, removing his hand slowly, holding his sack of tobacco and a packet of papers. He started to roll a cigarette. The guns lowered a fraction. With steady hands, he built his smoke. Reaching slowly into his pocket again he extracted a wooden match, striking it on the fender of the car beside him. He inhaled deeply, letting the smoke out slowly. He looked down at the glowing end. "You were not too bright, Sheriff. You disclaimed to me several times you had no interest in the treasure. A man in your position not interested? Yet, you kept a close enough eye on me because you felt I did have an interest. I'm still not sure why you ambushed me that evening when I was driving out to the S T Ranch. I must say, you're a pretty good shot with a rifle."

The sheriff's expression changed again. A flicker of a smile crossed his lips. "It was a little target practice," he said. "Perhaps I was a little angry with you at the time. I had strong feelings you knew where the money was, and I couldn't do a thing about it. I admit I wasn't thinking straight." He shrugged. "I am happy now that I didn't kill you."

"Why?"

"Because you will make us all rich." He moved his pistol to include El Gallo and the captain. He put one of his cigars in his mouth and lit it with a match scratched on his cartridge belt. His dark eyes never left Dick's face as he raised the flame to the end of the cigar.

"What about those men who ambushed me that night?"

"They were sent to me in case I needed them," he answered calmly. "Too bad they were no use to me."

"Did you arrange for that, Gallo?"

El Gallo started at hearing a question being asked of him. "Yes," he answered, simply and directly.

"Why are you in this, Gallo? For yourself?"

The Mexican shook his head slightly. "For my chief, Pancho Villa."

Dick turned his head toward Captain Galinda. "And you, sir?" He drew on his cigarette.

"I am also a Villista," he smiled quickly. "But," he continued after a slight hesitation, "my chief was General Rodolfo Fierro." He spoke with pride in his voice. "I want what my chief took from Urbina."

"Are you for Villa, too?" Dick asked the sheriff.

Armijo merely shrugged his shoulders slightly. He said nothing.

Little glanced at each in turn. He shook his head sadly. "Villa's cause is lost."

"What do you mean?" the captain demanded.

"The newspaper this morning," he replied. "Pancho Villa was assassinated yesterday in Parral."

"You lie!" The captain took a step forward. "You lie!"

"There's a copy from El Paso on the front seat of the car. You can read it for yourself." His eyes swung to El Gallo. He saw tears in the Mexican's eyes. This Dick hadn't expected at all.

"He speaks the truth," El Gallo said quietly. "There are many who wanted my general dead. This Panchito has told me himself many times. I believe it has happened. I know this man Leetle. He is my enemy, but he does not lie to me. Is it not so, *señor?*"

"It is so, Gallo," Dick said quietly. "General Villa is dead."

"Then—" El Gallo uncocked his pistol, sliding it into his holster. He turned on his heel, walking a distance, disappearing, it seemed, into the ground.

Dick Little spoke to Captain Galinda. "You were supposed to be my friend."

The captain shrugged elegantly. "Why not? When you told me you were a friend of General Angeles, I suspected you had looked at his part of the map. It was worth a gamble to become acquainted with you, to see where you would lead me. Now you will lead me to my general's treasure." He raised his automatic again.

"A couple of more questions before we get down to business, please," Little said. The automatic was lowered a bit. "What about the surveyor? You won't bother him?"

The captain shook his head. "I can't understand that. Why would your friend Oliver Lang wa—" His voice dropped off. "You did that. You hired the surveyor to pretend, to upset us." He smiled. "A very good trick," he said. "I was worried about him. I stopped and asked him questions while on my way back from Las Palomas where I went to arrange for transportation of the money when I'd need it. Very clever, Tiny."

"The sheriff fell for it, too, didn't you, Chucho?"

Again, the sheriff refused to answer a direct question. He puffed on his cigar, opening his mouth in a half smile, his teeth clenched on the end, the smoke rolling out as he exhaled.

"How did you get ahead of me to here? That really puzzles me."

"The sheriff," Galinda answered. "He saw you leave. He gambled you were coming out this road, as you've often done. But you had to drive south first to get on this road. We quartered you on horseback, just as a *banderillero* quarters a bull."

Dick nodded. He casually put his left hand in his trousers pocket. He nervously began to play with some coins. El Gallo reappeared astride a horse. He rode magnificently. He reined the horse behind the captain and the sheriff. He looked directly at Dick Little. He spoke to him in a quiet voice. "Tonight in Las Palomas I will get very drunk, and I will weep for my general and friend as many others have cried for their dead. I can no longer bring him the money. I do not need it for myself. I'm sorry, gringo. I leave you with these *cabrónes*. I know now they would not have given the money to the general, my chief. They are too greedy, Señor Leetle. They would have killed me when you showed us the money. They would kill you also." He shook his head sadly. "They will kill you anyway. I salute you." He touched the rim of his sombrero to Dick Little, spurring his horse at the same time away from the men.

Dick saw the captain begin to turn toward the rider. "Gallo!" he yelled.

El Gallo spun in his saddle, drawing his gun with lightning speed. Dick snatched his hand from his pocket and let gold coins fly into the air. Two shots were fired simultaneously—the captain cried out briefly, falling heavily backward from the force of Gallo's bullet. The sheriff shifted his eyes for a fraction of a second to the sun-glistening coins. He raised his gun at the same instant Dick drew his. Again, two shots almost as one. The sheriff twisted his body suddenly, taking a step backward as Dick felt a bullet crack past his ear. His revolver was cocked under his thumb for a second shot. It wasn't necessary. The sheriff was standing straight, his pistol at the end of his relaxed arm. As a look of pain crossed his face, Chucho's eyes bored into Little's.

"Gunner Marks will live," Little said quietly, evenly. "You couldn't even kill him by shooting him in the back." Richard Henry Little held up his gun so the sheriff could see it. "Billy Thomas's gun."

The strained look on the sheriff's face relaxed. He nodded slightly in understanding. He closed his eyes, his body folding slowly until he lay stretched upon the ground, his cigar still clenched in his teeth, his blood running into the dust of the road.

El Gallo guided his horse back slowly. He reined it beside the captain's body. He looked at it a long time while his horse pranced nervously, snorting with fright. "Thanks, friend," he said softly in Spanish. "I am at your service."

They loaded the bodies into the automobile. El Gallo tied his horse with the other two in the sink in the plains. The men drove to an abandoned mine in the foothills of the Floridas, around craggy rock, out of sight of the town. They placed the dead in the shaft of the mine. Dick worked about the shaft entrance, planting sticks of The Gunner's dynamite. The explosion was quick and not loud. The mine was closed forever.

They drove back to the horses in silence. "Turn them loose and let them find their own way back," he said to El Gallo.

The Mexican did so, mounting his own steed. He looked down at the tall man with a melancholy expression on his face. "Fierro's treasure is yours now, gringo," he said.

"Some of it," Dick admitted. "The rest goes to the Mexican government."

El Gallo nodded. "It is what we fought for," he said. "My general was a man of the people, for the people. That is why he never wanted to be president." He paused. "We'll meet again, friend." He rubbed a finger alongside his broken nose.

"In San Luis Potosí?"

"It is good."

El Gallo raised a hand to the tall man. He spurred his horse to the south.

Dick Little watched him until El Gallo was just a speck disappearing into the heat waves rising from the ground. He climbed into the automobile and sat for a long time, staring at nothing through the windshield. He sighed deeply as he started the engine. He drove slowly, and carefully, back to Deming.

EUFEMIO MARTÍNEZ picked up the belongings of "Mr. Smith" at the Park Hotel. He paid the bill. As far as the hotel clerk was concerned, he never thought of Mr. Smith again.

Dick Little visited the sheriff's little two-room adobe house that evening after dark. He pried open the door, closing it behind him. He used the beam from a small flashlight to look around.

The house was surprisingly neat, clean, and bare, containing only the essential furnishings for living with some degree of comfort. One room contained a bed, a small table beside the bed, a chair, a *ropero* for hanging clothes, a small two-drawer dresser and a mirror, and an Indian rug on the floor. In the other room, the kitchen, was a stove and wood bin, a table with two chairs, a small cabinet with a few dishes, two cups, and some eating utensils, an enameled washbasin, a bucket for water, and a towel hung neatly on a nail. Nothing more. The sheriff had been a Spartan. The clothes in the *ropero* were clean, neat, each item hung on its own hanger or hook. Two pairs of plain black riding boots were placed, side by side, on the bottom of the *ropero*. On top of the dresser were a brush and comb, a partially filled bottle of whiskey with an empty glass beside it, and a straight razor in a case. In the top drawer were white shirts, socks, two black string ties, all neatly folded, and his razor strop and stone. In the bottom drawer was underwear, also clean, and neatly folded. In feeling through the clothing, Dick felt something different. He opened the drawer wider, reached in further, and drew out a woman's diaphanous nightgown. He found, also, a bottle of very expensive French perfume. He held up the nightgown with one hand, shining the small beam of his flashlight through it. He carefully folded the gown, returning it to the drawer, closing it. He shined the light about the room. On the table beside the bed, he saw a box of thin cigars, a tin can for the ashes, and a few kitchen matches gathered together.

There were no books, no papers, no reading matter of any kind in the house. He noted the windows were uncurtained, but heavily shaded—all of them. For light there were candles stuck upright in saucers. That was all.

It was a squeaking board under the rug which called his attention to the floor. He pulled back the rug and pried up the loose board with a blade of his pocketknife. The Gunner's bag of gold coins was underneath.

When Dick Little left the house, there was no sign he had ever been there, except for a few scratches on the front door.

At first, the disappearance of Sheriff Chucho Armijo was taken as a matter of course. He was in the habit of absenting himself from Deming for days at a time; therefore, it was not unusual for him not to be seen. It was only gradually that some people became aware the man was long overdue to make an appearance. Inquiries were made to other lawmen around the state, and even into Mexico; but they all replied they knew nothing.

The chief of police of Deming called on Dick Little in a casual way, as did a mumbling young deputy sheriff with a worried look on his face. Beyond pleasantries, and admitting he had met the sheriff for business reasons, so to speak, Dick knew nothing. He was not bothered by the law again.

In the hospital, The Gunner made rapid progress. Dick was a daily visitor when he was in Deming. He finally persuaded the young doctor to discharge his patient before the morale of the hospital was completely disrupted. The old soldier perked up tremendously once he was again free and in the warm sunlight. He even started taking long automobile rides with Dick Little. Sometimes they camped under the stars, and, sometimes, they took the long drive to El Paso, to stay overnight and return the next day. Dick's metal trunk was always in the back of the automobile. The Gunner, riding beside the trunk as a nabob, carried a twelve-gauge pump shotgun. He gave everyone who noticed him the impression he could use it with deadly effect. Dick wore his pistol and always had the rifle ready on the front seat beside him. It was suspected they were moving Fierro's treasure to a bank in El Paso, but no one had the guts to go up to either of the men and ask. No one had the courage to try to follow them into the Floridas.

The Gunner put his pool hall up for sale. It quickly changed hands. One day, Dick drove him to the railway station to meet the train for El

Paso. They spoke a few words while waiting on the platform. When the
train arrived, they shook hands. The Gunner climbed slowly up the
steps into the car. They waved as the train started to move and the
conductor closed the door. Dick drove back to the hotel where he found
The Gunner had left two gallon jugs of his concoction with Charlie as a
surprise gift. That night, Dick invited the young doctor to take a ride
with him into the country where they could sample The Gunner's gift
deeply and in privacy.

A quiet event took place, which no one in Deming observed, and few
people in Columbus bothered to pay attention to. Again a Mexican
Central railroad boxcar was shunted onto the siding. Again soldiers, this
time in the brown uniforms of the Mexican Army, climbed from the car,
heavily armed. Dick was waiting in his automobile. He and the officer in
charge talked amiably for a while before they all piled into the automobile and took off up the road toward Deming. They never reached the
town, however. For the next few nights the automobile would reappear
with a couple of the soldiers riding in it, their armaments close to hand,
and drive up to the boxcar where wooden crates and heavy canvas bags
were unloaded into the open door. Soldiers were always near the boxcar,
always alert.

One day a Mexican Central engine puffed up to Columbus, turned on
the wye, hitched up the boxcar and puffed off, eastward; the soldiers
and their officer riding on the top and on the tender. Only Dick Little
and the officer knew its destination.

The Señorita Gutiérrez had remained in Deming, riding almost every
day, alone, into the countryside. When Dick met her occasionally, while
in town for supplies, she was apprehensive of the trips he took and the
long time he was away; but beyond a question or two, which he answered evasively, she did not pry. One afternoon, bathed, shaved,
rested, and again in clean clothes, Dick called for her. They drove into
the country to the cottonwoods where they could see the mountains.
Here the automobile was stopped. They lit cigarettes, smoking for some
time in silence. Dick reached into his jacket, taking from it a letter. He
handed it to her wordlessly. She opened the envelope, and read the
scrawl on the unfolded page. When she finished, she looked from the
letter to the envelope, noted the Mexican stamp, and reread the letter.

"What does this mean, Ricardo?" she asked.

"One million, three hundred thousand, six hundred and forty-one pesos—in gold—have been returned to your family's bank in San Luis Potosí."

She gasped. "That is not so!"

"It is so. Read the letter again."

Tiny, [it said]*I finished the business with the bank and am now a guest at the ranch. I have my own house and kids to tell stories to. There is a guy near here who was in my old outfit. We are thinking of buying a cantina in a little town near here. I will put in a couple of pool tables. No back room this time, but plenty of juice. The sun is good to my old broken bones. I am happy. Hope you are the same. See you soon.*

    Gunner

"The Gunner," he explained, when she had finished reading the letter for the third time, "took with him a certified check from the First National Bank of El Paso for the sum Urbina stole from your father. He made sure the money was restored to your bank. Those were my instructions to him when he left."

Impulsively, she threw her arms about his neck, and kissed him long and hard. He threw away his cigarette, reciprocating until they were both breathing irregularly. Finally, they drew apart. "If this keeps up," he said, taking a deep breath, "I'll compromise you again."

"There's nobody looking," she said huskily.

Sam Townsend had aged. His face was deeply lined, his gray hair had turned whiter. He still stood straight, but there was a lack of vitalness in his movements. Sam and Dick were enjoying a tall drink while sitting on the porch of the S T ranch house. "How is Stella?" he asked finally, after a long silence.

"Still very upset," Sam answered. "She's visiting friends in Las Cruces for a while." He paused to sip his drink. "I'm thinking of taking her back East for a visit. I think the change will do her good."

Dick nodded. "It might at that."

"Tell me, Dick," Sam began, slowly, after a long pause, "how did Stella get mixed up in all this? How bad was it?" He held up a hand. "I want to know everything, please."

Dick Little sighed. He looked at his glass, which he was rolling back and forth between the palms of his hands. "I can only guess some things," he answered quietly. "She was in love with Sheriff Armijo. When I came here the first time, to see Billy, you recognized who I was. You, and Billy, and The Gunner, were the only ones who knew me by sight. Yet, the next morning, Sheriff Armijo called me by my right name. Someone had to tell him who I was. Who? Who else but Stella? She must have called Chucho the next morning as soon as you left the house. She invited me here that evening I was ambushed. The sheriff knew that and waylaid me. He also had the Mexicans ready, just in case. They'd been brought up the day before from Las Palomas by El Gallo. It all had to fit, including my room being searched a second time. Stella did that. Charles Elliott, the clerk at the hotel, went to school with her. She must have bribed him somehow to let her in my room. I figure she was searching for parts of the map for Chucho. She might have even copied for him the piece I left in the desk. She even emptied some of my booze down the sink to make it look as if my room had been searched by a man who liked to drink." He did not mention that he thought strongly it was Stella who had laid him out when he had left the señorita's house, possibly to search him for pieces of the map for the sheriff. After all, *quién sabe?*

"The sheriff shot Billy?"

"Yes." Dick took a long drink. "He also shot The Gunner."

Sam Townsend shook his head slowly. "But why did Stel do it, Dick? Why?"

"She was deeply in love." He stopped there. He couldn't reveal to the rancher his search of Chucho's little house, and of the nightgown he'd found there; or of the way she had kissed him as she was leaving his hotel room.

"Poor little Stella." Sam's voice was sad and thoughtful. "No wonder she's been upset lately. All those killings she can blame herself for."

"Perhaps, Sam, you should take her East as quickly as possible."

Sam nodded. "As soon as I can make arrangements for someone to look after the ranch."

Dick said nothing.

"The sheriff has disappeared, you know about that?" Sam remarked.

"I've heard."

"If Stel was in love with him—." The rancher sighed deeply. "My poor, poor little girl." He puffed quickly on his cigarette. "Dick?"

"Yes?"

Sam asked slowly, "How did you get mixed up in all of this? The treasure—everything?"

Richard Henry Little was silent for a long moment. "Felipe Angeles, I guess," he answered softly. "He and I had a good friendship. I visited him a couple of times on his farm in the States. That last time I happened to be thinking of the old days and I mentioned Urbina and his robbing of Villa. Angeles carried the story on about the recovery of the money and it being shipped to the U.S. He told me then he hadn't the time or the curiosity to follow the clue he had, and he showed me his part of the map. Naturally, *I* was the one who became curious. Then, Galinda approached me in Guadalajara. There was something about him which clanged as a cracked bell. But I followed through to find out why he had taken the interest to make me a special friend of his. Maybe like I'd dropped a careless hint I had seen a part of the map. That must have been it. Anyway, I played along."

Dick Little rolled another cigarette.

"I checked up on the story with a couple of friends of mine on the *Trib* who had been in Mexico. One had heard of the story, but he hadn't much credence in it. Anyway, it was enough for me." He paused. "Actually, all I came here for in the first place was the story. It was a good one no matter which way you looked at it. Buried treasure—a torn-up map—the Revolution—Pancho Villa—Fierro—yes, it could have been one hell of a story. Instead, I walked into reality. That shot at me El Gallo fired. That was the first hard fact. Then Gunner's part of the map; and Billy Thomas. It began to prove too true."

He sighed deeply.

"I got caught up in something I couldn't get out of." He paused and shrugged. "Well, Sam, you know the rest."

The rancher nodded in agreement. "So much killing."

"Too much," Dick Little said sadly. "Those two poor Mexicans on the road—"

"Who were trying to kill you."

"Those were minor, Sam. There were the people Urbina and his men killed to get it. Urbina himself. Those Dorados I found with the treasure: too many."

"The sheriff—?"

Dick Little didn't answer.

"Well," Sam said, straightening up and moving his shoulders to stretch them, "how do you feel now it's all over?"

Dick Little thought a moment. "I don't know. I really don't know. I've seen too much death; but I never thought I'd cause any. Even when a person has to kill to protect himself it leaves a mark: not physically, but inside. I never thought I'd be capable of killing anyone. Now I know I can. It's upsetting. Very upsetting." He gave a short laugh. "I only hope it hasn't made me callous. I never want to kill again."

"You won't," Sam said softly.

"That's just it, Sam," Dick said, looking at his friend. "Now I know I can."

The tobacco and papers passed back and forth. New cigarettes were lighted. They sat on the fence in silence, both lost in thought.

"I've heard from Obregón," Sam said softly.

"Yes?"

"He thanks you. He's also made you a Mexican citizen and a retired army colonel—with pay. Quietly, of course. You understand."

Dick nodded. "Thank him for me." He chuckled. "Citizenship and an army rank will come in handy in Mexico when I go there."

"When will that be, Dick?"

Dick said, "As soon as I get married. Señorita Gutiérrez is waiting for a letter of approval from her oldest uncle, who now heads the family. It should be arriving any day now."

"And if he doesn't approve?"

Dick Little laughed. "He'll have to."

Instead of a letter of approval, the uncle from San Luis Potosí, a big, jovial man with a spade beard and a great mustache, plus several other minor relatives, and the Valencias, who appeared from limbo in Las Palomas, formed a large family group that not only approved of the marriage, but held a ceremony and fiesta just across the border which, even today, some of the ancients in the area still recall. For details, the story can be found in the back files of *The Headlight* as written by an enthusiastic editor.

The bride and groom left shortly thereafter to take up residence on her large ranch near San Luis Potosí, in the state of the same name. There, Richard Henry became known as Señor Ricardo Enrique Pequeño and his loving wife as La Pequeña Señora. A pun the Mexicans appreciated.

As for Deming, as time passed, the finding of the treasure became a legend and remains so; there are still a few who lived a part of it. Paco, for one.

Eufemio Martínez drove the bullet-ridden Studebaker for years as Deming's taxi. He never covered the holes in it, but would often tell tall tales about them for strangers who hired his services, producing large tips from his interested clients.

Stella left Deming first and finally went to live with relatives in the East. Sam Townsend returned and ranched quietly. One day, his face contorted, he grabbed at his chest and dropped dead of a heart attack. He was in the Manhattan Café eating a simple lunch. He was buried near Billy Thomas.

And the others, E. Thomas Mills, Charlie the desk clerk? They moved away. Dr. Smith passed on while he slept; *The Headlight* gave him a long obituary. The young doctor at the hospital eventually moved to California where he went into private practice. He sometimes takes down one of Dick Little's books from his collection and reads it—and remembers.

As for the Floriditas, they're still there: frowning in bad weather and beautiful in good. They have nothing to remember and, if they could, would not tell of the blasted mine shaft which hides the bones of two greedy men; and of a deep, lost cavern holding forever in silence the bones of four of Pancho Villa's Dorados and the secret of the treasure of Rodolfo Fierro.

St. George Cooke was born in Richmond, Virginia, in 1918. He attended the University of Richmond and was later a radio and television announcer. He also worked in the public relations field and had his own publishing company in New Mexico, where his interest in the notorious Pancho Villa was whetted. Mr. Cooke passed away in October 1987.